THE UNKNOWN

THE UNKNOWN

HEATHER GRAHAM

THORNDIKE PRESS
A part of Gale, a Cengage Company

**LIBRARY OF CONGRESS CIP DATA ON FILE.
CATALOGUING IN PUBLICATION FOR THIS BOOK
IS AVAILABLE FROM THE LIBRARY OF CONGRESS.**

ISBN-13: 978-1-4328-9198-5 (hardcover alk. paper)

Published in 2022 by arrangement with Harlequin Books S.A.

Printed in Mexico
Print Number: 01   Print Year: 2022

For Lorna Broussard,
with love and thanks.

PROLOGUE

The screech of sirens penetrated the depth of the forest, causing Sienna Murray to waken suddenly and jump out of her chair.

She was accustomed to another sound, the little buzzer warning her that her grandmother needed something.

She never minded the buzzer; she adored her grandmother. Granny K, as she had always referred to her father's mother, was the best grandparent any kid in the world could hope for. She had taken Sienna on amazing adventures, told her countless stories, and been her secret confidante many times. She was over seventy but looked younger — or she had until the illness had robbed her of her strength and enthusiasm.

But never her humor.

She had the gift of laughter and mischief, though never the kind that was harmful. But now . . .

She was sick. And they would lose her.

7

Sienna knew that, understood it, and still . . . caring for her grandmother was always time well spent.

The buzzer hadn't gone off, though. She'd been awakened by the sirens, though now they sounded far away, not loud enough to wake someone.

Granny K was awake and looking at her with concern, rising the best she could on her bed.

"It's down at the McTavish home," she said. "Sienna, you must go. Now! Quickly! There's a fire. The wee one is caught under the stairs . . . Her mother has fallen."

"Granny K, I can't leave you —"

"You can, and you must! The wee bairn is 'neath the stairs!"

Granny's accent from the old country only became pronounced when she was upset.

"But, Granny —"

"No buts, lass! Dearie, I've had a fantastic go of it, and I'm quite fine with me fate. Go save that baby!"

Sienna didn't want to go; she was so afraid to leave Granny K. But her grandmother was growing so upset it seemed she had little choice.

She would. She'd call her mom as she ran, asking her to please come over.

Then she'd have to explain that Granny K

had made her leave. But . . . she would deal with that when she had to.

The McTavish house was down the curving road. She thought she could see an orange glow in the distance.

Country roads in this area of Louisiana tended to curl around woods and marshes. It was no different here; and in the country, homes could be far apart.

She ran nearly a mile, grateful she was moving quickly.

There were only a few houses in their outlying region of Terrebonne Parish. She was vaguely aware of her neighbors: Terry Berger, shrimp-boat captain, was coming out his front door as she passed, confused and curious as he looked down the road. And Thayer Boudreaux, local hotshot football player, was emerging from his house, the same look of concerned curiosity on his face. The door was open, and his parents were standing behind him, staring down the street.

The Harrison family — parents and all three kids — were standing by their picnic table, staring down the street in shock.

Sienna reached the house as the sirens still wailed — in the distance, but getting much closer now. Fire was shooting out, but the front door was open. She was pretty sure that meant she wouldn't be caught in a back draft. Bursting into the house, she saw Eleanor McTavish on the floor in the living room.

And as Granny K had said, the baby, bundled in a blanket, had rolled under the stairs. Gasping, Sienna reached for the baby, certain that poor Eleanor was badly hurt or else she'd have heard the cries.

Smoke filled Sienna's lungs, but she knew she needed to act; the fire and rescue vehicles weren't going to arrive in time. She had to balance the baby and drag Eleanor. She might hurt the woman by dragging her, but if she left her, she'd die for certain. The flames had eaten half the stairway and were consuming the old wood-frame house with a fierce gold and bloodred hunger.

She couldn't grab both of Eleanor's shoulders and hold the baby. She tried setting the baby on Eleanor's stomach and dragging them both.

The baby rolled off.

She picked up the screaming bundle, tucked her under her arm, and dragged Eleanor by the collar of her pajama shirt.

It worked.

Somehow, she had the two of them out on the lawn when a fierce explosion sounded, and the house seemed to burst into one huge continuous flame.

Several vehicles pulled up into the yard: fire, rescue, and police.

Suddenly, Sienna started to cough and choke. She keeled over next to the baby and Eleanor McTavish. She felt strong arms around her, pulling her from the lawn.

"The baby . . . Mrs. McTavish . . ." she muttered.

Her head was light; she was gasping for air.

"We're helping them. They're safe," a voice told her. "They're safe. You saved them, little girl. You saved them."

Sienna awoke to the sound of her mother crying. She opened her eyes slowly, watching the world reel for a minute, then found she could focus again.

She was in a hospital room. Her parents were seated on chairs next to the bed; her mom held her hand.

"Baby!" her mom cried when Sienna opened her eyes.

"Mom, it's okay. I'm fine."

Was she?

She must have been, otherwise her mother's crushing hug might have hurt, but Sienna could see how distressed and worried she'd been.

"Precious!" her father whispered, emotion causing a raspy timbre in his voice.

"I'm fine, really," she said. The memories of what had happened surged within her. "The baby!" she cried.

"The baby is going to be fine, and so is Mrs. McTavish," her father assured her. He was quiet a second. "They and the entire McTavish family are grateful, my sweet, but Sienna, that was crazy! What were you doing at the McTavish house? You were supposed to be with your grandmother all afternoon . . ."

He choked on his words.

"Granny K told me to go!" Sienna said indignantly. "She's the one who —"

She broke off; both her parents had drawn back. They were staring at her worriedly.

"What is it?" she demanded.

"You have to tell her," Sienna's mother whispered.

Her father sighed, shaking his head, still looking at her with grave concern. "Granny K is gone, Sienna. Her doctor said that she died around three o'clock this afternoon."

The world almost turned to smoke and fog again.

"Darling, she couldn't have told you to run into a burning house," her mother said gently. "And I know how you loved her, how this hurts you, hurts us all, but she must have died in her sleep right after you went to sit with her when you got home from school today."

Sienna shook her head. "No, she sent me. She knew where the baby was, how I could find her. She . . . No!"

"Sweetie, I loved my mom. We knew we were losing her. She died peacefully in her sleep," her father said.

"We were terrified we'd lose you, too!" her mother told her. "I love you so much, my darling. You were an incredibly brave girl. It takes a lot of courage to rush into a burning building when you're only fourteen! The McTavish family wants to reward you —"

"No! People shouldn't get rewards for trying to do the right thing. Granny K knew that I could . . . that I would do the right thing."

The doctor came into the room then. Her parents excused themselves and spoke with him.

She was being treated for smoke inhalation. Just overnight. But the doctor must have explained that it had been a traumatic ordeal. She'd behaved admirably, above and beyond, and they should just humor her.

So, they did.

After the doctor was finished speaking to her parents, the sheriff arrived as well. She tried to listen to their conversation with Sheriff Patterson, hearing enough to give her chills. The fire hadn't been an accident. It hadn't been faulty wires or a burner left on. Someone had set the fire, using a mixture of gasoline and ethyl ether as an accelerant. Brian McTavish had been out of town on business when the fire had started; but he was here now, sitting in a chair in the room where his wife and daughter had been assigned to receive their medical attention together.

"Why?" Sienna's mother asked. "They . . . The family is lovely. She stays with the baby, and he works for a tech company. Why would anyone . . ."

"Hopefully, we'll find out," the sheriff said.

"Mom," Sienna said, when her mother returned to her bedside.

"Shh."

"But, Mom, I heard the sheriff —"

"And it's his job to find out what happened. It's your job to get better!"

"Dad —"

"Sweetheart, you did the best anyone could! Our parish has a fine sheriff and a good office. Let them take over now. You rest."

Her parents stayed at the hospital, taking turns in the chair-bed. She woke at one point to see her father in the corner, tears in his eyes, and her mother walked to him to hold him as they cried together. She knew her mother had loved Granny K, too.

But more than that, she knew Granny K could not have died when they said.

There was no sense fighting it. They were absolutely determined the doctor was right.

And Sienna was equally determined he was wrong — until the funeral.

And there, walking silently along a row where mourners sat, was Granny K.

She stopped where Sienna's dad was seated, tenderly drawing a line down his face with gentle fingers, then doing the same with Sienna's mother.

Sienna was never sure how she managed not to cry out — or pass out.

She saw her parents draw closer together, as if they had been comforted.

Maybe it was the words the priest so eloquently spoke.

Next, Granny K looked at Sienna. She had a mischievous light in her eyes as she drew a finger to her lips, warning her to stay silent.

Sienna blinked rapidly. Her grandmother remained unseen by all but her apparently.

It wasn't until later, when her parents decided she should be allowed a minute alone at the grave, that Granny K came and spoke to her again.

"Just bow your head, child, and let your hair fall over your face. That way you can answer me when you need to. But first, just listen. I haven't meant to frighten you, lass. Not at all. But that baby might have died. My body couldn't fight the ravages of the disease anymore, but my soul is strong, and my Higher Power must have determined that I may stay — and look after you. Now, you know me, love. I'll not just be hanging around. I have places to be!" She giggled softly.

"I know, but, Granny K, the sheriff said the fire was set! Someone was trying to hurt Mrs. McTavish and the baby. Who was it, Granny? I can try to tell the police or steer them in the right direction!"

Granny K sighed and shook her head. "Lass, I don't know. There was a moment when I realized I was not even a wee part of me body anymore. And there was a sudden flash around me, and I don't know. Maybe if you hadn't acted, the babe and her mum might have joined me. I saw what I saw, but nothing before it. But it's true that Sheriff Patterson is a fine man, and he'll be doing all he can. Now, go grow up and be a power out there! You're a fine, good girl, and ye'll be making the world a finer place!"

Sienna was never so sure she could *make the world a finer place.* The sheriff investigated; officers from the state investigated. Criminologists, psychologists, fire experts, and more tried, but the arsonist wasn't caught.

Mr. and Mrs. McTavish came to thank her, but then they moved out of the state.

He accepted a job in South Dakota, as if he wanted to get as far away from Louisiana as he could.

Time went by. The arsonist still was not found.

A year later, Mr. McTavish was killed by a hit-and-run driver outside of Atlanta, where he'd gone for a three-day tech convention. Mrs. McTavish and her child were going to stay right where they were — in an apartment in one of the casino hotels in Deadwood.

What remained of the McTavish house was demolished; a modern duplex went up in its place to the great distress of Sienna's father.

The new construction was still about a mile away so Sienna didn't really understand, but she knew her father loved everything old and traditional.

She spent the next several years in Terrebonne Parish, growing to adulthood, doing the kinds of things kids did and mostly staying out of trouble.

When she was eighteen, she headed to Loyola University in New Orleans. When she graduated in communications, she opted to stay on, being offered a great job with a new undertaking in the city, a museum that offered areas with wax characters relating the history of the city *plus* a petting zoo, wildlife rescue, and several other eclectic sections.

She was happy to go to work every day.

And life went on.

She fell in and out of love. She partied too hard — and learned how to pull back.

It wasn't until she'd been working in the city, living her life and loving it, for five years that she had a sudden and frightening visit from her grandmother.

She woke that night, not at all sure why.

And there, in the moonlight that filtered through her Garden District apartment window, was Granny K. "Listen. It's happening again. The killer is here, in the city! The Kimball house next door is going to go up!"

As the ghost of her grandmother gave the

warning, the entire house seemed to shake.

Searing red and blue flames shot up beyond her window, obscuring every essence of the gentle moon.

CHAPTER ONE

Ryder Stapleton had been in the Bywater area when he received the call about the explosion and fire in the Garden District.

He'd been relieved a situation that might have led to murder had been diffused, with Albert Greenway subdued and in jail, and his intended victim was at the hospital dealing with nothing worse than a minor injury to his shoulder.

He'd been contemplating his future as he drove, having recently accepted an offer to join a special unit of the FBI after passing all the requirements at the academy. He'd turned in his resignation to the New Orleans Police Department just that morning. He'd made the choice because he'd seen it as important, but he also knew he was going to hate to leave the city that was his home.

And since he still wasn't great at ignoring the dead in the company of others, joining the Krewe might also keep his coworkers and friends from — with the best of intentions — seeing him locked away in a mental institute.

He'd barely driven a matter of blocks on his way home when he saw the flames rising into the sky as the police radio broadcast the report about the explosion and fire.

The scene was far better than it might have been.

While the old Garden District house had burned to nothing more than a skeleton of the structure, no one had been killed.

The Kimball family had gotten out — he knew that before he arrived. The mother, Rebecca, and two children, Teddy and Sophia, were seated at the rear of one of the rescue vehicles, wide-eyed and frightened still. Martin Kimball was speaking with an officer and a fireman.

The fire marshal, John Beckett, saw Ryder drive up and excused himself, hurrying over even as Ryder got out of his car.

"Glad you're here," John said.

Ryder arched a brow, looking at the house. "It wasn't a gas leak, huh?"

John, a man with iron-gray hair who had been at his job for years, shook his head.

"I've just begun the investigation, but this thing was accelerated with gasoline. Possibly combined with ethyl ether. I don't have lab tests yet, but combined . . . well, you can guarantee a blaze."

"Someone got in the house and doused it with both?"

"That's what it looks like so far."

"Not an inside job?" Ryder asked. He'd seen a hell of a lot in his time with the NOPD. Recent months had been hell, not to mention the insanity of the year gone by.

But to think that a mother or father could set a fire that would kill their children . . .

"They all got out," he murmured.

"Mrs. Kimball said one of their neighbors came by. She smelled the gas before they did. But Mrs. Kimball, her husband, and the kids were sound asleep. At least, that's what she says. And while I'm hoping to not discover that we have an arsonist at work in the city, I can't help but pray to God that's true. We've barely got the flames doused, so what I've said is preliminary."

"And the neighbor smelled the gas?" Ryder asked.

John shrugged. "That's what Mrs. Kimball said. She told me she was half-asleep when she came downstairs to answer the door. But the banging and ringing woke up her husband, too, and he smelled the gas immediately."

"Interesting. Where's the neighbor?"

"I don't know."

Ryder nodded. "Okay. Thanks, John."

"We'll be investigating with all our resources, of course. We can look for signature aspects of the fire, but . . . Well, we haven't had an arsonist around here in a long time." He sighed again and looked at Ryder. "Think this was personal?"

"So far, all I know is that a brilliant fire marshal has told me that the fire was intentional and, thankfully, no one died. Like you, I'll be investigating."

"Right. Sorry. My people are good."

"I know. And thank you. I'll talk to the husband."

John nodded and stood back as Ryder walked over to where Martin Kimball stood.

He was about Ryder's age, thirties, a man of about six feet, medium build, with short fluffy blond hair that was standing straight up in the gentle breeze that had surely helped fan the flames of the fire. He looked at Ryder with red-rimmed sky blue eyes that were dilated and appeared almost blank.

"Mr. Kimball, Detective Stapleton. I'm grateful to see you and your family alive. And I'm sure you're in rough shape right now, but I'm afraid I have to ask you some questions, anyway."

Kimball nodded. Then it seemed to sink

in that Ryder would be investigating — and investigating him.

He began to shake his head. The motion was slight at first, then vehement.

"I didn't do this. I would never do this. My wife didn't do this. We love each other. We love our kids! I swear to you —"

"Mr. Kimball, please. Do you know who might have done something like this? And did you have a security system in the house?"

Kimball shook his head. "This is . . . Well, we're in the Garden District. The cops here are good. It's a safe neighborhood. We have a lock and a bolt on the front door and another set on the back door . . . or, uh, we did."

"Windows?"

"Yeah, um, they had locks."

"Were they all locked?"

"They should have been."

"Can you think of anyone who would do this to you?"

Kimball looked truly lost. "I work for Delaney Enterprises. We work on computer software. My job is probably pathetically boring to most people. My wife teaches grade school!"

"Someone wanted to hurt you," Ryder said, watching the man's reaction.

Kimball shook his head, baffled. "Detective, my wife and I were sound asleep until Sienna came to the door. Thank God for her or we'd be dead now. I can't imagine anyone who would have done this."

"But someone did."

The man was shaking badly. He needed medical attention, Ryder thought, or he'd wind up with a heart attack or go into shock.

"Mr. Kimball, I'm going to see to it that you and your family are brought to a hotel for the night. There is nothing to salvage here now. Tomorrow, we're going to have to talk again, but for now . . ."

He glanced over Kimball's shoulder. Shelley Anderson, a first responder he'd known for years, was waiting. He nodded to her and said to Kimball, "Sir, Miss Anderson here is going to escort you over to your wife and children. An officer is going to help you from there. For tonight, we're going to place you and your family somewhere we know you'll be safe."

Kimball nodded. "I'll think on your questions, but who would want to hurt us?"

He truly appeared to be baffled. Shelley started to help him walk away.

"Mr. Kimball!" Ryder called.

"Yes?" The man stopped and looked back.

"Your neighbor Sienna. What's her last

26

name? And where does she live?"

He pointed to the apartments just next door, with outer walls now covered in a residue of smoke. "Sienna Murray. The closest apartment," he said.

"Thank you," Ryder told him.

Kimball nodded and resumed walking toward the back of the ambulance where his wife and children waited.

Ryder stared at the building next door. An old, Victorian home like the one that burned to the ground. It had been turned into apartments.

He paused by his car.

No one in hell could be sleeping at this time.

He walked over to the house and read the names on the mailboxes: there were only two. *Mr. & Mrs. Craton* and *S. Murray.*

He hit the bell for Sienna Murray.

"Um, yes?" a female voice replied through the intercom. She didn't try to sound as if she'd been sleeping. Then again, seriously, there could be no pretense when the walls were all but scorched and the house next door had burned to the ground.

"Miss Murray?"

"Yes."

"It's Detective Stapleton. I'd like a word with you."

27

"All right."

"May I come in?"

A buzzer sounded. He opened the door.

The house had been divided just about evenly with a hall running from the front door to the back door, shotgun-style, and two main doors, one to the right, one to the left.

The one to the left opened.

Maybe she'd expected him; maybe she'd pulled on the jeans and T-shirt when she'd run next door, and after all that had gone on, she'd just stayed up.

Maybe she'd started the fire. The family trusted her.

She was an extremely attractive young woman with long, chestnut hair, dark green eyes, and a slim build. She didn't appear to be frightened of him but a bit wary.

She didn't look like an arsonist.

But looks could be deceiving. That was a given.

She stepped back from her door, indicating he was welcome to come into the parlor. It was a pleasant room with period furniture. A Duncan Phyfe sofa sat in the center of the room, facing the hearth and framed by two large upholstered wingback chairs.

She gestured toward the area.

He chose the sofa, and she chose a chair.

"You warned the Kimball family about the fire," he said.

She straightened and frowned.

Had she asked them not to say who had given them the warning?

"Yes," she said flatly.

"How did you know?"

She stared at him skeptically. "What do you mean, how did I know? I could smell the gas all the way over here."

"And you checked out this apartment first?"

"I . . . Yes."

"And your housemates, did you wake them?"

She frowned again. "I . . . No. I could tell it wasn't coming from that direction. I just ran out, and the nearest house was the Kimball one, and I knew the odor was coming from there. Of course, I know Martin and Rebecca and the kids, and I was scared for them, so I started banging on the door."

"You don't know how the gas got there, right?"

"What?"

"Did you see anyone at the house? Any suspicious cars in the neighborhood? Anybody going in or out that shouldn't have been?"

"Mister —"

"Detective Stapleton."

That seemed to tick her off. She went ramrod straight.

"Detective Stapleton, I awoke to a strange smell at two in the morning. At that time, I'm not usually out on the street watching my neighbors' houses."

"This is New Orleans. Tons of people are up at two in the morning."

"Detective, we're not on Bourbon Street or even Frenchmen Street or Magazine Street or any other street that has late-night or early-morning entertainment. This is a neighborhood. I work for a living. My neighbors work for a living. They have children. We're pretty quiet here when it's two in the morning!"

Ryder knew how to change his tone when necessary.

"Of course," he said calmly. "I was just hoping that you could help."

She shook her head, swallowing. "I'm so sorry. I didn't see anything or anyone. I'd love to help. The Kimball family is great. The kids are sweet and well-mannered. I would help, if I could."

"I may have further questions for you tomorrow," he said. "Is that all right?"

"Can I stop you?"

"No."

She shrugged. "Well, then . . ."

She stood, and he headed swiftly to the door, pausing there.

"Under the circumstances, I suggest you make sure to lock up."

She nodded.

"The main door will automatically lock behind you," she told him. "You'll hear this bolt slide," she added sweetly.

He nodded and went outside.

Sienna Murray. There was something the woman wasn't telling him. But he needed the fire department and technical crews to do their work.

And he needed to get some sleep.

True to her word, Sienna Murray slid the bolt as he left.

It had been a hell of a long night. A few hours' sleep and he could continue with a hell of a long day tomorrow.

"Granny K!" Sienna said, loudly and firmly.

But there was no response. Her grandmother's spirit was elsewhere. Well, as she had said years before, she wasn't going to be a continuous haunt. As in life, in death she was going to have her own social life.

"Hey! You get me in trouble with the police — and then you disappear?"

Again, no response.

31

"Well, I knew about the gas smell and the fire. They're going to think I had something to do with it!"

Still no answer.

"That detective, Granny K. Did you see him? Tall guy, built? Really, really, *really* intense gray eyes? He's the kind of guy who isn't going to let it go and move on. He's going to grill me to pieces. I mean, half the city can smell gas and smoke now!"

True.

The air conditioner wasn't doing such a great job. She knew she and the family across the hall should be grateful: the fire, as strong as it had been, had centered right where it had started. Outer walls were scorched and covered with soot, but no windows had broken, and no damage had been done. Amazing. But the fire responders in NOLA were amazing, possibly because, twice upon a time and years and years ago, fires had almost leveled the city — once in 1788 and again in 1794. Between the two fires, they had taken a thousand buildings. Of course, that had been long ago, and there had been fires since, but whatever the cause, the fire department was top-notch.

Thank God.

But . . .

She needed to sleep. She did work for a business, and like most other businesses, they were still busy rebuilding after the events of the previous year.

While the fire was going to affect the Kimball family and their friends, it wasn't going to change the rest of the city. And she needed to be at work. They were planning a major family day at the Oddities Museum. A fall celebration. She started every morning by first checking with Dr. Jared Lightfoot, head of their petting zoo and rescue area, and then moving on to speak briefly with Morrie Nielsen, their head docent. The museum was private, owned by Byron Mitchell, a wonderful man who had begun by rescuing an injured mule and slowly wound up with more creatures — living and not. A wax museum in a tiny town in Mississippi was going out of business, and Byron had purchased the wax figures to help the owner sell and then retire.

She loved Byron. He had made his money in real estate, but he used it wisely and was always good to his employees and the world at large. She was the museum's director of communications, but the title meant all communications, which also made her Byron's manager.

So she needed to sleep.

And she tried, but she never managed it.

When she left in the morning, half the neighborhood seemed to be in the street.

Staring at the remnants of the Kimball house.

Captain Ebenezer Troy leaned against the door frame to Ryder's office.

Ryder stood; Troy was a damned good man. In his midfifties, he had a headful of snowy white hair, bright blue eyes, and mahogany skin. He could be a no-nonsense man who got a job done — but never without thought and care. He could be hard-core, but he was respected by his detectives and he respected them in turn, without taking any kind of guff from anyone. New Orleans was a tough city; the captain knew the ins and outs of both it and the people, and he ran it well.

"Sir!" Ryder said.

Captain Troy laughed. "Son, at ease. I'm here to try to talk you out of leaving." He walked in and took the chair in front of Ryder's desk, indicating Ryder should sit again.

"I can't tell you how long I've weighed this," Ryder told him.

"Yeah, I didn't think I could talk you out of it. You spent a lot of time working with the agents who were down here on the Axe-man's Protégé case, and the Display Artist murders ripped apart the whole area. I just hope you're the man they send down here during our next fiasco. Speaking of which, I understand the fire that burned up a house in the Garden District last night was arson."

"That's what the fire marshal told me, yes," Ryder said.

"And you were the detective on scene?"

"Yes. I was on my way home, but got word on the police band, reported in, and headed straight out."

"I need you to think this through. I know you feel you need to go." He paused and grinned. "So, I'll accept your resignation — when you've discovered who set that fire."

"I —"

"Please."

Ryder nodded slowly. "I . . . Sure. I'm waiting on the report from the investigators on the fire itself. I sent the family to the Trudeau Hotel last night. I seriously don't think word is out that the police make use of the place. Not enough people know. I'll go through the family contacts, but the husband swears he leads a bland life, and his wife is a teacher — they have young kids — and he can't imagine anyone is an enemy. I don't believe he's lying. But I'll still investigate all possible angles."

"You don't think the husband or wife set the fire? No crazy kids who failed a subject and decided to get even?" Troy asked.

Ryder shook his head. "She teaches grade school. Then again, those kids have parents. There are dozens of angles, but she doesn't teach at a school with a waiting list where someone might have been furious their child didn't get in. There is nothing obvious to grasp onto, but we'll go through every conceivable motive."

"The family lived. We're lucky on that," Troy said. "They smelled the gas?"

"No, a neighbor smelled it and came and woke them up."

"A neighbor?" Troy said. His mind was ticking.

Ryder couldn't help but be equally suspicious, though he had met the neighbor. He still intended to bring her in.

"For the family, it might have just been a lucky break. I talked to the young woman briefly. Sienna Murray. I intend to question her again. I looked her up seconds before you came in. She's young. Her title is director of communications for the Oddities Museum. It hasn't been open long, just a few years. Uptown. I was there once — my sister and her husband were down from

Philadelphia with their kids." He hesitated, then shrugged. "It's a neat place. There are wax displays, interactive exhibits, an animal-petting area, an animal-rescue area."

"Director of communications," Troy repeated.

"I imagine that means press releases, interviews, interoffice communications, and who knows what else. I'm sure she writes to donors and manages the advertisements and invitations for special events as well."

"Doesn't sound like an arsonist."

"How many arsonists sound like arsonists?" Ryder said.

Troy laughed. "Well, the kid who lit the tails of cats on fire and grew up to enjoy things burning, for one."

"Well, I'll try to find out if she lit any animals' tails on fire. I doubt it."

His computer was in front of him. He swung it around for Captain Troy to see. "I looked her up on social media and the museum's website. That's her, there, helping the vet bandage a rescued gray-fox cub. Its leg was ripped to shreds from a rusted makeshift trap."

Troy looked at the picture, his brows rising. "Hmm."

"Hmm?"

"She's pretty."

"And as we all know, being pretty doesn't make a man or woman innocent."

"Nope. Doesn't make them guilty, either. I'd like to chat with her, too, when you bring her in."

"All right."

"Anything else? Did anyone see a car or anyone suspicious in the neighborhood? Anything weird? I suppose everything is weird in this city. Weird is normal."

Ryder shook his head. "There was a motive behind this. If we find out the motive, we can find out who it belonged to."

"Get on it, then," Troy told him. He left the room, pausing at the door. "Hey, sooner you solve it, the sooner you can kiss this place goodbye."

"Captain, it's not like that," Ryder protested.

"I know it's not. Just giving you a hard time." He grimaced and then grew serious. "A fire like that — one that could have killed a husband, wife, and two kids — well, that's not just arson. That's attempted murder. Somebody wanted at least one member of that family dead. Use anything and anyone you need. Get this bastard."

Ryder nodded and watched the captain leave.

He keyed into different law-enforcement

38

files, starting with local cases and then beyond.

Then, he extended the timeline. A year back. Five years.

He'd need to go further. Not that arsonists weren't busy in the country, but they seemed to be attacking churches and synagogues and mosques along with banks and other financial institutions.

He found a house fire in Gretna that had occurred five years back: arson.

The couple had been in the middle of a vicious divorce, and the police had proven the wife had set the fire but with no one in the house.

Officers had been house-to-house in the area of the fire; they reported back to him. So far, no one had seen anything — not until the flames shot up in the sky. No one had been spotted fleeing the scene.

He leaned back in his chair. He had nothing. A fire, deliberately set, and gasoline and ethyl ether used as accelerants. Luckily, no deaths.

He needed to expand his search. But he stared at the screen: he had nothing further from the fire inspector. He had nothing.

Except for Sienna Murray.

He rose suddenly, grabbing his jacket.

He had enjoyed the Oddities Museum. It seemed as good a time as any for a trip back.

"He's beautiful, and you're amazing," Sienna told Dr. Lightfoot, their resident veterinarian. He was young but one of the best vets Sienna had ever known. Sandy-haired, slim, and wiry, he often looked like an overgrown teenager, though he was in his midthirties. He'd gotten his degree at the College of Veterinary Medicine at the University of Florida, spent five years with a local city vet, and run his own practice for a few years before being lured into being the museum's resident doctor for the petting zoo — and the rescue branch.

Lori Markham, his tech, felt he was wonderful. "I've seen vets be not callous but careless with their patients," she had told Sienna once. "But he goes a step above. Animals hurt like people, in his mind. So you do everything you can to keep them from pain while you're treating them."

"He came in last night," Jared said, stroking the nose of the Louisiana black bear cub he had just injected with an antibiotic. "His paw is pretty mangled. Stupid trappers!" he added angrily. "These guys just came off the endangered-species list. We may have to keep him."

"Maybe not in the petting zoo," Sienna said, joking. "But if we need to keep him, of course we will."

Jared smiled at her. "Thanks."

"Don't thank me. We're lucky. Our owner is a good guy."

"Yep! Aw, this poor baby. Traumatic night for him," Jared noted. He looked at Sienna. "But I heard it was a traumatic night for you, too."

She grimaced. "House next door burned to the bones. But everyone was all right."

He nodded, still watching her.

Thankfully, he didn't know she had gotten the family out of the house. With luck, no one — except that detective — would know. She hoped to God the family wouldn't say anything to anyone else. It didn't sound as if her part in the event had made the news.

"Well, I'd better move on," she said cheerfully. "I'm going to do an email release to members about this little guy, though. Can I snap a quick pic?"

"You look better hugging our critters than me. I look like that Beaker guy from the Muppets. You're a lot cuter."

"You look fine, a handsome fellow, and you're the vet," she reminded him.

"Okay, okay. But you're a liar."

41

"I am not."

"Wild hair that sticks straight up, nose the size of Kansas —"

"Stop! That's a great nose, and Artie, one of our docents, said you have a nose that belongs on a Greek statue, so let's just go with that, huh?"

Sienna had her cell phone ready to take the photo. "The Greek god of nostrils," Jared said, but he lifted the little bear cub close to his face, and she quickly snapped a picture.

"Thanks, Jared!" she said, ready to walk out. But the little bear cub was adorable. At this stage in his life, he seemed as loving as a new puppy. She had to give him a stroke goodbye before leaving Jared's on-site animal hospital.

"Hey, call Byron!" Jared said. "I'm horrible. I just remembered. He wasn't sure you were coming in, and he didn't want to bother you. Said to call when you felt up to it."

She smiled; her phone was still in her hand. She dialed her boss quickly.

"Sienna? You're all right? News about the fire is everywhere," Byron said. "It was right next to where you're living, right?"

"Byron, I'm absolutely fine, and so is the family. The house is a loss, and our place has some marks on the walls, but that's it."

"Still, you should have taken the day off."

"Byron, I'm fine. What would I have done? There is nothing I can do."

"Some might have cuddled up with a drink and spent the day watching TV."

"I love my job. I'm fine, and all is good."

"Of course it is. Anyway, I am taking the day, fishing with friends. I'm lucky that I can take lots of days because I have you and Lightfoot. Anyway, glad you weren't hurt in any way."

"Nope. I'm good. And thank you."

They ended the call, and Sienna headed in, feeling odd that it was such a beautiful day after a horrible night: the sky was a crystal blue with just puffs of clouds.

Well, the world always did go on.

She passed the petting zoo. It was early, but families were out. There were two miniature horses, two sheep, two goats, one small donkey, and a ridiculously affection-ate albino skunk — descented at birth ap-parently and left on the doorstep of the museum one morning.

Smiling, she headed to the back door that led to the animal sites. The hall she entered was filled with handsome wax figures. There was a display on the founding of New Orleans, another on Jackson and Lafitte,

43

and another on the signing of the Louisiana Purchase, plus several more displays depicting the history of the city. Then there was another wing with displays that reminded one of condemnable events. In that hallway, a few displays included the horrors of slave trade, including one on the infamous Madame LaLaurie who, with her doctor husband, had performed despicable medical experiments on their slaves and were to eventually flee the city after a slave chained to the stove had set fire to the house, willing to die to stop the torment.

But that opened into a hallway that offered up Mardi Gras splendor and colors.

The wax-display portion of the museum was eclectic, for sure.

She knew the figures well. They had been excellently crafted. So well crafted that many of them were downright creepy, especially those in Murderers' Row.

Sienna never looked at them when she was hurrying through from the back — especially at night.

It was too easy to imagine they were staring at her.

That they might even jump down from their displays.

"Ridiculous," she muttered aloud, hurrying along through the How Things Work hands-on section for the kids toward the front and her office.

But before she reached it, she stopped abruptly.

The detective she'd met after the fire was there, waiting by her office door.

Of course, he had seen her. She took a deep breath, wishing his eyes didn't seem quite so intense, that he wasn't quite so tall, that . . .

Tall, dark, and deadly! she found herself thinking.

"Granny K?" she said quietly. "Where the hell are you?"

To her surprise, she did hear her grand-mother behind her then.

"What? I'm supposed to let those ador-able little kids die in that fire?" her grand-mother demanded. "Buck up, girl! Hmm. I like him! Good-looking fellow. Very good-looking. Be nice to him. You haven't had a decent date in ages!"

"Granny!"

"I'm going! You didn't do anything wrong. You did everything right. You're going to be okay."

Sienna felt her leave.

"Deserter," she hissed beneath her breath, just in case she could still hear her.

Then she walked to her office, not bother-

45

ing to smile as she headed toward the man, a brow arching as she reached him.

She didn't speak.

She stared at him and waited.

He smiled slowly. "Well, you're not happy to see me. Sorry, Miss Murray. You're all I've got. And you *are* going to help me."

CHAPTER TWO

Ryder wasn't surprised by the way Sienna Murray stared at him. If hostility could be bottled, she could have filled a few dozen gallon jugs with the look in her eyes.

"There has to be something," he said quietly. "Something you saw that you don't realize you saw. Something you heard that you don't realize you heard. It's there, in your mind. And you also know the family, right?"

She turned and walked into her office. She didn't try to shut the door on him but walked around behind her desk and indicated he could take the chair in front of it.

He did.

"It's true what they say," she said.

"And what's that?"

She stared at him with eyes that were almost a forest green they'd gotten so dark. Then she shook her head and sighed.

"No good deed goes unpunished."

"I'm not trying to punish you. The family is grateful. I'm grateful. I'm sure all sane people who know about the incident are grateful that an entire family didn't perish in a fire."

She shook her head again. "Don't you think I'd help if I could? That I would tell you anything that I knew?"

"I don't think we always know what we know," he told her. "I'd like to spend some time during which we just talk. And I'll ask you about the neighborhood —"

"I'm at work. I really can't talk right now. Unless you're going to arrest me —"

"All right."

"What?" she said, startled and frowning.

He grinned. "No, I'm not going to arrest you. And I'll leave your place of business now. But I will be back to talk with you in the future."

"That's foolish. I don't know what else I can tell you."

He stood and said, "Thank you. Please think back about any cars in your neighborhood that didn't belong there."

She sighed deeply again. "The entire Garden District is a tourist zone. All kinds of cars are in the neighborhood. If I paid attention to every car —"

"Just think about it."

"I'll think about it."

"And the family, if you ever heard them talking —"

"We're neighbors. I haven't known them forever. I throw balls back to the kids. Believe it or not, I have borrowed sugar. We chat now and then. They are not lifelong friends."

"I know. But I also believe you have something."

"Once more, if I had something, I'd give it to you."

"Again, you might not know what you know."

She stared back at him and then shook her head. "You said you were leaving. Did you come to my work just to torment me?"

"No. To start you thinking."

He stood, smiled grimly, and left her.

He would see her again, whether it made her happy or not.

He wondered about the brief glimpse of *something* he'd seen with her in the hall as she had walked his way. A presence, there and gone so quickly once she'd been in his sight that he couldn't be sure.

But did she have something — some ability — that allowed her to see the dead?

He couldn't be sure. Until his own experience with the Krewe, he would have thought it all crazy. And in spending time with Krewe members, he'd learned there were those who also sensed the dead but couldn't communicate the way that certain people could.

Of course, not even the Krewe could explain it. Still, it was something to explore when he saw her again.

Her office was close to the front of the museum, near the reception/ticket area.

It seemed like a nice museum. The concentration was on the animals and the wax figures, but there were great hands-on exhibits for the kids, too.

The wax tableaux were great, ranging from great historical scenes to the creepiest history of the city. Of course, one exhibit was especially disturbing to him now: the Axeman of New Orleans. They had just dealt with a murderer determined to one-up the long-ago killer.

They had, at least, brought the more recent situation to a successful conclusion. Of course, it couldn't bring back the dead.

He smiled at the receptionist as he prepared to leave. She was in her late fifties or early sixties, he thought, a slender dark-haired woman with her hair cut in a swing that hugged her face, dark-rimmed glasses, and a cheerful look about her.

"Thanks," he said.

"Of course, Detective!" she said. "You found Sienna okay?"

"I found her heading back to her office, so, yes. Thank you again."

"We're always happy to do anything that's helpful in any way. Poor Sienna. What a traumatic experience. But she's a strong one, our girl! She deals with whatever falls her way."

She was chatty, nice. Getting to know the receptionist here could be a good thing. He could find out more about Sienna.

"Well, it seems like a great place to work," he said. "I'm sorry. I don't know your name."

"Clara. I'm Clara Benitez," she said. "And yes, it's a wonderful place to work. So many places are corporate, where every question needs a meeting for an answer. But this museum is privately owned, and it all started because our owner is an animal lover and . . . Well, Byron Mitchell is a good man, fair and giving to all his employees. Oh, he expects us to work! But during our recent bad times, he saw that we were paid, and if we needed anything, we knew we could call him. You don't get that from a small business all that often. Of course, we don't have that many employees. We do have a resident

51

veterinarian, though, which many small places don't have either."

"How many employees are there?" he asked.

"Well, let's see, Byron himself, though he usually rules from afar. Sienna, our VP, handling media and any problems that pop up day-to-day, but we don't really have problems. No one here is a micromanager. Then, there is me — I deal with the tickets and memberships. Then, we have Dr. Jared Lightfoot and his assistant, Lori Markham, for the petting zoo and the rescue area. And then, Artie Salinger, our historian in residence, who gives speeches on the tableaux, and Morrie Nielsen, all-around guide, excellent with the hands-on section. He was a teacher for years, and we're lucky to have him. He's great with kids."

"Nice. Well, I can see that this place is as much a labor of love as it is a job," he said. "I have only visited the museum once, but I plan to come back and see more. I do admire the tableaux."

Clara laughed. "Not me! The wax figures scare me. I steer clear of them. But I'm weird. I don't like dolls, either."

"Ah, too many movies about evil dolls," he said.

She laughed. "You haven't had to arrest

any, have you?"

"No, the perps I've dealt with have tended to be human. I get it, though. Dolls can be creepy," he agreed.

He left the museum, irritated to discover he was at a loss. It wasn't that others weren't working — the fire had been fueled by gas and started by a stove burner. That meant someone had been in the kitchen. The family had locked up for the night. That meant someone had broken in. Or someone in the family had set the blaze. But he didn't believe that. He'd worked with people so long there were things about them that could be read in their looks, their manner, and their behavior.

The kids in that household were loved. They were precious. Even if the husband had wanted to do in the wife or vice versa, neither would have taken the kids with them.

He headed to the Garden District, parking next to the burned-out shell of a house.

Two firemen were still there. They waved to him, wearing gloves and masks, going through the debris. He saw one of them was the fire marshal, John Beckett.

The street was quiet, and Beckett walked over to him. "We're on it, Detective. Sifting through for an answer as to how . . . Well, looking for locks. I know you want to know if someone broke in."

"Of course. And thank you for being on it yourself."

Beckett nodded, looking at the house. "This is bad, but I can't help but hope it was an isolated event. Personal. I hate the idea of an arsonist running around the city. Fire here . . . Well, it's better now, of course. But the French Quarter and other areas can still burn out of control. Building was so much better after the fires that raced through at the end of the 1700s and in the early 1800s, but no matter what man does, fires can spread."

"I'm grateful for anything you give me, and you know I —"

"I know you. You won't stop. And you won't be an ass if they bring the FBI in. Of course not. I heard you're leaving us, going to the FBI."

"Not until this is over," Ryder assured him.

"Then I'm back at it. So what are you up to now? Checking up on me?" Beckett asked with a grin.

"I'm going to visit a few neighbors. Our men and women in uniform did a lot of house-to-house already, but you never know what someone may have remembered."

"You never know," Beckett agreed. "We had a fire in the Irish Channel not long ago. The people were completely dazed afterward. Then when we traced it to an electrical wire, the man remembered his idiot cat had been chewing on something behind the couch. He'd yelled at it and dragged it out but never thought to check if it had been a wire."

"It happens. Well, I'm off."

"And I'll tell you as soon as I can if we find a lock that was compromised."

"Thanks."

Ryder first went to the house that was a single-family dwelling to the right of the fire.

An older woman answered the door, after asking to see his credentials as she looked at him through the peephole. He'd done some research and knew that she was Grace Wooldridge, the homeowner, and that her adult daughter, son-in-law, and two young grandchildren lived in the house as well.

He produced his badge, and she opened the door.

She had curly gray hair and was plump and bubbly, asking him if he'd like to sit down and have tea.

He decided he would. He waited just a minute: she must have had the tea brewed and ready before he'd gotten there.

The house was lovely, and he complimented her as he took a seat on the sofa in her parlor. The mantel was handsomely built of stone and held a dozen family photos.

"Beautiful home, beautiful family," he told her.

"Oh, thank you," Grace said. "I love my home. I'm so grateful my daughter and my son-in-law are here, and the kids, too." She laughed. "I'm the default babysitter, but that's fine. It works for us. The home will go to my daughter when I'm gone, anyway. But we both know I'm not planning that for a long time!"

"That's great. With your energy, I see you as being with us for many years," he assured her.

"And you're here about the fire."

"Yes. I'm hoping someone saw something."

She sighed. "Not here. With kids in the house, even if we mean to stay up and watch something on the television, we fall asleep early. We only woke up when the cops and the fire department started to show up. I heard Sienna smelled the gas and warned the family, and I am so grateful. I don't know the girl that well, but she is a true

56

gift! If there hadn't been such an early warning, I don't know what might have happened. My grandkids love those kids."

"Have you seen anyone around who . . . maybe shouldn't have been in the neighborhood?"

"Oh, that's hard! I did see a homeless fellow on the corner down the street a few days ago. I gave him a sandwich, and he was grateful. He wasn't a money-grubber looking to buy a fifth of tequila or anything."

"What was he like?"

"Uh . . . homeless?"

"Young, old, clean, worn, dirty?"

"Oh, long hair and beard. Jeans and a T-shirt and a jacket. It was a denim jacket, beige, and yes, worn-looking."

"You saw him only once?"

"I think. He might have been there on other days. I don't drive around too much. I like to stay home, and yes, I knit, and I love to yell at politicians on the news."

"Well, thank you. I'll ask your daughter and son-in-law, if I may."

"They don't get home with the kids until six or so each evening. But, Detective Stapleton, you're welcome back anytime."

"Thank you." He produced a card. "If they'd like, they can call me. I'd appreciate it."

"Of course."

He thanked her for the tea. As he rose from his seat, he asked her, "You said Sienna Murray is a *gift*. In what way?"

"Cheerful, sweet. In times of trouble, she asks if she can help. I once saw her pick up a dog someone had hit and left by the road to die. They have a vet at her zoo-museum or whatever it is, but I saw a lot of people walk around the poor thing. She was great during all the stay-at-home times, masked, gloved, carrying sanitizer, going shopping for others. She's . . . a gift."

Great. The woman who might hold the answers for him sounded like Mary Poppins.

Except she wasn't very pleasant to him.

"Well, there is one thing."

"What's that?"

"She's a little crazy."

"Oh, how?"

Grace lowered her voice as if there was someone near them who might hear.

"She talks to herself now and then!"

He smiled. Well, now. He had suspected she had something he could use, and now he knew it.

He thanked her one more time and left at last.

He had another stop before an interview with Martin and Rebecca Kimball and then

58

was off to the office for some research on whatever discoveries he might make.

But before he left the area, he wanted a chat with the other neighbors, Judy and Ronald Craton, who shared the other house next door to the burned-out shell that had been the Kimball home.

Artie Salinger appeared at Sienna's office door about an hour or so after Detective Stapleton left.

She was still working on the design for an invitation that should have taken her about fifteen minutes.

"Hey, you doing okay?" Artie asked.

"Yes, I'm fine. All is well with the world."

Artie grinned and plopped into the chair across from her, where Stapleton had been seated not long ago.

"Right. All is well with the world! We're going to get you a pair of tights, a bodysuit, and a cape. You're a heroine, kiddo. You saved a family and possibly prevented half the neighborhood from going up in flames."

She shook her head. "Artie, please!"

"Aren't you happy?"

"I'm thrilled people lived. I happened to smell something odd."

"In your sleep?"

"Well, I guess so." She grinned. "What,

there aren't enough people crawling around the museum to ask questions? You came to torment me?"

"No." He grinned. Then he threw back his head and howled out a song. "I want to go ou-out tonight!"

She had to laugh. Artie was a good guy, a brilliant historian who had gone to Harvard, dabbled in law, and then determined that history made him happier. He had been working as a ranger before Byron had found him and convinced him to come to the museum. He was in his early thirties and liked to sweep his fingers through his rich dark hair and loved it when they all suggested that he'd have made a great Gaston if he'd ever wanted to work for a Disney park.

Early on, he had been flirtatious, even suggestive. But Sienna had let him know they were only friends. They worked together, and for her, that was where she drew the line.

And they were friends — good friends. She had discovered her relationships at work were great ones. She and Lori Markham had a special bond: Lori was a cousin to friends Sienna had known before, growing up in Terrebonne Parish. And Morrie Nielsen, their docent and Artie's sidekick, was wonderful. Morrie was in his early fifties; he had spent years teaching before he'd come to the museum. He often listened to Artie go on and on — rolling his eyes behind Artie's back. Artie, in turn, liked to call him Old Man. And while Morrie didn't join them every time the younger group of employees went out, he did now and then. So did Dr. Lightfoot on occasion, but his true love was the animals, and he wouldn't leave unless someone else was staying on the property.

The museum had cameras, and they captured footage every day, but they weren't a big-budget operation — nothing like the National WWII Museum, one of the finest museums to be found anywhere, in Sienna's opinion. Not that *they* weren't a wonderful museum; they were just different. Small. So the cameras were checked out each morning — either by Sienna, Clara, or sometimes Byron himself — and they were programmed to start over once a week. Naturally, the local police toured around the area, but they didn't have a security department. But Byron liked to come in and work at night sometimes — specifically so that his vet in residence could go out and enjoy life with "animals without fur or feathers," as Byron liked to say. Sometimes, Lori

61

would insist on staying, and the others took turns as well. No one there begrudged it when they went well over the forty hours specified in their contracts.

"Ou-oouut, tonight!" Artie repeated. "I didn't do it well, huh? Guess it's a good thing I liked history and hated drama club. Not that I don't like a good play. But music . . . there's the ticket. Musicals!"

"Is *Rent* playing somewhere?" she teased. She knew it wasn't; she loved the city's drama group, and would have known.

He made a face at her. "There's a new group playing at that place on Magazine Street you like going to. You know, where you get those sweet-potato chip-and-dip things you love so much? I say we go out. I say you need to go out."

"Hm. I'm tired. Not enough sleep."

"As they say, you can sleep when you're dead. And you won't sleep unless you get tired. Dr. Lightfoot is fascinated with his new rescue, so he doesn't want to come, and Clara is knitting something for her new grandchild. But Morrie, Lori — hey, that rhymes — you, and me. Sound good?"

"I should —"

"Oh, stop with 'should.' You won't sleep. Oh! An old friend of yours is coming, too. Thayer — the dude who owns the art gallery. The one you grew up with."

She grinned. "I didn't actually grow up with Thayer. He was the big football hero — older than me — and back then, I'd have probably been akin to a fly in his life."

"Hey! He's been out with us before. And he likes you — thinks you're hot, by the way."

"He turned into a great guy, from what I can see. It's just we were never really friends. I was closer with Lori's family. I was the same age as Lili, Freddie was a year or two older, and Sam was a year or two younger than me."

"You're not answering the question. Are you in?"

"Sure. Except we're not going to talk about the fire."

"We won't talk about the fire," Artie promised. He grinned and hurried out of her office, yelling, "I'm holding you to it!"

"No, I'm with you guys. It will be great!" she called to him.

Yes, and she'd get out of the office as fast as she could, before Detective Stapleton had a chance to come back!

"Honey?" Judy Craton called, meeting Ryder at the main door.

The door to their half of the house was

63

open; she had left it so, apparently, when she'd come to meet him. She was a petite woman in her midthirties, with no makeup, nice brown eyes, and curly brown hair framing her face.

She smiled at Ryder. "Ron isn't usually home this time of day. He stayed today because of . . . well, because of last night. We took the kids to school, but school is out early, and he wanted to make sure they were feeling okay."

Ronald Craton stood at the doorway to their half of the house. "Detective Stapleton, right? Please, come in."

Ryder did so. Two kids, a little girl of seven or eight and a boy, probably just in kindergarten or first grade, were jumping on the couch in the parlor area.

"Hey!" their dad said firmly. "No jumping on the furniture. You fall off the wrong way, you break your neck. Go to the back, turn on the TV. Something educational!"

"Sure, Daddy!" the little girl said. "There's a cool monster show on!"

"Do not scare your brother, Whitney!"

"Noah's not scared of no monsters!" she said happily.

"Noah's not scared of no monsters!" Noah repeated.

Ron Craton frowned fiercely, and the two

64

raced off. "Detective, please, sit down. I'm sorry — we tend to be a bit of a mess."

"I think I got the jelly all picked up," Judy said.

"I'm fine, thanks, and for having two kids, this place is neat as a pin," Ryder said politely. "I'd like to ask you —"

"Yes, that's what you said on the phone. But we were asleep. We never heard Sienna go out," Ron said.

"We didn't hear anything or wake up until we heard the commotion. Everyone heard it when the place exploded in flames. Then we grabbed the kids and raced out and . . . I'm not sure that was the smart thing to do," Judy said.

"It was the smart thing. We could smell fire by then," her husband said. "I guess someone had called it in."

"But not you."

"Not us," Ron said. He glanced at his wife. "Maybe Sienna called it in."

"I didn't see her this morning," Judy said. "And last night . . . Well, we all milled on the street, and then we all got back into our homes when the fire department said it was under control. Around here, of course, we worry about flames traveling."

"Of course. Well, I'm sure you've heard that the fire was set on purpose," Ryder said.

"Yes, and let me tell you, it was not set by any member of the Kimball family!" Judy said.

Ryder smiled. "No, I don't think so."

"Oh, my God!" Judy said, gasping and staring at him wide-eyed. "You don't think one of us . . . No, no, no, not any of us, not the neighbors! We like each other on this block!"

"And we sure as hell wouldn't want our own homes catching fire!" Ron said, frowning as he looked at Ryder. "If you came here to —"

"I came for help," Ryder said calmly. "The fire was deliberately set, and we have to keep fearing for the family — and perhaps the neighborhood — until we discover what happened. Frankly, in my mind, we're looking for a monster. An entire family might well have died. What can you tell me about Sienna?"

Ron stared at Ryder. "Trust me. That young woman did not set that fire!"

"Do you know her well?" Ryder asked.

"Yes and no. She was living here when we moved in. We don't see her that much — *hello, goodbye,* mostly in the morning, though we also cross paths at night. She's great with the kids, she brings them little toys — oh! And she brought us all in for a special tour at the museum where she works. Noah was thrilled meeting the veterinarian there. She's great. I mean, she saved the family, right?" Ron demanded. "You can't possibly think —"

"I don't," Ryder said.

"You know, the cops came and talked to us after the fire. It's just . . . Well, it was night! Everyone was asleep. I just don't see —"

"What I'm looking for is anything unusual you might have seen during the day — or days and nights before the fire. People who shouldn't have been in the neighborhood. Cars driving by too slowly. Anything like that," Ryder said.

Ron and Judy looked at one another. They both shook their heads.

"It's hard," Judy said softly. "We're not far from Commander's Palace and Lafayette Cemetery and the great bookstore and . . . it's the Garden District. People like to just look at the houses. Even when they're privately owned, they like to look from the street. 'That's where Jefferson Davis, only president of the Confederacy, died. That's where Anne Rice lived.' Stuff like that. There are always people around."

"That homeless guy on the corner was weird . . ."

They were all startled by the voice. Little Whitney, looking grave and mature despite her chestnut pigtails, was staring at them.

"The homeless guy?" Ryder asked.

She nodded. "Mom, remember? You drove around the block to get away from him." She looked at Ryder. "My mom is a nice person. She gives people dollars all the time for food but not for booze or drugs."

"Judy!" Ron said, clearly uncomfortable.

"That's what you told Aunt Carol on the phone." Whitney looked at Ryder. "Even when we were staying in because of the sickness, Mom gave money to people who needed it if we passed them. But she went around this guy."

"Judy?" Ron addressed his wife, frowning. "You didn't say anything."

"Well, he was probably harmless. But he was . . . ranting. And he wasn't dirty, and I was afraid he was pretending to need money to . . . I don't know. He scared me. I do remember now. I just went around the block to pull into our drive instead of going right past him. I'd forgotten it, and I don't see what he has to do with the fire."

"If I sent a sketch artist out here, would you be able to describe him?" Ryder asked.

"Maybe, but, um . . . Sure. Send someone out."

"Grace Wooldridge saw the man, too," Ryder said. "And we'll be asking her to contribute to a likeness as well. If nothing else, we'll find out if he might possibly be a danger to anyone and, hopefully, help get him off the streets." He stood, glancing toward Whitney. "Thank you, young lady. And Mr. and Mrs. Craton, thank you."

"We will do anything we can," Ron Craton said, rising to see him out.

He led him to the main door. Once outside, he heard the bolt click.

Maybe they were scared.

Another possibility was that someone had chosen the wrong house. Had the arsonist possibly been off when he — or she — had set fire to the Kimball home?

Not likely, since the Kimball home was a single-family dwelling and the Cratons and Sienna lived in clearly marked apartments.

He had to talk to Kimball, and he had to get back on a computer and look into police files, expand all his searches.

Most likely someone had been after Kimball. Someone had wanted the man dead so badly it hadn't mattered if they'd killed his wife and children as well.

Had the strange homeless man, a street beggar, been there to watch the house, to learn what he could, while hopefully not being remembered?

The arsonist had to have known the house and the family's habits. Cruising the sidewalks and streets on foot as a beggar was certainly one way not to be suspected of any coordinated plan.

To find the killer, what he really needed to find was the motive.

As he headed to his car, he was dead set on finding one. He looked back at the dwelling he had just left. Sienna had saved the lives of the family members. *How?*

Maybe it had something to do with the presence he had noted at the museum.

Whatever or whoever the hell it was, he or she just might be the help Sienna didn't know she had.

His phone rang as he headed to the car.

It was the captain.

He answered it immediately.

"We've got something that may or may not be related, but what the hell . . . I need you on it. A couple of kids found a floater down in the Ninth Ward."

"All right. I'm working the arson at the Kimball place, but I'll head out. Any cause of death yet? Murder, suicide, drowning?"

"I can tell you it wasn't a drowning," the captain said. "Not unless a man can drown after he's been charbroiled to cinders."

"I'm on my way," Ryder assured him.

CHAPTER THREE

"Now, here's the thing!" Artie said cheer-fully. "The child is weird — despises sweet potatoes. I mean, who the hell hates sweet potatoes? But we come here for sweet-potato chips!"

"Uh, not so bizarre," Lori said. "I don't particularly like onions — but I love little onion straws on salads and things. And they've got those here, too."

"Yes, but seriously, who wants to just eat a whole raw onion anyway?" Artie teased.

Morrie yawned. "So drinks . . . and ap-petizers. And the band has done a set. When are we ordering dinner?"

"Soon," Artie assured him. "Thayer Bou-dreaux is on his way, and he's bringing someone with him. A surprise guest."

Morrie sighed. "Kiddies, I'm not up for surprises. Dinner!"

"Dinner sounds good to me, too," Sienna said. "We have to work tomorrow."

" 'After all, tomorrow is another day,' " Morrie quoted.

Sienna laughed. "And maybe a long one." She glanced nervously at the door. They hadn't told anyone where they were going — except for Thayer, who was supposed to have met them by now — but she still expected Detective Ryder Stapleton to come walking in.

And she was so tired.

"Let's order," Artie said. "They should be here any minute now."

But they didn't order; Thayer arrived then along with his surprise guest.

Lori jumped up with surprise and pleasure. Sienna smiled, too. The surprise guest was another old neighbor: Lori's cousin Freddie Harrison.

They all stood to greet the newcomers. Sienna saw Thayer often enough, stopping in his gallery now and then, and he'd stop in at the museum to say hi to her and Lori, and sometimes they'd be at a gathering together.

He'd been expected to go the football route, but a torn rotator cuff had stopped him from pursuing the game. He had told her once he hadn't really cared; he'd loved art since he'd been a little kid, and while others might have seen pro football as a dream for him, he was living something more akin to his own dream. She was glad for him. He was still a big, good-looking guy and a nice friend to have in town.

Freddie Harrison had also gone the art route. Sienna had heard he didn't like the city and preferred staying out in Terrebonne Parish, but he did come in occasionally. He'd find a spot at Jackson Square to sell some of his pieces. He was a decent artist, and Sienna really enjoyed his caricatures, though she wasn't quite so sure about some of his modern art. She supported him and his efforts, nonetheless.

She gave him a hug and loved the grin he gave her. "Kiddo, you grew up really cute. Still weird, but really cute!" he told her.

She laughed. "You, too." He was cute: still skinny, with tousled brown hair and a quick smile. She had grown up playing with the Harrison kids, and she liked them all, but Freddie was her favorite. He always tried to be upbeat.

Greetings went around, they all sat again, and food was ordered.

Freddie was having a show at Thayer's gallery, and that was why he was in town. He sat next to Sienna.

"Are you staying at Thayer's house?" she asked him.

Freddie shook his head. "Nope. I'm at a little boutique hotel in the Irish Channel. Thayer's place above the gallery on Royal Street is too much city for me!"

"Hm. I should have known. When is the show?"

"We're opening tomorrow night, and it will run two weeks."

"You're staying in the city for two weeks?" she asked him.

"Hell, no!" he said with a grin. "I'm just here for the opening, and maybe I'll stay on a few days . . . to see friends." He grew serious suddenly. "Sienna, I hear you were a savior again, that you got a family out of their house before it went up in flames?"

She winced inwardly.

"So, it's true! The fire department should bring you on."

She shook her head. "Freddie —"

Thayer cut her off, lifting his bottle of beer to her. "Hear! Hear! A toast to our local hero, Sienna!"

"Remarkable," Lori agreed, smiling at her.

"Guys, really —"

"How do you do it?" Thayer asked. "I mean, years ago you saved a family. Sadly, the husband was killed in a car wreck a few years later, but . . ."

"Sienna — this happened with you before?" Morrie asked.

"Hell, yeah," Thayer answered for her, and he went on to explain how Sienna had saved a mother and her baby.

"Please, guys," she moaned. "We weren't going to talk about this," she reminded Artie.

"Hey," Artie protested. "It wasn't me."

"Fine. We're not going to talk about it," Sienna said.

"Okay," Thayer agreed, but then immediately asked, "How the hell do you do it?"

"I don't even remember the one when I was a kid, and with the Kimball house, I just smelled the gas. I don't know how. Maybe I have an acute sense of smell? Whatever. Please?"

"Okay, come on now," Lori said, giving the others a stern look. "Let's talk about art."

They did. Freddie smiled at Sienna when he said this show was going to be caricatures of famous people with their pets. He thought they would all really get a kick out of it.

"Dogs, cats, horses, parrots — you name it. Oh, and one with a skunk!"

Sienna listened; she promised to come to the opening. Then, she begged off as she needed to get some sleep.

The rest of them were still there when she left.

The neighborhood was quiet when she drove into her space in front of the house.

It still smelled of the fire that had been doused.

But the street was empty as she headed inside. There, it was quiet: her housemates had gone to bed. Easy to understand with small children in the family.

She went into her own half of the house, up to bed, and to sleep within fifteen minutes.

When Ryder arrived at the scene, the body was just being lifted onto a gurney for its trip to the morgue. The ME on duty was Dr. Peter Philbin, a seasoned medical examiner who had worked through the devastation of Katrina, the virus, and more. He saw Ryder coming and strode to meet him. Slim and athletic, he approached his job with care, determined he would always do his best to speak for the dead.

"This is ugly. There's not much I know yet, including method and cause of death, but this fellow was burned to a crisp before he went in the water," he told Ryder.

"Surely, he couldn't have burned like that

here. There are people who would have —"

"Smelled human flesh burning?" Philbin asked.

"Right. Maybe he was burned upriver and came down," Ryder said, answering his own question.

"That's what I'm figuring. It's not going to be easy, given the state of the corpse, to determine cause of death."

"And I can't really get anyone trying to calculate the movement of the river if I don't have a starting point," Ryder said, more to himself than to the doctor.

"I'll get you something. The organs might still tell me something," Philbin said. "We'll get him into the morgue tonight, and I'm going to start on this first thing in the morning."

"I'll be there," Ryder promised.

Philbin nodded grimly and headed out with the corpse.

There were four patrol cars in the area and a van from Crime Scene Investigation. Lights had been set up, but Ryder didn't think that they'd find much. The corpse had been delivered into the Mississippi somewhere else. With the size and power of the river here, it could have rushed along from a great many places, and they were probably lucky it had snagged by the shoreline

78

where it did.

He saw that Captain Troy was there, and he moved around the crime-scene tape at the river's edge to reach him.

"You're willing to take this on?" Troy asked him.

"You called me because of the fire in the Garden District," Ryder said.

"Yes. I mean, this guy was . . . It looks like he's been cooked, rotisserie-style, over an open fire. Hope to God he was dead first. The murder and the house fire might have nothing to do with each other, but we haven't had a fire problem like this in . . . Well, we have fires, but not like this." He took in a deep breath and let it go. "Hell, I've been around, and I've seen a lot. Human tragedy. The results of Katrina and the levees breaking. But it still disturbs me to no end when I witness just how great our inhumanity can be. Anyway, I talked to your almost-boss."

"Jackson?" Ryder asked.

Troy nodded. "I don't want to officially invite the FBI in. I'm just on speculation at the moment. And I know you. You'll be looking all over the place for connections. But I thought he'd lend me someone I knew you could work with. He's got Fin Stirling coming down. Figured you might want someone you've worked with before and will be joining in the future."

"Great, thank you. Yes, I work well with Fin. Where are the kids who found the body?"

Troy nodded in the direction of a police van. Two teens sat on the edge of the back of the vehicle. Ryder nodded to Troy and walked over to them.

The young girl was stunning, with sienna skin, large dark eyes, and long dark hair. The boy was seated, but even so, he appeared tall. He was also mixed-race, Ryder thought, though the kids looked quite different from each other. The boy had a protective arm around the girl's shoulders as they waited.

She was still shaking.

"Hey, I'm Detective Stapleton," he said, introducing himself.

"I'm Barry Tremaine, and this is Sue Jenkins," the boy said. "They said they wanted us to wait for the detective, but I don't know what I can tell you."

"You two found the body?" Ryder asked.

"We were walking along the edge of the river, talking," Barry said. "We both started college this fall and, anyway, we thought the . . . the body was a log at first. It was snagged on a root that was curling around the wall here, and Sue noticed what an intriguing shape it was, so I looked closer. And I wasn't even sure then, the log didn't have eyes, but the shape . . . I called the cops."

"Thank you for waiting. I'm sure you want to get home."

"Yes, please," the girl begged, her brown eyes wide. "The way it was there . . . I remember thinking at first that nature was so great, it made such interesting shapes and colors and . . ."

She broke off.

"Thanks again for waiting." Ryder produced two of his cards, handing one to each. "If you think of anything —"

"Yeah, though I'm not sure what I could think of," Barry said. "I mean . . . that's kind of it. We were walking. We found the body. We called the cops."

Ryder gave him a grim smile. "That body might have kept going all the way out into the Gulf if it hadn't been for you. So thank you. Do you have a car nearby? Do you need an officer to drive you home?"

Barry gave him a broad smile. "Thankfully, I have a car. We're both still living at home to save money, and if I came home in a cop car, my mom might have a heart attack. But thanks for the offer."

Ryder grinned. "Sure. Thank you again. And keep those cards. You can call me if you need anything, any help along the line, too."

The kids both nodded and jumped off the rear of the vehicle.

As he'd expected, the boy was very tall. Ryder was six-four himself, and Barry Tremaine was a good two inches taller than him.

There was nothing else to be done. Ryder waved to the crime-scene techs he knew and headed home. He was tired, and he damned well meant to be at the autopsy bright and early.

But when he reached home, he was too restless to sleep.

He went back on his computer and started searching. He couldn't help but believe that there was something going on that stretched further than he could see.

Someone out there liked to play with fire.

As accustomed as Sienna had become to Granny K just showing up, the ghost of her grandmother startled her when she woke up.

Granny K was just sitting at the foot of her bed, waiting.

Sienna groaned.

"I thought you loved my visits, my dear," Granny K said, hurt.

"Yes, I love that I get to see you, but —"

"Not all the time."

"No! It's just that you startled me."

Her grandmother laughed with delight. "Aw, I'm so sorry, my fine lass. Indeed, I am! And here's the thing. I don't ever mean to infringe on your life with friends or special friends — not that you've had any of those in a while — but there's something not right here."

"Could we leave my personal life out of this? No offense, but it's not something I want to discuss with my grandmother."

Granny K lowered her head, grinning. "Well, honey, at this moment, you don't have much to discuss with anyone, do you?"

"Granny K!"

"I would like you to be happy."

"I am happy."

"True. And better alone than with some creep. You haven't always chosen the best!"

"Okay . . . Please."

"Anyway, I'm here because I want you to be careful."

"Careful of what?"

"I was following that handsome young man around —"

"What handsome young man?"

Granny K let out a long sigh. "The only new handsome young man in your life! The detective."

Sienna rewarded her with another groan. But her grandmother stared at her, and so she asked, "Okay, you followed him. And?"

"And there's something going on, something very bad, and I'm afraid . . ."

"Afraid of what?"

"Not of *what. For.* I'm afraid for you."

"What? He's going to arrest me for smelling gas?"

Granny K shook her head. "No. It wasn't something I had thought of before. But . . . I did send you to save that baby when the McTavish place was burning. And I did send you to warn the Kimball family. But I didn't *see* what had happened. I certainly don't know how to explain any of this, and I doubt if I'm really still smelling anything, but I am sensing things. I *sensed* the fires both times. And I sent you. Now I'm afraid I did the wrong thing."

"The wrong thing? No, no, no! You did the right thing. People would have died if you hadn't sent me," Sienna assured her, incredulous that her grandmother could be worried. "Granny K, he can arrest me if he wants. I didn't do anything wrong, and no one could possibly prove that I did."

Granny K shook her head. "I'm afraid I've put you into danger."

"Me? How?"

"As I said, I followed that detective. He was nosing around here, which is fine. It's his job. But he got a call last night. He's going to an autopsy this morning. Sienna, they dragged a charred body out of the Mississippi last night. Someone *burned* someone to death or burned their corpse after murdering them. I don't know if I should be heading to that autopsy . . . Oh! I can't imagine the horror. But you've been involved twice when someone set fire to houses. And now . . . there's a corpse charred to bits!"

"Granny, the fires were ten years apart. And while it's horrible that someone was murdered and burned, none of this may be related."

"I want you to be careful."

"I am careful."

"Don't go pushing that detective away when he can help."

"Wait a minute. If you're trying to —"

"Stop right there, young lady. I lived a full and beautiful life. But your life is just beginning. I don't want you to be . . . like me."

Sienna was silent. "Okay," she said softly. "I will be very careful. I promise. But I need to go to work. Last year was brutal on the entire world, and I'm in a place where we try to take people out of their problems for a bit, where we help animals and maybe even people. I can't hole up in my apartment —"

"That would be stupid."

"I'm confused."

"Be careful! I can't shop for you. Buy a stun gun or some mace. Or better yet, be decent to that young detective, and he'll protect you."

"I will be careful. I'll even make a point of seeing the detective. And I'll help him in any way that I can. Okay?"

Granny K nodded and stood, coming over to run a ghostly hand over her hair and cup her chin.

"Thank you. Love you. Must run!"

And then she was gone.

Sienna groaned and got out of bed: she did have to go to work.

But she turned the TV on as she dressed, and the news was broadcasting the same information she had just heard.

A John Doe had been discovered in the Mississippi the night before.

Charred beyond recognition.

Investigators would be seeking the man's identity as well as the cause and method of death. Anyone with any information was encouraged to call the number on the screen.

The morgue was, ironically, not as dreary as it sounded.

Those who worked there usually had empathy; they had respect for the dead.

But they were living, and sometimes they joked — though, Ryder had yet to see a medical examiner chewing on a sandwich near a corpse.

But two of the morgue assistants in the hall, just off from night duty, were discussing a new restaurant in town as they prepared to leave. The receptionist apologized to Ryder after he politely waited for her to finish a call with her babysitter.

Life went on. Even around the dead.

He probably didn't need to be here, but Dr. Philbin had seemed to think he should be. It wasn't his first autopsy. He'd learned that, though it wasn't frequent, the dead sometimes attended their own autopsies as well. But this case was difficult. In his experience, a body was seldom burned so completely and then left to the ravages of the river.

He arrived late enough for the photographs to have been taken along with the

87

X-rays he knew were being ordered. The state of the body was such that anything would help.

He was directed to the proper room by one of the assistants.

When he arrived, Philbin nodded his way. He was speaking into the mic strung above the body. He'd made the incisions that allowed him to examine the remains of the inner organs.

He looked at Ryder, shaking his head as he switched off the recorder for a minute.

"This is just about impossible. One would have thought he had been seared up well-done for a variety of seabirds and fish."

"You don't know how he died?" Ryder asked.

He couldn't see Philbin's mouth beneath the mask he was wearing, but he was sure the man grimaced.

"I said it was just about impossible. Thankfully, the skull is one hell of a hard thing to burn. He was struck from behind." Philbin pointed to an X-ray on the wall. The top of the head had been crushed. "It gets way more technical, and that will be in my report."

"So he was killed before he was burned."

"Small mercies," Philbin said.

He flicked his recorder back on. Ryder

listened as he gave what information he could on the organs. The fire that had charred the man had burned so fiercely that even the heart, lungs, and stomach were affected. There was little chance of identifying him through a last meal.

"What about the teeth? Fingerprints?"

Ryder knew that, even burned, the skin could sometimes be removed, fit over another finger, and therefore provide prints.

"No prints. What wasn't burned on his fingers was . . . gnawed. The left pinkie is gone altogether. Birds are so pretty, but they can be nasty little creatures when they're hungry. We also have a host of critters in the Mississippi," Philbin told him.

"Method of death, blunt object against the skull. Cause —"

"Traumatic brain injury."

"Teeth?"

"Yep, we've got those. We're searching dental records."

"Age?"

"I'm saying this man was between thirty-five and forty-five years old. He stood about six feet even."

Ryder thanked him. He got close to the corpse and felt nothing, and he was glad. The scene here was horrible. No one should see themselves like this.

Ryder waited patiently for any other information. Philbin promised him a copy of the report as soon as possible. The detective thanked him and left.

He called to make sure the police were visiting Sienna's housemates, the Craton family, with a sketch artist. Little Whitney might have a good description of the homeless man, and they would need to stop in on Grace Wooldridge, on the other side of the burned house as well.

Then he headed to his car.

It was just about lunchtime, though he had a feeling Sienna Murray would probably tell him that she didn't take lunch and she was busy.

But then again, he'd pin her down.

He'd made interesting discoveries online last night.

And he was rather sure he was being watched and followed as well. In visiting Sienna, he might at least find out just who the shadow in the hall might have been . . .

And if he could get Sienna to admit the truth about her strange ability to smell gasoline and/or accelerants and fire from so far away . . .

The morning went along beautifully. Sienna managed to write and design several of the museum's invitations and ads, and she also spent time with Dr. Lightfoot, helping him treat some of the injuries on the cub's paws. She thought he was amazing. Even the little cub loved the vet.

Artie stopped by midmorning, happy they'd all gone out. "And you know what tonight is, right?"

"Friday night," she said.

"Opening for Freddie's show at Thayer's place. We should all go and, when it closes for the night, have dinner."

"I don't think it will close until at least midnight," Sienna told him. "Maybe later."

"So? It's New Orleans. We'll find something open! You said you were going."

"Yes, I'm going. I'm just not sure I can wait until midnight for dinner."

"I'll bring hamburgers to the show, slip you into Thayer's office in the back to eat, and then you can have dessert wherever we go — or dinner again. It's your choice."

"Let's see how it goes. You don't need to get me hamburgers. I'll make it — or I won't. I mean, I'll be at the show. I'm just not sure I'll make dinner."

"You will," Artie assured her. "Hey, I have a school group in there now. If I can handle thirty teenagers today and then make the show, you can, too!"

He left her office.

She thought he had come right back when she heard someone enter. Artie had left the door open, so he walked right in.

Detective Ryder Stapleton.

She winced, and he surely saw it. But at the same time, she was remembering her grandmother's words about her being in danger.

She couldn't be in danger. That was too preposterous.

"May I?" Stapleton asked.

"What if I said no?"

"Well, I'd just come back at five. But I thought maybe it was your lunchtime. And you might like to talk away from here."

She frowned at that, but he added, looking around, "Is your friend here?"

"What friend?"

"The dead one."

"Pardon?"

"I couldn't really see who it was the other day, so my apologies. But yes, your dead friend."

"You're crazy."

"At one point, I might have been convinced that I was. Except I have friends and coworkers with the sense or ability or whatever it is," he said.

"I don't know what you're talking about,"

she insisted.

"But you do," he said, and his gaze was intense as he confronted her.

She stood, grabbing her bag.

"There's a sushi place just down the block. We can walk."

She practically ran out of the museum, promising Clara she'd be about half an hour.

He followed behind her but she moved fast, wondering if Granny K was anywhere around and if Ryder Stapleton was on the level or pulling her chain to get something out of her.

The sushi place had outdoor seating.

Stapleton had never been more than a step behind her; the man had long legs.

"I'm going to suggest one of these tables," he told her.

She arched a brow to him.

"In case your friend wants to join us," he said.

"I still don't know what you're talking about."

"You do."

"Are you always so ridiculously annoying?"

He shrugged, a twisted smile on his face. "I can be even more annoying sometimes," he told her. "Please, honesty is going to be important. I'll start. I'm leaving the force here."

"That may be a relief to many," she said.

He smiled again, holding a chair for her. She sat. He sat across from her.

"I'm going to the FBI academy."

"Lucky them."

"I'm joining a special section of the FBI."

"How nice."

"The agents in this unit have special talents."

"Do you play the kazoo?"

He just kept smiling, and then his smile faded.

"They see the dead," he told her softly.

She froze.

"Um . . . they visit graveyards and cemeteries? They work in morgues —"

"You know exactly what I'm saying."

She remained still, stunned.

"All right, let's go at this from another perspective. I'm sure you're going to remember the name McTavish. Brian and Eleanor McTavish, and little Gwen, who is now ten years old, thanks to you. Their house was also set on fire. But you raced down from blocks away, burst in, and dragged out Eleanor McTavish and her baby. You did so in the nick of time. Brian was later killed by a hit-and-run in Atlanta,

Georgia, while he was there on business. The responsible party was never found. No one was ever arrested for the house fire, and it was suspiciously similar to the house fire the other night."

She stared at him, her mouth dry. She was unable to speak.

Finally, she shook her head. "You think that I could have done something like that? You think I was there for two fires and so I'm connected? I was fourteen when that first fire happened! I was at home. I was watching my grandmother . . ."

A cheerful waitress came out, setting menus down before them. Sienna smiled; she knew the young woman from the many times she'd come to the restaurant with her coworkers. The place was close, had delicious food, and was always fast and efficient.

"Hi," Sienna said, trying to force a smile and sound normal.

"Hey, nice to see you. The day is really pleasant, isn't it? Outside seating — good idea! What can I get you to drink?"

"Water and some of your tea, for me. Sienna, would that work for you?" Ryder Stapleton asked politely, his head arched slightly as they awaited her reply.

She nodded; it was the best that she could do.

The waitress left to get their drinks.

Sienna stared at Ryder Stapleton.

"I don't think you're guilty of anything . . . except lying to me," he said.

"Lying to you? How dare you? I saved lives and . . ."

Her voice trailed. Granny K came up to the table, grinning. She perched on the far end of the table and said, "Ryder Stapleton. Detective Stapleton, I should say. What a pleasure to meet you," she said.

Sienna stared at her grandmother's ghost, frowning.

It made no difference. Ryder Stapleton saw her — *saw* her.

"The pleasure is truly mine," Stapleton said. "But I'm afraid —"

"Katherine Murray, sir. Granny K, as the kids called me."

Yep. It was true. He saw her. Ryder Stapleton saw her grandmother — or her grandmother's ghost — and Granny K was just sitting there, delighted to meet him, as casual as if she were still living and just joining them for lunch.

"You were the one who warned Sienna to help the McTavish family in Terrebonne Parish, and the one to have her warn the

Kimball family, right?"

"I was," Granny K said.

"Then can you help me? Who is doing this? How did you know?"

"Well, easy enough with the McTavish family. That house went up in flames. I saw that poor woman and the baby. But this time . . . I saw someone running away from the Kimball house. A shadow, moving like a streak in the night."

"A shadow?"

"Oh, a living person," Granny K said. "But I don't know who it was. I have no idea if it might have been the same person . . . I mean, there was never much evidence from the fire in Terrebonne Parish. But that poor man was later killed in Atlanta. That's suspicious to me."

"Yes, very," Stapleton said, nodding gravely at Granny K.

Well, the good thing, Sienna thought, was that neither one of them seemed to care if she joined in the conversation or not.

"You saw nothing but a shadow?" Stapleton asked her.

Granny K sighed. "Here's the thing. I'm dead. I'm not omniscient. You should know that, Detective Stapleton."

"Please call me Ryder."

"And I'd be proud to be your granny, son,

so you call me Granny K."

"Thank you. How kind," he said politely. Then he fell silent and turned to smile at the waitress who was bringing the tea and water.

"Have you had a chance to study the menu?" their waitress asked. "But then, you know it by heart, honey, don't you?"

Yes, she knew the menu. She ordered a small platter with sushi and sashimi, aware she sounded like a zombie as she tried to be normal.

The waitress was too polite or too busy to notice. But she was certain Ryder Stapleton was smirking.

When the waitress left them again, Sienna finally found her voice. "So now you know, Detective. I see my dead grandmother, who gave me warnings about bad things happening. I can't help you more than that."

"But she may be in danger," Granny K said.

"Granny K," Sienna muttered.

"She's right. But I also believe you can help. I know what happened here. I can investigate people here. I can't do much except read the records regarding something that happened ten years ago, and those records don't go anywhere. A crime of arson — and it went unsolved."

"But that was so long ago," Sienna said.

"The BTK Killer stretched out his murder spree between 1974 and 1991," Granny K said sagely.

Ryder kept looking at Sienna as he nodded.

She shook her head again. "Detective —"

"Just Ryder is fine."

"Okay, *just* Ryder, you think this person started —"

"Person or persons," Ryder interrupted.

"Okay — *person or persons* started a fire intended to kill ten years ago and has done the same thing now?"

"It's a solid possibility. And I also believe this person may be responsible for the corpse we just pulled out of the river."

"I'm sorry. That just seems . . ."

She stopped speaking. She could see the waitress coming with their sushi. They thanked her as she set down their food and asked them if she could get them anything else.

"Just the check," Ryder told her. "That way you don't have to keep coming in and out since we're the only ones out here."

"Aw, that's sweet. Thanks!" Ryder handed her a credit card.

"You don't have to buy me lunch," Sienna murmured.

"It's all right," he said, smiling at the waitress. She smiled back. Sienna realized the detective did have a killer smile. He was a striking man with piercing gray eyes, eased somewhat by the fall of sandy hair over his forehead. He might have been an actor, she thought, or a sports hero. He had that kind of presence about him.

But he wasn't. He was a cop. Out to drive her crazy.

"She's a smart girl, Ryder," Granny K said, shaking her head and sighing softly. "But not smart enough to realize her own danger. I didn't realize that danger myself until . . . well, until after this last fire, and then . . ."

"You've been following me."

"Yes. You knew?"

"I suspected."

"Would you both please stop?" Sienna said. "Why would I be in danger?"

Ryder leaned across the table, and she felt the intensity of his gaze.

"Because, Miss Murray, you might have thwarted a killer. A killer with an agenda. Twice."

He leaned back, still staring at her. "And anyone who is willing to accept a baby and children as collateral damage — condemning them to horrid deaths — wouldn't think

100

twice before swatting an annoyance like you right off the map."

CHAPTER FOUR

Ryder was delighted to have met Granny K. He could only imagine the woman in life: she must have been one hell of a firecracker.

She was also what he needed.

Sienna Murray was stubborn and in denial, and maybe she had a right to be. Ryder knew he was going on an unproven theory, but he'd served as an investigator a long time. He'd witnessed a hell of a lot just in the last half year, let alone the years before.

Most of those who had been born in New Orleans or had moved to the city were good people who loved the music and the food and everything the city had to offer. But there had always been a criminal element; there were drug dealers, those who came from other places, and those who were homegrown. But there was a magic to the city, too, a mystique. The best thing about the city though, in his mind, was that for the most part, people cared about other people, no matter what their ethnicity, color, or creed.

Crimes were domestic sometimes, and other times they were gang- or drug-related. He hadn't been on the force yet when Katrina had hit; he had just started high school. But his dad had been a cop, and he'd learned then that natural disasters brought out the best and the worst in people. He'd seen looting, and he'd seen people risk their own lives to help others. It had been the same when the virus had ravaged the city. He'd seen a woman at a pharmacy insist on paying for supplies for a man ahead of her in line when his credit card didn't work, and he'd seen a man throw down his mask and gloves on the floor before leaving a grocery store. The latter hadn't been a terrible crime, but it had been rude and careless behavior, and he knew the harried, masked clerk would have to leave her protected area to pick up the mask and gloves.

It took all kinds to make the world.

But it took a special kind to attempt to kill, heedless of those caught in the fallout.

And he — or they — had to be stopped.

Thanks to Granny K, he was able to walk Sienna back to the museum. And thanks to her, he knew Sienna intended to head to a gallery opening that night. She was friends with the gallery owner and the artist, who were from her old neighborhood.

With Sienna back in the museum, he stood on the street with Granny K.

"Please. She's stubborn. But don't let anything happen to her," Granny K whispered.

"I'll do my best," he assured her.

"The gallery will be busy tonight. I could just be crazy worried because Sienna . . . is Sienna. But will you be there?"

He pretended to adjust a phone wire in his ear and turned to her with a smile.

"Me? I love art! I love an opening. Yes, I'll be there," he promised.

"Thank you," she whispered.

He nodded and headed down the street toward his car. As he did, his cell phone rang.

It was the ME.

"I have a name for you. Dental records on the corpse gave us a match."

"That was fast! Thank you."

"Fast because our victim was listed as a missing person by his wife ten days ago — and his last known destination was New Orleans," Dr. Philbin told him. "Captain Troy has a copy of the original report, sent to all precincts in NOLA. Seems he'd been working really hard and headed here on his own while his wife was watching the kids. He was a doctor, Ryder."

"A doctor from where?" Ryder asked.

"Charlotte, North Carolina. His name was Dr. Lester Mahoney. Father of two, sixteen-year-old daughter and fourteen-year-old son. His wife thought he'd been working way too hard, and she made him take a few days off. Seems the good doctor loves craps so he headed here for some casino time. But when she tried to reach him after he checked in with her his first night, she couldn't get him. And she knew he'd never go that long without calling her and checking on the kids, so she filed a report. Police in Charlotte are notifying her . . . but I have a feeling this lady will be down here, maybe even already knows he's dead. I wanted to let you know as soon as possible."

"Thank you, Doc. I promise, I will follow through on this," Ryder assured him. He made a mental note to get to the casino himself. Someone there had to have seen the man.

He ended the call and moved quickly to call Captain Troy himself. Troy assured him he would get officers to the casino and the hotel, hoping someone might have seen Dr. Mahoney after he checked in and before he disappeared. While no cell phone had been found on the dead man, with an ID they could summon phone records. They'd get a recent photo of the man in life and scour area bars and restaurants, hoping someone might have seen who he met up with once he left the casino.

Ryder hurried to his car. He wanted to head back to the office and read the report himself.

He had plans for the night.

He had to get to that art opening.

But what the hell was the connection between a fire in NOLA, a long-ago fire in Terrebonne Parish, and a doctor from Charlotte?

"Hi, Sienna!"

Leaving her car and heading toward the house, Sienna saw Whitney and Noah Craton in the front yard of the house. They were playing with a plastic water toy that had gears and levers and showed how water moved and could move machinery.

"Hi!" she said, walking over to join the children. "That looks like a cool toy!"

"Yeah, it's fun — and refreshing," Whitney said sagely.

Noah gave her a smile; he didn't speak. He was too involved with running a little

106

water wheel.

"I saw the cops today," Whitney told her, lowering her voice to something like a whisper. "I helped them draw a picture."

"Oh?"

"Yeah! There was a homeless guy hanging around here a few days before the fire. I told that cool detective I'd seen him, and I helped them draw him!"

"That was good of you, Whitney. I'm sure they were grateful."

"I think so. After, they went to see the granny on the other side." She frowned. "I miss my friends," she said, indicating the burned-out shell of the Kimball home.

"I can imagine. I'm so sorry," Sienna told her.

"That's okay. Mommy says we're lucky. You probably saved our house from catching on fire, too."

Judy Craton came out of the house as they were talking, hurrying over to the kids. She looked at Sienna. "I'm sorry. I should have asked if you minded that we put up this contraption before we did —"

"I think it's great. No problem," Sienna assured her.

Judy gave her a smile that quickly faded.

"The police were here today," she said. "Whitney worked with a sketch artist."

"She told me. I hope it helps."

"And quickly," Judy said. She looked at Sienna then. "Do you think it will help? Do you think they can get whoever did this quickly? I'm sorry, I can't help it. I wish Whitney had never spoken. If someone meant to start a fire that could burn up two kids . . . Well, now I'm worried."

Sienna thought quickly to come up with a true but reassuring reply.

"I think whoever did this had a personal agenda, and it was against either Mr. or Mrs. Kimball. I don't think they'd want to just hurt a child," she said quietly, glad Whitney was again fascinated with the water toy. "And I'm sure she helped. But if you're worried, maybe we can speak to the police about watching the house."

Judy Craton sniffed. "The police are pretty busy most of the time."

Sienna hesitated. "Well . . . we can ask Detective Stapleton, right?"

"Maybe. He was just here, and Whitney told him what she'd seen . . . It might have just been some poor homeless guy. But still . . ."

"I'll talk to him," Sienna said. "See if he can't make us all feel a little better."

"Thank you. That would be great," Judy told her. "I'm not much on guns, but I went out and bought mace and pepper spray, and I make sure to lock the main door — oh! Sienna, you're being careful about that, right? Locking the main door?"

"Always," Sienna assured her. "And if you need me at night, I am right across the hall."

Judy gave her a weak smile and nodded. "Thanks. Please, let me know what Detective Stapleton says."

"I'll call him first thing tomorrow," Sienna promised.

She went into her house. It had been a long day at work — not that she didn't love it — but she'd been playing with the animals as well as working in her office, and a shower was in order.

She headed out at about seven thirty, knowing the show would be open, Thayer and Freddie already greeting guests.

She was lucky to find street parking near Esplanade, and then she just had a few blocks to walk. As she did, she smiled. It was good to see places up and running again. She paused in front of her favorite wig shop.

They were amazingly creative at Fifi Mahony's. Even when she didn't need anything for a party or occasion, she loved looking at the window displays.

But she didn't linger long; she was certain

other friends would be there already.

Freddie's caricatures dominated the windows, and she paused in front before going in, smiling. He had been right.

This was the kind of art she loved.

He was never mean in his work: he had the tendency to emphasize smiles or hairdos, silly things that added to the charm of his chosen subject.

When she went in, smiling and thanking a young woman who swept by with a flute of champagne, she saw a woman pointing to one of Freddie's pieces and speaking with Thayer, before heading to his counter to buy the piece.

Then Freddie, standing not far from the door, came over almost as if he'd been waiting specifically for her.

"You made it!" he said.

"Of course," she told him. "Freddie, I love these!"

"Thank you, my darling!" Freddie said enthusiastically, grinning as Artie joined them, lifting his glass of champagne.

"Hey, that lady over there just bought your caricature of that 1950s movie star. She's in love with it."

"Excellent!" Freddie said. "Thanks."

"And the gang's all here," Artie said, smiling at Sienna. "Morrie and me, Lori, and even our good doc!"

"Are you kidding? Jared Lightfoot left his animals?" Sienna asked.

Artie made a face. "Only because the big boss is holding down the fort."

"Nice," Lori said, coming up to join them. "Can you believe it? Dr. Lightfoot and I in the same place at the same time? I'm so glad he came out. He's toward the back. And a pretty woman who comes to the museum is talking animals with him."

"I didn't know the boss was coming in to the museum," Sienna said. "But I'm happy to hear it. Nice of Byron Mitchell to ensure everyone could come out. That's pretty cool. He's a great boss, for sure."

Artie shrugged. "Byron showed up right after you left today. I was heading out to my car. He is nice as hell. He said he'd heard about this, said we should all take the time to come in. He knows Lori is a Harrison cousin and that you grew up in the same neighborhood. He wanted everyone to have a night off. Even Clara is here with her daughter, son-in-law, and granddaughter. It's wonderful!"

Sienna laughed softly. "That's great, but what is even greater is that this place is crowded to the gills. That's so wonderful, Freddie."

"Even my family came in," Freddie told her, pointing across the room.

Joel and Mary Harrison were there, as Freddie said. They were in conversation with a small group by one of Freddie's political caricatures. Joel, a big man with a headful of graying hair, was enthusiastically talking; Mary — a bit plump — was looking bored. Freddie's younger brother, Sam, was flirting with a blonde, and his younger sister, Lili, was pretending to listen to a long-haired man who was pontificating with grand hand gestures.

"Nice that they all came!" Sienna said.

"It is. And look. Recognize him? Who is that old dude over there?" he asked. "Do you remember him?"

"I have no clue," Lori put in.

"That's because you weren't actually from the old neighborhood," Freddie told her.

Sienna looked over to where Freddie was pointing. "Oh, wow!" she said. "Yes, I remember him. Terry Berger. He was . . . a shrimper and a charter-boat captain back in the day. He lived about a half mile from me. He hasn't changed a bit! He was always a bit crusty. I do remember we were all afraid of him. We knew he'd tell our parents if we stepped out of line."

"Good memory," Freddie said, applauding.

Thayer joined them, grinning. "That old dude still works as a shrimper and a charter captain. Loves to take people on bayou tours, especially when they shut up and listen to him. He says that the *young'uns* these days don't know how to do a bayou up proper."

"Ah, you've been in deep philosophical conversation with the man," Artie said.

Thayer shrugged. "He's buying a piece."

"Really?" Freddie said. "That's great."

"He's pretty sure he was your inspiration for the one piece," Thayer said.

"Well, he was —" Freddie broke off.

Artie wasn't looking at them. He was staring across the room. "There's that guy," he said, before looking over at Sienna. "Are you dating him, Sienna?"

"I'm not dating anyone —" she began.

"Well, you could be dating me," Freddie said, grinning.

"Why ruin a good friendship?" Sienna asked lightly. Freddie was the last person she would ever date. Being the high-school hero had stayed on as part of his personality. He was a flirt, which was fine: women liked him. But he liked women, too, and didn't seem to care too much about which

113

one he was with.

"He's a detective, isn't he? He was at the museum," Artie said.

"He is a detective, and yes, he was at the museum," Sienna said. "He keeps hoping someone might have seen something the night of the fire."

"But nobody did."

She almost mentioned the fact that her neighbors had seen a homeless man wandering in the days before the fire, but then she chose not to. It wasn't that she distrusted any of them, but people said things offhand all the time. While the homeless guy had probably been just that — a person with no home — she didn't want to take any chances with the safety of her neighbors.

Then she remembered she had promised she would mention her neighbors' concerns for their safety to Ryder Stapleton.

Well, here was her chance.

"He thinks you're an arsonist?" Thayer asked.

She shook her head. "No, he just thinks I'll think of something. Or," she glanced at Freddie, smiling, "maybe he likes art. I think I'll go over and talk to him, if you all will excuse me."

"Only if you come back," Freddie said.

"If we need to keep our eyes on detectives," Lori teased, "I don't mind keeping my eyes on that detective. He's . . . What's the word?"

Thayer groaned. "Hot?"

"Oh, Thayer! That is so high school!" Lori said. "Be more eloquent! He's tall, he has presence, great bone structure . . . and body."

"Yeah, she's hot for him," Freddie said.

Lori groaned, rolling her eyes.

Sienna smiled and excused herself. As she approached Ryder Stapleton, he turned to see her coming, offering her a welcoming smile. She had to admit she was becoming more accustomed to him — and not feeling quite so hostile toward him. Lori was right: he had a presence. Strangers in any room would notice him. He somehow compelled respect by just being.

"You're an art critic," she said, coming to his side.

"What's not to like? This is a great, fun likeness of one of our great New Orleans Saints. He's got sports figures, movie stars, and political figures. I noticed he has a few of his sculptures on display, too. And the champagne is good."

"Aren't you working?" she asked him.

"Ah, well, living and breathing is work, in a way, isn't it?"

"Not for most of us. Is there a particular reason you're being an art critic tonight?" she asked him.

"Who is to say that I don't love art?"

"But you are working," she said flatly. "Watching . . . me?"

"I'm not working. Just watching."

Sienna shook her head. "Detective Stapleton, you need to be finding out what business associate might have been after Mr. Kimball. You need to be looking somewhere else. I know the police were at the Craton house, and that Whitney helped them draw a likeness of a homeless man she'd seen in the neighborhood —"

"Whitney is a great kid," he told her.

"Yes, she is. And now that you've made it known she helped the police, you need to make sure she's safe."

"Yes, of course," he said.

"Then do something!"

"I have done something."

"Besides put a target on her."

He smiled. "Not to worry. Your place and the house on the other side are being watched, too."

She frowned. "I didn't see anyone —"

"They're not very good if you see them," Ryder said.

She arched a brow at him. "You're saying

someone is watching the house? Police officers?"

He looked at her and then around the room. "They're being safeguarded," he said.

"Okay, exactly what are you doing here?" she demanded.

"I told you. I really do enjoy an art opening," he said. "But I'm also intrigued. I'm looking forward to meeting your friends."

She inhaled, staring at him incredulously. "My friends? Oh, please! You're putting the two fires — ten years apart — together again?"

"And maybe even a murdered man, burned beyond recognition and thrown in the Mississippi."

"I'm going to walk away from you, and if you come near me, I'm going to have security throw you out."

"No, you're not."

"There is this thing called co-incidence . . ."

"I love art and literature. I was always a fan of Sherlock Holmes. I'm just not a big believer in coincidence."

"You want to meet my friends? Sure, great —" But she fell silent. Clara, their receptionist, was walking up to her all smiles, her granddaughter, eight-year-old Kelsey, in tow.

"This is wonderful! It's so fun to all be out together, celebrating the work of an artist we actually know. So nice of Byron, too, helping Jared come out. And," she added, lowering her voice, though no one could have possibly heard her with the many conversations going on, "he's interacting with a young woman."

"It is nice that Jared is out," Sienna agreed. "Kelsey!" she said, addressing the little girl. "Are you having fun?"

Clara beamed at Ryder Stapleton then. "Detective, even you're here!"

"What can I say? I like funny faces."

Kelsey giggled. "I like the funny faces, too. And they have good stuff to eat."

"Where are my manners?" Clara said to herself. "You know Sienna already, Kelsey, but I want you to meet Detective Stapleton."

"Hi," Kelsey said shyly.

"A pleasure," Ryder said to her. He hunkered down to smile at her. "Which was your favorite funny face?" he asked.

Kelsey grinned and pointed across to one of the caricatures of a popular football player.

"Mine, too," he told her.

Kelsey giggled. Ryder Stapleton had won her over, Sienna thought.

"I've got to get her home. I hope you guys enjoy," Clara said. She waved a hand across the room. Her daughter and son-in-law were waiting. They waved to the others, who waved back.

Clara and Kelsey left, Kelsey watching them as she followed her grandmother.

"So I see you got to know Clara," Sienna murmured.

"She's a very nice woman," Ryder said.

"Have you been looking into who might really have wanted to do this to the Kimball family?" Sienna asked him. "I'm trying to figure out the motivation for a gallery owner, an artist . . . A docent at a museum wouldn't want to hurt anyone."

"Ah, well, motives can be twisted."

Sienna shook her head. "I think you're crazy."

"And I think you're naive."

She let out a sound of frustration but then quickly fell silent. Lori Markham was coming toward them, smiling broadly. "We're going to take off soon. Going to grab some snacks, coffee, drinks. Detective," Lori said to Ryder, "would you like to join us?"

Ryder glanced at Sienna. She thought there was a glint of triumph in that glance.

"Sure. I'd love to. Thank you."

"Meet by the door in ten minutes," Lori

said and whirled off to make her way through the crowd.

"Why don't you just ask them all if you can question them over a Sazerac?" Sienna asked dryly.

"I don't want to question them. I want to get to know them," he said pleasantly. "Excuse me. I'm delighted I'll see you soon, but I have a few people to say goodbye to."

"To question, you mean."

"To get to know," he rephrased.

Then he was gone. She thought about refusing to join the group, but she knew she wasn't going to. Whatever he was up to, she wanted to be there for it.

She noted he managed a few polite words with just about everyone in the gallery, from Terry Berger to Freddie's parents, Mary and Joel.

Norman and Kathy, Thayer's parents, were there, too. They stayed in the background with Thayer for the most part.

She realized, feeling a little bit guilty, the neighborhood — or their small section of it — had all come out except for her parents. She'd talked to them, of course, avoiding any conversation that might make them worry. They'd known about the show — her mom had said they would support Freddie by buying something — but her dad had an all-day meeting and getting into the city for the opening would just be too hard.

She saw Freddie was talking to someone who seemed to have a keen interest in one of his caricatures. Thayer was behind the counter with his folks, but he was speaking with Freddie's family.

Sienna certainly knew them well enough to join them.

Mary looked up with a beaming smile as she saw Sienna, taking a step to give her a hug and then letting her husband, Joel, give Sienna a hug as well. Freddie's siblings waited their turns but grinned at her as they did so.

"Great to see you!" Lili told her. When they'd been young, they'd been close. "I'm so glad you came."

"I wouldn't have missed it," Sienna assured them. "This is really nice. Your family and Lori and me and Thayer's folks, too. And even Terry Berger!"

"Have to support our children!" Mary said.

"Always," Kathy said.

Sienna smiled again. Mary had always been fierce when it came to being a mom. She'd been strict with her kids — and with everyone in the neighborhood if they ventured into her yard. But if an outsider attacked anyone, she was hell with a mop.

Kathy had been a neighborhood mom, too. She had always seemed older and wiser than the other moms, but she and Norman had married late, and Thayer was their only child. He'd been what others called a *last-minute child,* since Kathy's first husband had died in the military, and she hadn't remarried until she was forty. They had taken a chance, but they'd been lucky, and Thayer had been a great son. She was seventysomething now, Sienna thought, but slim and straight, well-dressed, and almost elegant.

Thayer's parents doted on him, sometimes so much so he would roll his eyes, breathe for patience, and remember they drove him crazy because they loved him.

"Of course, Freddie's art . . . Well, it seems I was wrong. He's going to do okay with it," Joel said.

"Some of his pieces are amazing!" Norman Boudreaux said. He was in his mideighties, but time had been good to him. He had beautiful gray hair that enhanced friendly, bright blue eyes. He was a big man, just as Thayer was, but he had kept himself fit, and his size was more muscle than fat.

"Oh, Dad! Not everyone can be a chip off the old block," Lili told him. Lili was an attractive woman, tall and, if anything, too thin, the opposite of her mom. She'd been awkward in high school, but she'd followed her father's wishes. Sienna had heard that she was doing extremely well as a stockbroker, even from Terrebonne Parish. Sam had gone into computers, though she wondered if his dad was happy with that. He created video games.

"Still loving the museum?" Sam asked Sienna. "I know Lori loves it — and Dr. Lightfoot! He seems like a great guy. I got to spend some time talking with him tonight."

"Me, too, but we managed to slip away," Lili said. "Lori told us that his life is his animals. She seemed excited he was enjoying time with human beings."

"Yes, it's nice to see him out," Sienna said. She noted Ryder Stapleton was speaking with her old neighbor, the shrimper.

Terry Berger didn't seem to have changed at all: he'd been older, thin, gray-haired, and grizzled when they'd been kids. He looked good, though, dressed in trousers and a fawn jacket rather than his usual well-worn jeans and T-shirts.

"Old Terry," Mary said. "Gruff, but a good old guy. He's always been happy with shrimp!"

"Hey, come on," Joel argued jokingly. "He

takes people out in the bayou on his boat, and he's equally fond of crawfish!"

"That's an interesting young man," Kathy said, nodding toward Ryder. "Thayer said he's some kind of detective."

"Right. I met him after the recent fire by my place," Sienna said uncomfortably.

"Well, he may be a detective, but he knows his art," Norman said. "He chatted with us for a while. I was impressed. You know, you kind of think of cops as muscle people, rough and hardy —"

"Like football players, Dad?" Thayer asked dryly.

"Yeah, well, football players, cops . . . But that guy, light, easy to talk to. Pretty cool."

"That probably helps him," Mary said. "Maybe he was really questioning us all tonight!" she added.

Kathy laughed. "In truth, the man was speaking with Norman most of the time about various artists. Seems both he and Norman love the artist Rodrigue, and the *Blue Dog* series of work."

"It's a shame the fellow has passed," Norman said. "Now I love my *Blue Dog* works more than ever."

Sienna saw that ten minutes were up and Ryder Stapleton was headed toward the door along with Lori. The two were laughing together.

"I guess I'm leaving. It's great to see you all," Sienna said.

"Hello and goodbye!" Kathy teased.

"The group from work and I are grabbing a bite to eat. Anyone is welcome to join us."

"Hey, don't go stealing Freddie's and my dinner party," Thayer said from behind his sales counter.

Mary laughed. "Thanks, sweetie," she told Sienna. "We're staying until the bitter end."

"Bitter end," Thayer protested. "*Beautiful* end!"

"Of course!" Sienna said, and waving, she headed to the door. Lori apparently didn't care her aunt and uncle and cousins wouldn't be joining them. She was going to leave with her work crowd.

"Am I horrible?" she asked Sienna softly as Sienna joined the group gathering just outside the door.

"Um, no, you mean —"

"I mean, I love my aunt and uncle and cousins, but . . . we have Jared out tonight!"

"Yes. Looks like he's joining us solo," Sienna said. She twisted around to see who was congregating by the door: Jared, Morrie, Artie, and Ryder Stapleton.

The place they wanted to go was one block up on Bourbon Street and one block closer to Esplanade, an easy walk.

And it wasn't what Sienna had expected.

Ryder was between Lori and Jared as they moved at a leisurely pace to the late-night bar and restaurant.

Sienna knew and liked the place they were going. While it was on Bourbon, it was farther down and didn't tend to be as crazy as some other places. The owner was local and owned only the one establishment. The building was old and reminded her of Lafitte's, with its old wood and big fireplace and mantel, and seating that wasn't shoved together.

She'd been certain Ryder Stapleton would find a seat next to hers.

He didn't.

After politely pulling Lori's back for her, he sat in a chair that was beside her and to the other side of Artie. Morrie was next to Artie, and Sienna was next to Morrie, with Jared winding up on her other side.

They ordered appetizers and desserts and drinks. Sienna noted Ryder Stapleton ordered coffee.

Because he was working.

Always working.

Observing.

For a while, they all listened to Jared, who was extolling the virtues of his bear cub.

Lori piped in about care for the other animals, telling Ryder they were so careful about how they kept their petting zoo and rescue. If an animal could be let back out into the wild, they tried to limit human contact, not wanting to make the transition difficult for the creature. When an animal would never survive in the wild, they worked to get all the employees involved so the animal would become accustomed to human contact.

They talked about Freddie's art.

"Oh!" Artie said suddenly. "We should have asked Mr. Berger if he wanted to join us."

"If anything, he's probably going to join Thayer and Freddie and Freddie's family when they close up the gallery for the night," Lori said. "The older generation knew him a lot better than we did."

"Well, it was nice to see him there," Artie said.

Appetizers arrived and were passed around. The desserts appeared: three different kinds of bread pudding and Key lime pie. Then Lori looked at Jared and said, "I'm going to call it a night. Byron might be a great boss, but I work for a tyrant of a manager."

She was teasing, of course. Jared didn't

realize it at first. He looked at her, puzzled.

"Jared," Sienna said, touching his arm lightly, "it's a joke."

"Seriously!" Lori said. "Just a joke. You're an amazing boss."

"Oh, good. Thank you. You scared me! And in truth, everyone manages themselves. I'm around for problems and scheduling."

They all laughed, but Jared rose, too. "Hey, we need to get the check."

He started to reach for his wallet and the others quickly protested, but Jared shook his head. "Byron wanted his people out together tonight. He's picking up the tab."

"I'm not one of his people," Ryder reminded him.

Jared shrugged. "My boss isn't going to resent you having a cup of coffee, a few shrimp, and a few bites of bread pudding. Let me keep it easy. I hate making servers split up checks."

"Well, I wouldn't have split it up, I would have picked it up," Ryder said.

"Byron is rich. I'm sure he'll be fine with it," Sienna said, rising herself. "Tomorrow, as we all know, is another day. I think we're all ready."

They were. They talked about where their cars were; Artie was going to walk Sienna to hers. Ryder Stapleton didn't protest. He said he'd make sure Lori got to her car okay.

Sienna was on her way down Canal toward her home in the Garden District when she realized she was being followed. For a moment, she felt a ripple of fear.

But then she knew.

Ryder Stapleton was following her home.

He had to find street parking, and she thought about running in and locking the door before he could get to her.

But she waited.

It was late. The street was quiet. She looked around, wondering what he meant about someone guarding her and her neighbors.

She leaned against her car and waited for him, watching him warily as he pulled up to her.

"I don't see anyone," she said.

"No, you don't," he told her. "And once you're in, it's not likely you'll see me."

"What?"

"I'm on now," he told her softly.

"And you're going to stand out here to see that people are protected?"

"I won't be standing."

She let out a sound of aggravation and headed to the door. She hesitated and stared at the lock. It was a bolt system, but it wasn't a round knob that might have marred the aesthetics of the old house; it was a long handle that pulled the door clear once the lock had been turned.

Is there a new scratch on it?

Ridiculous and paranoid. He was doing that to her.

She opened the door and turned to him. "You're going on guard duty *now*? How will you be an effective police officer in the morning?"

He smiled. "As soon as you're at work, I'll head home for some sleep. I don't need much."

"Of course you don't," she said. "Are you coming in? Are you going to check out my place?"

"I don't see your grandmother around, so it would be a good idea."

She realized she hadn't seen Granny K all night. But it wasn't all that surprising.

"Not to worry," she said dryly. "She told me from the first she intended to maintain a social life. She's somewhere being social, I guess."

"Or somewhere . . . observing," he said, smiling. "She's something. I wish I had known her in life."

"She was always wonderful," Sienna murmured. "So okay, come in. Look around."

He did. He went through the parlor and

kitchen and dining area, checking all windows before he went upstairs and checked under beds and in closets and everywhere anyone might conceivably try to hide.

When he was satisfied, she followed him back to the parlor, disturbed to discover she was glad he was so thorough, and bizarrely wishing he'd been closer to her at dinner. He was an intriguing man. His looks were striking. He'd also been comfortable with her friends and seemed to be gentle with children.

She didn't want to like him.

She didn't like him. No. She couldn't like him. Not when he was using her to probe into the lives of others and seemed certain she, or someone she knew, was part of a conspiracy.

But she was sexually attracted to him.

She didn't think before she spoke.

"Look, you don't have to stand in the front yard —"

"I won't be standing in the front yard," he assured her.

"You're welcome to stay in the parlor. I can bring down sheets and blankets, and while that sofa doesn't come out as a full bed, it's really cozy."

"The sofa would be fine," he said. "But I need to speak with some people, and there's a second house I need to be watching as well. I'll have other people on it, too, of course. It won't be just us."

"You're bringing in . . . someone else?"

"I'm joining the FBI, remember? A special unit of the FBI. I worked two cases here with them recently —"

"Oh, lord! The Axeman's Protégé and the Display Artist or whatever?"

"They're exceptional," he said with admiration. "Anyway, one Krewe member is . . ."

"Coming down?" she asked.

He shook his head. "He's here," he said softly. "They know New Orleans and the surrounding areas. Almost as well as I do," he added dryly. "Ah, they may say more. Anyway, the best law-enforcement agencies will be looking out for these houses. I wouldn't put Grace or Whitney in danger for the world."

"But you did," she reminded him.

"Only if someone knows . . . and what would make you think that they know? You haven't told anyone, have you?" he asked politely.

"Let me lock you out," she told him.

"As you wish."

He went through the door on her side of the house and then the front door. He still seemed amused; she was torn.

He stepped outside. "Let me hear the bolt slide," he said.

She slid the bolt. Then as torn, as bitter, and as drawn as she felt, she couldn't help herself from calling out, "I hope it rains!"

CHAPTER FIVE

Ryder moved his car down the street, finding a place by a giant magnolia tree where he could sit in the driver's seat and have a clear view of the burned-out shell of the Kimball place and the houses to either side.

But first he leaned against the hood, waiting, glad to see Fin Stirling as he headed across the street to him.

They greeted one another with a quick embrace.

"Thanks for coming," Ryder told him. He'd known Fin had been out watching the street that night, and the local office of the FBI was on call for staffing along with the police department. Because watching over someone for contributing to a sketch on a possible witness to an event wasn't considered high priority when other crimes might riddle the city, Ryder had called in all the favors that he could.

"Hey, you'll be a Krewe agent soon

enough," Fin told him. "Jackson Crow, our great field supervisor, and Adam Harrison, our great director, are both huge believers in Krewe helping their own whenever called."

Fin had been an exceptional agent to work with, and beyond that, he had been key in helping Ryder accept what he saw when he had realized he could see the dead.

The Krewe was an amazing entity.

"And technically," Fin continued, "Adam has seen to it you're already listed as a *consultant* with the Krewe. He likes to use that term to get people quickly on the team when necessary." He hesitated, studying Ryder. "Have to say, though, this has been a tough spell for you. The Axeman imitator, the Display murders, and now a firebug. But I'll see you at your office tomorrow before we head out to the streets. I want to see everything you have."

"That's a plan. And those last cases, well, they became Krewe cases, so there you have it," Ryder protested.

"All solved through working with a damned good detective."

"I'll take that," Ryder said, grinning. "Anyway —"

"Nothing so far tonight. No one came near either of the houses. I don't think

135

they've published the police artist's sketch yet, have they?"

"It's going out tomorrow with a caption that police are looking for him just to help with their investigation. There's not going to be mention he's under suspicion for setting the blaze."

"That sounds best." Fin studied Ryder again. "You're really convinced the blazes ten years apart might be related?"

"I know. It sounds crazy. I can't help but think there's an underlying agenda behind what has happened. Not a crazed serial killer, but someone with a real agenda. I don't think it's jealousy, love, hate, or revenge. I can't find anything to suggest such a motive. But years ago, Mr. McTavish and his family survived the fire, then he was killed a few years later in Atlanta by a hit-and-run driver. I don't think the killer cares he didn't kill the wife and kids. They weren't the targets. And that's why I feel like I need a few of us. I want to follow Kimball and see if anyone is following him. And we have a body pulled out of the Mississippi, burned and dumped. We did get an ID on him, and I'll be speaking with his widow when she makes it down here." He hesitated. "Fin, could you do another hour or so? I know Troy sent good officers to the casino, but I want to head there myself and see if I can't find someone who might know something about the dead man found floating in the river."

"I can be here as long as you like," Fin confirmed.

Ryder thanked him.

"Hitting the craps tables?" Fin asked.

"Something like that." Officers had already spoken with the craps dealers and personnel, and several had remembered the man.

But he hadn't mentioned anything about anyone he might be meeting or anyplace he might be going. Maybe Dr. Mahoney had said something to someone that hadn't seemed significant that might mean . . . something.

Ryder left Fin and headed straight to the casino. He had a picture of Lester Mahoney — not from the morgue, but in life — on his phone.

He quickly discovered, by checking with security first, that footage had been pulled, and the last anyone had seen of the man, he was heading out to find a spot still open for some food in the middle of the night.

He knew the officers would have been diligent, and he wasn't sure what he'd expected to get here. But then he did, talking to one of the cocktail waitresses, who told him she'd waited on the doctor several times. "A nice man, big tipper. Even on free drinks. We wound up chatting. He showed me pictures of his wife and kids."

"You know his body was found, right?"

She nodded grimly.

"We know he played craps until very late and then went out looking for food. Did he ever say anything about knowing people here or looking to meet up with a friend?"

"Oh, sure, yeah! Said he was involved in some research and hoped to meet up with the people working a different angle of it." She frowned for a minute. "Oh! He got a phone call once when I was bringing him a beer. In fact, it was that night. He'd already left the craps table and was just sitting at a machine. I think he was looking something up on his phone when it rang. He seemed aggravated, said something like, 'They just don't stop, do they? You'd think the world would be grateful! Nothing is going to change me!' Then he saw I was there and thanked me. Then he left. Everyone here has been whispering about the man, and I know they traced his movement via our cameras, but . . . I didn't think his being annoyed meant anything. Maybe I should have spoken up."

"I'm sure you hear all kinds of things here. You did nothing wrong. But thank you," Ryder told her. She hadn't really given him anything solid, but he felt he was right. Dr. Mahoney had been doing something someone didn't want him doing. And he'd left the casino and met up with that person somewhere out of camera range.

He headed back to Sienna's street. He had to take over from Fin.

He told Fin what he'd learned from the cocktail waitress.

"So, he did leave the casino and meet up with his killer right here in NOLA."

"I can't go further than that right now. Thank you again. I'm on. Get some rest," Ryder told him.

"All right." Fin glanced at his watch. "I'll go catch some sleep. You have two local agents on tomorrow morning by six. Don't forget to sleep, too. We all have to remember we're not worth much if we don't fit that sleep thing in there."

Ryder nodded and thanked him again. With a wave, Fin headed down the street to his car, ready to call it a night.

Ryder slid into the driver's seat of his car and leaned back. He had a great view of both houses.

All he had to do was stay awake.

And he did. Through the night, he kept a sharp lookout while running the facts of the case through his mind over and over.

He thought about Sienna's group of friends and coworkers. Most of them had been very young ten years ago. Too young to have wanted to burn down a house with a family in it and then discover a way to get to Atlanta with a car to kill McTavish after he hadn't died in the fire.

Now another one. And a dead, burned man in the river.

There was a connection.

He was convinced.

He had to find out what it was.

That morning, as Sienna left for work, the wrecking crews were out next door.

There was a policeman in uniform watching the proceedings, arms crossed over his chest, sunglasses in place.

She waved as she went to her car. He waved in return.

Ryder Stapleton, she imagined, had gone. She winced, remembering she'd offered him her sofa. She had wanted him to stay. She still felt at odds with him, but she was glad he had really seemed to care.

"He was out here all night."

She jumped. By now, she should expect to

see Granny K at any given moment, but her grandmother never seemed to mind startling her.

She crawled into the car ahead of Sienna, smiling at her.

"I'm going to pop out at Rampart Street and stroll the Quarter to see some friends," Granny K told her.

"You go where you want when you want so —"

"Sure. But it's nice to drive with you, love. And I am impressed. Do you know, with his experience and rank, there's no reason that nice, young detective has to be sitting outside all night by himself? I think he cares."

"Well, his wanting a sketch of a homeless man might cause danger for Grace and Whitney."

"Yes, there's always danger in helping the police, but they're good people. You help so other people don't wind up hurt or killed. You may feel he put them in danger, but he's willing to work to make sure they stay safe."

Sienna sighed and kept her eyes on the road.

"He's not just good-looking, you know," Granny K said. "He's solid, stable, determined, rugged . . . and yet kind. Truly strong men are kind and generous, you know."

"Granny K!"

"He likes you."

"Leave it alone."

"Again, you could do worse. You have done worse!"

Sienna groaned aloud. "Seriously?"

"Oh, yes, seriously!"

"Granny K, if he's right, there's someone awful out there who will do more terrible things to people. If there's any way I can help him, I will. But —"

"The more I listen to him and observe him, the smarter I think he is. Well, for one, he sees the dead."

"I have a feeling the ability might be genetic, like an unusual color of eyes or strange toes or the like, Granny K. Not sure it has to do with being smart."

"Maybe, maybe not. All right, he has *instincts,* then."

"Do you really want to walk around the French Quarter or just torment me?" Sienna asked.

"Good lord, lass, someone must torment you. A beautiful thing is looking you straight in the face, and you're going to let it all just slip through your fingers."

"We're not dating!"

"You should be."

"Okay, Granny, the man has not asked me on a date. Does that make you happy?"

"Of course not! He needs to ask you on a date, and you need to say yes."

"Don't you dare suggest it to him."

"Never. I promised you I'd never interfere and, certainly, never be around when . . . Well, I will never be too close when I shouldn't be. I solemnly swear that."

Sienna made a turn off Rampart and stopped the car.

"Is here good?" she asked her grand-mother's ghost, pulling to the curb.

"Lovely, lass."

She stepped out of the car to allow her grandmother to exit from the driver's side. Granny K was perfectly capable of getting out on her own, but she often complained that doing so was difficult and wearisome, while also explaining she was a talented ghost. Sienna should definitely appreciate the fact she had mastered pushing the brew button on the coffee machine.

"See you later," Sienna told her.

"You be careful, dear, you hear me?" Granny K said.

"I promise."

"And date or no date, hang around with

the tough guy as much as possible. Promise?"

"Sure."

She refrained from telling Granny K she had offered her sofa to the man, and he'd rejected the idea. Which, of course, still left her feeling awkward and uncomfortable.

She needed to forget it.

Sienna slid back behind the wheel, ready to move on. But her grandmother remained next to the driver's-side window, looking at her.

"What?" Sienna asked. "Granny K, I love you. I love seeing you, I love that you care and that you help people, but . . . ."

"You don't see it."

"See what?"

"What that smart detective sees. That something long-range and determined is going on."

"Granny —"

"You talked to him about your neighbors. You're smart enough to be worried for them."

"I'm careful. And I'm going straight into work now. And I'm sure I'll see Detective Stapleton later. Okay? I promise you, nobody at my work is in on this. They're not even remotely associated —"

"Lori Markham is related to the Harrison family."

"And I'm to think Lori is evil because of that?"

"No. You're to stay safe in crowds."

"Well, there's no crowd in my office, but I will do my best. I promise."

Granny K stepped back at last, and Sienna drove to work.

Clara greeted her with a smile when she came in. "What a lovely show that was last night! I'm so sorry I couldn't join you guys afterward. But I'd made plans with my family, so —"

"Clara, you see us all day, every day, and we do get out. When you're with your family, enjoy your family. Kelsey just gets cuter and cuter, by the way!"

"Aw, thanks. I think so. But I'm biased."

"As you should be," Sienna affirmed. "I guess I'll head out back and check with Jared and Lori, then I'll be in my office." She paused for a minute. "It's Saturday, isn't it?"

"It is, dear."

"Thanks. Losing track of things lately," Sienna said.

She first headed to her office to toss her bag and went through the hands-on exhibits and toward the wax-tableaux area. She went by several scenes depicting history and founding fathers, and then down Murderers' Row.

The characters were good. Too good.

The tableau featuring the original Axeman of New Orleans, whose killing spree went from May of 1918 to October of 1919, featured a dark, cloaked, and masked figure carrying a massive weapon. He stood above a bloodied bed with the figure upon it mercifully hidden in the pile of red sheets.

Another tableau featured a more recent crime, in gruesome detail. Zachary Bowen took his own life in 2006 but had left a suicide note that had led police to his girlfriend, Addie Hall. He had strangled and dismembered her, leaving her head, hands, limbs, and feet in various pots and cookware.

Thankfully, most of the scenes pictured days long gone and weren't quite so graphic.

Not that a scene about a horrific and bloody stabbing was any better.

In 1863, the Union held the city, but Southern prostitutes did well. One prostitute had a handsome brothel and a boyfriend — Treville Sykes. Later, she fell out of love with him and in love with someone else. But Sykes proved to be annoying to her, and she threatened to kill him. Instead, he killed her, stabbing her again and again.

"Ugh!" Sienna muttered aloud, reminding herself that if she didn't look at the figures, they wouldn't look at her.

She wouldn't imagine they moved, either.

"Dumb," she said to herself. There was another way out to the petting zoo and the rescue area. Byron had been adamant children were not to come through Murderers' Row. But the children's entrance was down the long hall from the entrance and through the area that held a number of the waterworks where the kids played. She seldom took it; it meant a longer walk and more time. But since she was beginning to feel a bit on edge, the longer walk sounded appealing.

The last of the tableaux featured the so-called vampire brothers of New Orleans, John and Wayne Carter. The brothers had led regular lives, day jobs in labor, and behaved quite normally — most of the time. Police knew nothing about them until a young woman escaped from them. The men had been holding her captive to drink her blood. Her wrists were cut, she was in terrible shape, and the police went to the brothers' home. Four people remained alive, tied to chairs. Fourteen were found dead. Of course, the brothers were arrested. The

147

story went that they were two average-sized men, but it took dozens of police officers to hold them down. And when they were executed and interred, their bodies disappeared. Legends abounded that the Carter brothers still roamed the streets of the city, abducting victims to slowly drain them of their blood. In the tableau, the brothers were seated, both dining on the wrists of beautiful young women, while others lay about the room, dead or dying.

"Yeah," she said aloud, "I think I have to start taking the kids' entrance."

"Sienna?"

She nearly jumped a mile high when she heard her name said with worry and concern.

The light from outside was blinding as she looked up. It was just Jared Lightfoot, wearing his white veterinarian's cloak and a confused frown.

"Jared! Doc, I'm sorry, I —"

"Oh!" he said. Then he smiled. "These guys are getting to you? You know, Byron told me once he hadn't been sure when he'd made this hall lead out, but he thinks it might have been his best idea ever. Wax figures can creep people out, but most of the time, animals make people happy. So people are freaked out . . . and then relieved.

And then if you head back out to exit the museum this way, you get creeped out, and then you get history!"

"And so we have the children's-wing exit," Sienna said. "I was just coming back to check on you. Anything needed? Everything all right?"

He laughed softly. "I was just coming in to report all is well. We haven't had any call for a rescue. Our little cub is doing great, and the donkey, goats, miniature horses, and sheep have all been given their exams, and they're in good shape."

"That's great. Thanks, Doc," Sienna said. "I've finished up a report for our members on our little bear cub. It's going out today."

"I'm still on the fence where he's concerned. I'm hoping he's going to be well." He hesitated and shrugged. "I'm not keen on keeping an animal that should be in the wild, not unless we absolutely have to. But time will tell."

"Thanks. We all bow to your wisdom."

Light was coming in from outside, and Sienna was glad. Of course, wax figures didn't seem quite so horrible when there was a live human being in front of her and sun poured in from outside.

"Okay," he said. "I'm taking a break for a bit. Lori is here, if anything is needed. I'm going to have coffee and pancakes."

"Sounds like a plan," she told him.

Sienna made her way out of Murderers' Row and back toward her office.

She opened her computer and tried to concentrate on the finishing touches on the design of their latest newsletter. She was thus engaged when Morrie poked his head into her office.

"Hey, kiddo."

"Hey, Morrie. Everything all right?"

"Yep, fine. I was just checking in. It's Artie's Saturday off, and I just wanted you to know we have a special tour group going through around noon, so if you're looking for me . . ."

Sienna laughed. "We're just not that big. If I needed you, I'd find you."

He nodded and smiled. "Hey, kid, are you ever going to take a Saturday off? Or any day for that matter?"

Sienna shrugged. "Yeah, when I need to, I will. I don't stay all the time. I just check in a lot of days."

"All right, but remember, *all work and no play* . . ."

"None of us feel this place is really work, anyway," Sienna said.

"True," Morrie agreed. "We do work for a great boss. That was nice of him to insist

Doc go out with the rest of us last night. And I saw the man actually flirting!"

"I know. Cool, wasn't it?"

"Yep. So, okay, I'm here if you need me."

"Good to know."

He left, and Sienna returned to her newsletter.

Her mind wandered, and she wondered what Ryder Stapleton was doing.

Without thinking, she switched to news online, just to catch up on the day.

And there, first up on a local news site, was a sketch.

It was of a ragged-looking man with shaggy hair and whiskers, slim, and wearing worn clothing. The whiskers were the kind that covered a great deal of his face; it was hard to see much else. The structure of the face couldn't be seen, and the whiskers even obstructed the nose.

The article went on to say the police were looking for the man as a possible witness to a crime in the city.

It didn't mention anyone's name in connection with the sketch.

It didn't even mention the fire.

Beneath, there was a short article on Freddie's art opening.

Nice.

Neither article offered much.

She remembered she was doing her own newsletter and went back to work.

She wondered if she had passed the man while driving in her neighborhood, but she knew she hadn't.

Even if many agencies considered it wiser to support foundations than give money directly to the homeless because they might just use it for drugs or alcohol, she was a sucker for someone down on their luck. She kept bills just for that purpose, and for the musicians and buskers who played in the city, too. Actually, it was easy to go through a lot of money just contributing to acts along Bourbon or Royal Streets.

But this man wasn't familiar. She would have remembered him. She would have given him something.

There was something about him that just wasn't right.

Ryder met with Martin Kimball at a small coffee shop near his office.

While Kimball was grateful for the temporary housing for himself and his family, he had insisted he had to get back to work. When Ryder spoke with him on the phone about meeting, Kimball had assured him the spot he chose for coffee and lunch was just down the street from his office in the

CBD, or Central Business District. This meant plenty of people, and Kimball seriously doubted anyone was going to walk up and set fire to him.

Ryder sighed inwardly at the flippant way Kimball seemed to think about the danger to himself, but he decided he'd see the man in person and tell him about McTavish then. And like many others, he might think an incident ten years ago had nothing to do with him.

Ryder wasn't sure why he was so convinced. But he wanted the meeting with Kimball, because after, he'd be meeting with the widow of the man who had been nothing but a charred corpse by the time he'd been pulled from the Mississippi.

The coffee shop was a nice, clean place at the bottom of the tall buildings on Poydras in the CBD. Kimball arrived just a few minutes after Ryder and ordered himself a breakfast plate with salmon and a bagel.

"You're just having coffee, Detective? You should be keeping up your strength," Kimball told him.

"I've eaten. Thanks. Mr. Kimball, I've asked to speak with you again because I need you to think about any possible enemies you might have, and also to remind you to be extremely careful as we continue to investigate."

Kimball almost had a forkful of food to his mouth. He paused and then ate it.

"Detective, I'm just a regular guy who got lucky with a lovely wife and beautiful children. Never in my life have I been a threat to anyone. I didn't play sports, and I didn't compete on a debate team . . . I'm not a competitive man. In fact, I like working with others."

"Mr. Kimball, I'm going to tell you about an event that may or may not mean anything to you," Ryder said. "Approximately ten years ago, there was a fire just like yours in Terrebonne Parish. The house was broken into late at night and a mixture of gasoline and ethyl ether was used as an accelerant. The fire was purposely set. The family escaped, but the father — who also worked in the technical field — was later killed by a hit-and-run driver in Atlanta, where he was attending a tech convention."

To Ryder's surprise, the man set his fork down.

"*Mc* or *Mac* something," Kimball muttered.

"Pardon?"

"I was at that convention, and there was an announcement on the last day that we'd lost one of our own — killed on one of the

Peachtree-named streets by a hit-and-run driver."

"His name was McTavish."

"His house was set on fire, too?"

Ryder nodded. Kimball shook his head again. "That was all ten years ago. Honestly, Detective Stapleton, I don't mean to be difficult in any way. But I think you've just got a firebug on your hands. I mean, the accelerant for one. Gasoline or a mixture of gasoline and ethyl ether. Anyone can get either. I mean, sure, this is some sick puppy, ready to burn up little children, but . . ."

"As you noted, McTavish was in tech, as are you. We've also discovered the body of a man. He was pulled out of the Mississippi, burned as if someone had left him on a rotisserie. His name was Dr. Lester Mahoney, and he was from North Carolina but had come to New Orleans for a little R and R."

Kimball shook his head. "A doctor, not a tech man. A medical doctor?"

"A medical doctor."

"A computer nerd and a doctor are miles apart," Kimball said.

"Mr. Kimball, what are you working on?" Ryder asked.

"I can't give you details — you know that. We all sign agreements not to share anything

155

about our work. You must know the tech industry is one that involves billions of dollars."

"I don't want details. I just need to know if your work involves the financial field in any way, banking, the stock market, anything like that?"

Kimball seemed relieved. "No. Um . . . I mean, I'm not sure I can say anything at all, but no. Not money. Well, everything is money, right? But I'm not working on any kind of software that would be used in a bank or by a stockbroker. I'd like to help, but, Detective, it's crazy to think I was targeted." He lowered his voice. "What I'm working on is medical, okay?"

"So there is a connection, given a doctor was murdered," Ryder said.

"Um, yes, but still . . ."

"You don't know of anyone you're competing with?"

"We're always competing. Anyone in the tech field is competing."

"But you don't know of anyone in particular who might be after your research?" Ryder asked. "Do you know of an individual who is jealous of your work, or a group that might be after your work?"

Kimball leaned back, shaking his head. "Detective, if there was anyone after my research, they'd hopefully be smarter than sneaking into a house and using something as common as gasoline to accelerate a fire."

"Maybe this way it looks like random violence."

"Or maybe it looks like random violence because it is random violence."

"Mr. Kimball, I'm asking you to think of anything, anything at all, that might be suspicious as far as your work dealings go, that might be related here in any way. I'm asking you to watch out for yourself. We haven't found anything, except for a trail of death and destruction. I don't want you to be part of that trail."

"I'm careful. I'm out with tons of people during the day. My work has security. When we find a place to live, I promise you, it will have security, too, the best alarm system I can find."

"Even the best alarm system can be beaten. Trust me, I'm not arguing you out of it. An alarm system is a good thing. But the best way to beat this is to find out who did it," Ryder said.

"What about the homeless man? I saw the sketch on the news today. Could he have done it?"

"We're trying to find him to question him. Maybe he saw something. I still believe you were targeted. And anything you can think of might help."

"I will think, I promise." He hesitated. "My wife is a schoolteacher. A grade-school kid didn't do this, but maybe a parent, angry with her method of teaching?"

"Has she ever had any complaints?"

"No, but people can be strange."

"Yes, they can." Ryder shook his head. "I doubt this has to do with your wife. Ten years ago, it was Mr. McTavish who was killed in Atlanta. His wife and child are still alive."

Kimball nodded. He'd finished his food, and he looked at Ryder uncomfortably.

"Look, Detective, I know you're working this hard. And I'm grateful. But I just don't think this is anything more than a coincidence."

"You said yourself the field you're in is highly competitive."

"Yes, but . . . McTavish and I were in different areas of the field."

"I understand that. I don't have answers yet, but I do truly believe you were targeted. You need to be careful."

"Thank you. I will be. And I've got to get back."

"Sure thing."

Kimball rose and drummed his fingers on

the table for a minute. "No dark alleys, I swear."

"Thank you."

He started to walk away but came back. "My wife and kids . . ."

"There's an officer at the hotel at all times. As long as they're not venturing out yet, they're in good hands. And I don't think they're targets."

"But you could be wrong."

"That's why police are watching the hotel."

Kimball nodded. "Thanks."

Ryder watched him head out the door and down the street, then rose and followed him quickly.

He kept a half-block distance between them. They weren't far from Kimball's building, and Ryder just wanted to see he reached it.

They'd gone about a block when Ryder first noticed the man in the dark jacket and wide-brimmed hat. At first, he just looked like anyone in the CBD, someone hurrying to or from a meeting.

But he moved closer and closer to Kimball, not with long strides, but by quickening his pace and almost pushing a woman out of his way.

So much for subterfuge.

Ryder burst into a run, briefly excusing himself to people, then just shouting, "Get out of the way!" as he saw the man draw a knife from his jacket, a knife with a solid six-inch blade.

Kimball didn't turn at first, but as Ryder gained on his would-be attacker, the attacker heard him.

He had the presence of mind to draw his hat low as he looked back.

Then he pocketed the knife and shoved past Kimball.

"Hey, buddy, what the hell?" Kimball began.

Then he saw the man racing down the street and noticed Ryder hot on his trail. Color drained from his face.

There was no time to say so much as a word to him.

Ryder ran; the man was ahead of him. Again he looked back, but the hat concealed everything but his lower jaw.

The man ran harder as he saw Ryder gaining on him, and he caught a woman by the shoulders, throwing her into Ryder's path.

She screamed, slammed into Ryder, and fell at his feet.

He paused long enough to help her up, identify himself as a cop, look into her terrified eyes, and ask if she was all right.

She nodded, and he hurried around her, hard in pursuit.

By then, his subject had made his way to Canal Street. He ran out into the road, dodging cars, heedless of them as stunned and irate drivers slammed on their brakes.

A streetcar was coming.

The man ran to the tracks and looked back briefly. Ryder was almost on him.

He used his old ploy, this time grabbing a little boy, wrenching him from his mother's handhold and throwing him down on the tracks.

And there was no choice. The mother screamed in panic. Ryder reached for the boy, knowing there was no way the driver could stop in time.

He swept the kid up and leaped off the tracks just in time.

And when he got the kid to safety, the tram managed to stop. He thrust the panicked child back into his mother's arms and tore around the streetcar, but it was too late. The man was no longer in sight; he could have headed down Chartres, Royal, or Bourbon. He could have rushed into a hotel. He could have gone in a shop . . .

He pulled out his phone to call for backup, but he knew it would do no good.

His suspect had changed by now. The

161

jacket would be gone, discarded somewhere out of sight. The hat, too. And the person wouldn't be recognizable among those out on the street. The man Ryder had been chasing could even be the kid whistling as he walked by a popular breakfast spot on Royal Street.

He swore to himself, frustrated. He'd been so close, and now he had nothing. He put a call through to Captain Troy. He described the items he was sure had been discarded and asked that patrols search for them. He also asked that an officer be discreetly assigned to Kimball. He worried about the man, even working alone in a lab, but when protected research was involved, all they could do was monitor who went in and out.

Investigating coworkers might yield information. He decided he'd have Fin Stirling get the Krewe offices working on that; they were able to obtain much more information than local authorities, or so it seemed.

Something, he was determined, would come of this.

He had just finished speaking with Fin when Captain Troy called him back.

"Ryder, she's here. You want to come back into the office?"

"Dr. Mahoney's widow?"

"Yes. I'm assuming you want to talk to

162

her yourself. She's a basket case of tears, so I'd hurry."

"Will do."

Ryder ended the call quickly and headed for his car.

Martin Kimball was a target. Brian McTavish and Dr. Mahoney had been targets, he was certain.

Something connected the three of them. He had to discover what that something was.

CHAPTER SIX

The museum had a small staff, but they were open seven days a week, and to give each other days off and work something that resembled normal hours, they'd all fill in for each other when necessary. Sienna certainly knew the museum and the history of the city of New Orleans and of Louisiana well enough to cover for Morrie or Artie, and that afternoon, she took over one of the groups so Morrie could break for lunch. She didn't mind; her tour group consisted of families mostly, many of them tourists. Those with young children looked forward to reaching the water area and the petting zoo, while those with teens were eager to reach the wax tableaux.

She talked about Jackson and the pirates Lafitte and his brother, the city at the time, and the Battle of New Orleans. Most of the teens wanted to believe Lafitte sailed off into the sunset and lived happily ever after, but she had to tell them all records indicated he had died off Honduras from wounds received while trying to seize a Spanish merchant vessel and he was buried at sea.

"No!" one teen told her. "He only pretended to die!"

She smiled. "I can only tell you what history has told us."

"But history lies sometimes. Because it's told by the victors, right?" the boy asked her.

"Hm. Interesting!" she said. The kid had a point.

But she moved on.

It was late when she wound up back in her office. She noted she had a message on her cell phone.

Ryder Stapleton had called.

She hesitated and then called him back.

"Hey. I'll be there soon. I've got a guy in the parking lot now, plainclothes cop. It will look like he's just waiting for someone."

"What? Why?"

"I just met with the widow of the man who was fished out of the Mississippi. Her husband was a nephrologist."

"A kidney doctor?"

"Yes. He had been asked to be part of trials in the future. He's worked with a new form of dialysis machine, and apparently,

165

he was truly beloved, and people came from all over to see him. He was at the forefront of what worked best with his patients, providing the longest lives with the best possible health."

"Okay," she said, puzzled.

"His widow is in bad shape. She insisted he take time off, but she couldn't come with him because they have school-age kids and they had full calendars, but Mahoney had been working around the clock, and she wanted him to take time. Seemingly, he had no vices except he loved to play craps and hadn't been down here in forever. She thinks it was her fault he was murdered here."

"I'm so sorry. But —"

"Kimball is working in the medical-tech field."

"Lots of people work in the medical-tech field."

"Seriously?"

"I'm sorry, I just —"

"I'll be there as soon as I can. Please."

"Okay. You do know I have a car here."

"Yeah, we'll get to that."

He abruptly ended the call. There was a tap at her door. It was Morrie.

"I'm out of here! Clara has already left. The front door will lock automatically when you leave, as usual. If you need to come back in, just make sure you lock up."

She laughed softly. "Got it! Have a nice night, Morrie."

"Will do," he said. "I can't wait. Netflix-bingeing on the sofa with my cat, and seriously, that will make me happy as a clam tonight. People-overload today!"

He made a face and left. She glanced at her phone. It was after six. Closing time was five thirty, but they knew it took a while to get everyone out. But by now, Morrie would have seen to it their guests had all departed.

Ryder was on his way, and there was a policeman in the parking lot. Sounded good. She stood quickly, wanting to run out to see Dr. Lightfoot and the bear cub before leaving.

She was halfway out the door before remembering only the auxiliary lights were on, since they were closed.

She thought she heard someone whispering. Or was that just because she was becoming unnerved by so much?

A movement of air.

But in her mind, definitely a whisper.

She knows . . .

It was nothing.

But when she reached Murderers' Row, it was downright eerie.

She looked at the scene of Madame La-Laurie and her husband, about to flee. Of course, she was being ridiculous, but she thought the wax figure moved.

She stopped and then swore softly to herself. She wanted to see Jared and the cub, to tell them good-night, to make sure everything was all right.

But as she moved in, her paranoia grew worse. And as she neared the large, caped, and hooded figure that represented the Axeman of New Orleans, she was suddenly certain that something did move.

"Hey! Who is still here?"

There was a rustle in the fabric of the cape.

And it seemed the rustle sent something moving through the exhibits. She thought she heard a whisper and laughter . . .

"Not funny," she snapped.

But the laughter she heard wasn't *fun* laughter. There was something throaty and malicious in it.

She loudly barked out just exactly what the prankster could do with themselves, determined as she was to walk through the hallway.

By the vampire brothers exhibit, she again swore she saw movement — one of the wax corpses rising from the ground.

She heard a thump. And then the wax figure was *definitely* moving. It was preparing to leap off the tableau.

And come straight for her.

Ryder ran into Morrie in the parking lot. He was just leaving.

"Hey, Ryder!" Morrie said, smiling and friendly. "Oh. Is it okay if I call you that?"

"It's my name," he said, nodding. He didn't know Morrie well, but he liked him. During the little they'd spoken, he'd found him enthusiastic about his work and life in general, and very fond of history.

Morrie laughed. "Yeah, I mean, I didn't know if you preferred for us to call you Detective Stapleton."

"No, thanks. My given name is fine. Is Sienna still inside?"

"Last one. She should be right out."

"Is the front door locked?"

"No, it's set to lock as soon as she's out."

"Thanks. Think it's okay if I go on in?"

"Yes, just leave that little wedge. Well, it's no big deal. Sienna has keys. I just leave it with the wedge to make life easy. Anyway, good to see you!" Morrie said, waving and heading for his car.

There was a man standing by a blue sedan, reading a comic. He waved to Ryder, and he returned the gesture. The plain-clothes man was Tim Busby, and he was great at looking like he belonged anywhere: today he was in jeans and a T-shirt from a Trombone Shorty gig. He'd worked with Tim frequently and had been glad when Captain Troy had told him earlier that Busby would be covering the museum.

Right after he'd entered, careful to leave the wedge, Ryder heard the scream.

It was Sienna; he knew that immediately.

He'd have recognized the sound of her voice, even in a scream, even if he hadn't known she was the only one left in the museum.

The sound had come from the left of the two main halls, he thought.

He catapulted over the turnstile from the reception area to the exhibits. He tore past the halls with the hands-on exhibits, bypass-ing the one that led to the children's play area and racing toward the wax museum.

He had just made it to the tableau of Jack-son talking to Lafitte before the Battle of New Orleans when he saw someone hurtling toward him.

Sienna.

He caught her as she crashed into his arms, screaming again as she felt his hold, meeting his eyes and gasping for breath. She

170

was shaking.

"The figure . . . It moved!" she said. "No, not the figure . . . Someone . . ."

She blinked, took a deep breath, and seemed to realize she was clinging to him as tightly as if she were a sloth on a tree. She pulled back, looking over her shoulder.

"Someone . . . Probably a joke, but . . ."

"Get behind me," he said.

He thrust her back as he drew his Glock and headed purposefully down the hallway. He'd have liked to have brought her out to Tim Busby first, but in that time, a person could escape.

Followed by her, he went exhibit by exhibit, crawling up into each, searching everywhere.

One of the vampire brothers had toppled over. It had displaced several of the other figures in the scene, including the waxen victims on the floor.

It appeared either something in the construction of the exhibit had just given way to time and gravity or someone had been up on the tableau.

There was no one anywhere in the hall except for Sienna, and she was looking at him defensively. "I swear, I'm telling you the truth," she said.

"I believe you," he told her.

He hopped down from the scene just as the door leading to the petting zoo and rescue area opened, and Sienna let out another startled scream.

It was Dr. Lightfoot; he was wearing his white lab jacket and appeared to be irritated.

"Sienna? What is going on? What the hell is going on?" he demanded. "The museum is closed for the day. I thought you guys made sure that everybody was out!"

"I thought Morrie had done so," Sienna said. "I was on my way back to check on you and our creatures when —"

"Damn it! We have to get better at this, then," Lightfoot said, shaking his head.

Ryder already had his phone out, calling Busby and telling him to get back there.

"What happened?" he then asked Lightfoot.

"Some idiot just came tearing out of the building," Lightfoot said angrily. "He burst into the paddock with the petting animals and left the gate open and went flying over the backfence, up on the roof of Mr. Nelson's barn next door! He left a gate open! Sure, the fencing is still there, but Harry the falcon goes after the lambs if given half a chance, and they're strictly kept apart! We run a tight ship here, and —"

There was no time. Ryder went tearing across the yard as well, high-stepping his way through the sheep and goats, to leap up on the neighboring barn roof as well and search for any sign of anyone.

But again, he was too late.

He heard Lightfoot shouting to him from behind the wall that separated the two properties.

"Mr. Nelson doesn't have a shotgun or a big dog, but I'll call him and let him know you're in his yard!"

He hopped down from the roof of the barn and hurried into it, ignoring the protests of chickens in their roost and two horses stabled there.

But there was no one.

He raced through the paddock and around the house, but he could see no one on the sidewalks, no one anywhere around. Heading back, he tapped on the door to the house. The Nelson property was about an acre and a half. The perp might have headed toward the residence.

Mr. Nelson proved to be around seventy, nice enough, and seemed happy to let Ryder look around.

"They need a better security system over at that place," Nelson said. "Okay, so I don't have one. But I'm an old geezer with two

173

old nags and some chickens. That place . . . I love that it's there. Doc Lightfoot lets my grands come in, even after hours. And Byron, well, he's honestly one of the good ones. They say the rich get that way by being cheap jerks. Not Byron. That man is the real deal."

"Good to hear," Ryder replied.

He looked through the house. No one had come asking for entry, and no one was hiding there.

He thanked Nelson and managed to climb his way back up to the barn roof to return to the museum the way he had come, landing back with the goats and the sheep, meeting up with Jared Lightfoot and Sienna and Busby.

Busby was helping Sienna and Lightfoot herd the animals back where they were supposed to be.

"Anything?" Lightfoot asked anxiously. "It was a kid, I'll bet, playing a prank. It would take a kid to pull a stunt like that and haul himself up on a roof."

Ryder cleared his throat. "I'm not a kid." He looked at Sienna. "Are you all right?" he asked her.

She nodded. "I'm feeling a little foolish. It probably was just someone playing a prank. I'll be honest, the wax figures freak me out a little. I should have turned the lights back on, and then I would have seen someone prowling around and been in a position to call the police. Or at least call for Officer Busby," she smiled over at Tim, "who has been a huge help."

"Thank you, miss," Busby said, smiling. The plainclothes officer obviously liked what he saw with Sienna. Ryder was annoyed with himself for being irritated that Sienna and Busby had hit it off so easily in a matter of minutes.

"There are cameras, right?" Ryder asked Sienna.

"There are," she said.

"I'll need the footage."

"I'll have to call Artie. He handles all that," Sienna said.

"Then call him. Someone was in here after hours, and you don't know the intent. I'm going to get a crime-scene crew out here, too."

"But —"

She stared at him, but Jared Lightfoot interjected.

"Sienna! I have animals out here. We don't need someone in the museum after hours, pulling pranks and causing problems. At least the exhibits aren't living creatures, but out here, my wards are!"

175

She turned and headed back to her office.

Ryder followed her. She paused for a split second in the Murderers' Row area, long enough to let him know she had been unnerved by the experience.

He wondered, too, if the person pursuing her from the vampire exhibit had disappeared because he'd known someone armed was after him. Might it have gone differently otherwise?

He stayed out in the hall and called Fin Stirling while Sienna tried to reach Artie.

He told Fin about the break-in at the museum.

Fin told him everything had been quiet in the Garden District.

"I've been in the neighborhood most of the day. I spent some time at the bookstore, talking to people. Others in the neighborhood vaguely remember seeing the man in the sketch, but apparently, he was around for a few days and hasn't been seen since. The people I talked to said they did call the police to report what they'd seen but felt they hadn't been very helpful."

"Captain Troy would have alerted me immediately if there had been anything useful, though it's been a busy day. Kimball was almost attacked earlier, and we have twenty-four-hour protection for him now. But he's fighting it. There's a connection here, Fin. I know it."

"And you're probably right. I have another one of our people watching the houses on either side of the Kimball property. Wrecking crews were here all day. I imagine they'll finish up tomorrow. Angela at the home office did background checks on the crews. Nothing there."

"I need her to do something else. I know all kinds of tech is übersecret, but I need her to find out everything about Delaney Enterprises — that's where Kimball works. And maybe more importantly, dig up info on any competition, anyone who might want what Delaney Enterprises has."

"We'll be on it," Fin promised. "And as for tonight, as I said, we have a really good team watching the houses. Special Agents Mary Langdon and Vic Dulcet."

"Great. I'll probably still hang around myself a bit, but I'm glad they're on. That does free me up when necessary. I'm hoping someone found something having to do with the attack on Kimball today, too. I know the man who meant to stab him ditched his coat and hat to blend in with the crowd. If we could find that evidence and it hasn't been compromised, we might get a print or some DNA. A hair off the hat, maybe."

"Keep me posted. I'm going to get something to eat and some sleep, but I'm a call away at all times, you know."

"I know, and thanks," Ryder told him.

He ended the call to find that Sienna had come from her office and was staring at him.

"Don't you think this is a little bit much? It was probably a kid, I probably overreacted, and we're dragging out a dozen people for . . . a prank."

"Is Artie on his way in?"

"He is." She hesitated. "We have remote viewing, but he's coming in."

"Good."

She was still hesitant, but then she said, "He got a bunch of static on his remote-viewing system. He thinks someone hacked into it and turned off the cameras."

"Of course," Ryder said. "Yeah, your casual prankster does that every time."

They could already hear sirens, and Ryder excused himself abruptly to go out and meet the arrivals.

Sienna begged them to be careful in the exhibits — nicely.

Jared Lightfoot, indignant, spoke with them as well, since they'd be going through his paddock to follow the trail of the trespasser.

Artie arrived, but was quick to shake his head.

"I'll see what I can do, but it looks like whoever did this was smart. That said, don't get me wrong — plenty of tech-savvy teens might have managed it."

Artie found nothing on the cameras. The crime-scene experts found nothing in the exhibits. Even the cleaning experts who came in regularly to keep the exhibits in a good state of maintenance wore gloves.

The trespasser, prankster, or would-be assassin had apparently worn gloves. While the paddock yielded hundreds of smudged fingerprints, a hundred people might be touching them on any given day.

All they gained was a single footprint from the paddock.

Eventually, the work was finished. There was nothing else to do. Artic fiddled with the computer forever, trying to figure out how the system had been hacked. He wanted to stay longer: Tim Busby was staying with him, and the NOPD would be watching through the night.

It was now late. Sienna had stood silently by Ryder throughout, with little to do but watch others do their work.

"Food," she muttered.

It was late, but it was New Orleans. There

was always something open somewhere.

"All right. And I'm sorry, I'm not letting you leave here alone. For now, your car can stay in the lot. I'll get you wherever you need to go, and I'll get you to work in the morning, assuming . . . Do you work on Sunday?"

"Unless I have specific plans or I'm out of town, I check in every day. Officially, I'm off Sunday and Monday, but Sunday is still the weekend, so I usually go in and take more time during the week. I love going to jazz mass, so I usually go in late. I mean, I do take time off, too."

Ryder doubted she took much time at all, but that was her choice.

"All right, so we'll leave your car."

He was afraid she would object, but she didn't.

"So," he continued. "Food. Anywhere in particular?"

"I know a great place."

"Oh?"

"My house. I'm not a gourmet chef at all, but I have fresh shrimp, cheese, and grits — if that works for you. It's a dish I eat too often, but I like shrimp and grits."

"All right. I'll get you to your place."

She stared at him strangely. "My cooking isn't that bad."

He laughed. "If that's an invitation, I accept."

They headed out at last. He paused to thank Tim Busby for being there, watching over Artie.

Sienna thanked him, too. He smiled at Sienna and told her it was a pleasure to do anything at any time that might help the museum, the city of New Orleans — or her.

The drive was just a few minutes, but he realized he hadn't had a chance to tell her much yet.

He glanced her way.

"I met with Martin Kimball today near his place of work. We were at a coffee shop just a few blocks from his building. He was almost stabbed to death on his way back."

"Almost?" she asked.

"I followed him."

"Then you caught —"

"No."

"Oh."

"The guy was clever. First, he threw a woman into me, and then he threw a kid on the streetcar tracks. He got away."

He didn't realize how bitterly he spoke.

"And you think he meant to . . . kill Martin Kimball?"

"He had a nice big knife ready for him."

She was silent until they reached her

181

house. "Have a seat and I'll get started," she said once they were inside.

"I can help."

"You don't have to," she assured him.

"I'd rather help than sit around."

He followed her into the kitchen, telling her he could wash lettuce and get a salad together. He did, watching in silence as she sautéed the shrimp, cooked the grits, joined them with the cheese and then the shrimp, and was eventually satisfied with the seasoning she had added.

They set the table together, brushing against one another awkwardly now and then.

Then they sat down. He complimented her shrimp and cheese grits, and she commended him on his salad. They ate together in pleasant silence for a while.

Then it felt awkward again as they finished their food.

"Um, so, the officer who was there tonight . . . he was the one already watching the parking lot?" Sienna asked.

"Yes."

"He was great."

"Yes, I noticed you like him."

"Oh, really?"

"Well, you do, don't you?"

"I like most people. You're the one who is

jaded, certain everyone you meet has an underlying motive for everything."

"That's not true at all."

She shrugged.

He leaned across the table, closer to her. "Sometimes people do have underlying motives. I'm not certain you want me around at all. The only reason you listened to me to begin with was because the ghost of your grandmother would have driven you crazy if you hadn't. And let's see. Tonight you let me drive you home. And eat here. And watch over you. Because you're finally smart enough to be scared."

"You think I invited you in for dinner because I'm scared?" she demanded.

"Maybe."

"Talk about people with underlying motives!" she said. The color of her eyes deepened when she was angry. They were as deep and green as a forest as the sun fell.

"Me?"

"The reason you're worried about me is you think I'm some kind of key that's going to unlock this case for you. You're obsessed with this situation, determined you're going to solve an old mystery and — I don't know — make yourself the hero of the hour or something."

He sat back, staring at her, jaw locked,

slowly steaming inside.

He forced himself to speak clearly and without shouting, determined not to betray his anger.

"Crazy as it sounds, I became a cop because I like helping good people and stopping bad people, or even bad behavior by good people. And when this is cleared, I'll be joining the FBI's Krewe of Hunters unit because I still believe in helping the innocent and apprehending the guilty. If I'm right, and I believe today proved me right, whoever killed McTavish after failing to do so when they set his house on fire has struck again here and murdered another man in cold blood. And he — or they — will kill Kimball eventually, if we don't find out what is going on!"

She was silent. Dead silent.

"I'm sorry," she said quietly.

He lowered his head, breathing. He should get out. Right away. Even when she was angry with him, calling him out . . . part of him wasn't listening. Part of him just felt the touch of her eyes, and they had brushed by one another often enough tonight that he knew her skin was soft, and he knew, too, from just being near her, that her scent was subtle and fragrant and . . .

"I guess you'll probably want to turn me

down again, but . . ."

"Yes."

"I — I didn't ask you anything yet."

"You're going to ask me to sleep on the sofa. Yes, we have other agents out there tonight, through the night. I can sleep on the sofa."

"Uh, great."

She stood, ready to take the dishes from the dining room back to the kitchen. He stood to help her, and they nearly knocked into one another. They managed to give each other space and pick up their plates. He rinsed them, and she put them into the dishwasher.

They had just finished the cleanup tasks when they both started in different directions again, this time colliding face forward, with Ryder catching her shoulders and meeting her eyes. There was something in them. With no thought whatsoever, he leaned his face down. Her lips were damp, parted in a strange invitation . . .

He kissed her. Softly. Felt the sweet, liquid give of her mouth. And he winced and drew away, because he wanted her so desperately, but he wasn't thinking about being professional.

She was looking at him, seeking, searching for some truth.

185

He managed to speak.

"I don't want you coming to me like this because you're frightened. I'll be here."

She smiled. "Hey. If I just wanted protection, I could call on Granny K."

He smiled. "She does tend to sense danger."

"I don't want you to . . . Well, I mean, the other way, you don't need to be . . . I mean, honestly, you don't have to — oh, wow! I'm doing this terribly," she muttered.

He smiled. "We're touching because you want to touch?" he asked softly.

"Yes. But physical attraction doesn't mean I like you."

He pressed his lips to hers again, loved the silky wet feel of their mouths touching.

"What is it you don't like about me?" he whispered against her mouth.

"You're arrogant."

"Not really."

"You think you know everything."

"I often do. Hm. I like you. Except, of course, the naivete and refusal to see danger."

"Hm."

She moved against him, tasting his lips again, allowing her fingers to thread through his hair as she stepped closer against him.

"But it's all right," he whispered. "I'll do?"

he teased.

"I don't get out much," she told him.

"Ah, so any port in a storm."

"Something like that. Except there is no storm, and I'm not here because I'm afraid. I mean, honestly, I'd call another cop if . . ."

She didn't finish. She pulled his head down to hers. The kiss they shared then wasn't tender or sweet but deep and long and desperate. His hands slid along her back, cupping her buttocks, pulling her ever closer. Her fingers trailed through his hair and then down his back, and when she broke away, she smiled ruefully and turned to head out of the kitchen.

When he didn't follow immediately, she turned back, and now her voice was teasing.

"I did say you would do," she told him.

He followed her quickly then, catching her in the parlor and sweeping her into his arms.

"Luckily," he assured her, "due to careful searches of the residence, I do know how to find the bedroom."

"Don't you dare drop me on the stairs!" she told him.

"Please! I'll do, remember? And we have a gym where we cops work out, you know," he said mock-indignantly.

She laughed at that. And from that point,

any awkwardness, stuttering about longing to do what they were about to do, and wondering if it was right in so many ways slipped away like cast-off clothing. She was laughing when he all but bounced her on the bed and eased down to join her. They disrobed as they rolled on the bed, kissing in between, touching. With all the rolling, she wound up beneath him with them both breathless, staring at one another. And then he kissed her again, long and deeply, and allowed his lips to roam to her throat and breasts and below. He felt the touch of her fingers on his flesh, his shoulders and back, like a whisper of magic. Their words became slightly unintelligible as they entwined and broke away, each exploring, tender, passionate, their lips meeting time and again before moving to more intimate and erotic zones.

At last, when they came together, his mouth found hers again, and his body thrust into hers. They moved with passionate urgency, the intensity of their physical bond growing greater and greater until their need consumed them.

There would be time to explore, to be tender again.

Climax seemed to sweep them both away, something as desperate and strong as the force with which they had come together.

And they held together, locked in an embrace at first, letting the winds that had swept them subside.

Then he rose above her, met her eyes, and told her, "I'm not usually this easy, you know."

She laughed, punched him in the arm, and then rolled to his side, her head resting on his chest.

"I was worried about . . . feelings, I guess. I mean, you are the detective on this case."

"Well, I can't be fired. I've already resigned," he told her.

"To join the Krewe," she said.

He nodded, stroking her hair.

"Was this just tonight?" she asked, and he thought the question was directed to herself as much as it was directed to him, and maybe she hadn't even meant to speak aloud.

"Hey, I like you, remember?"

He couldn't see her face, but he could feel it on his skin when she smiled.

"I don't dislike you as much as I did at first," she assured him.

"That's okay. I thought you were a spoiled brat."

"Really?"

"But you saved lives," he said.

"Granny K saved lives," she murmured.

189

His hand froze on the top of her head. "Granny K," he said with a groan. "You don't think —"

"I can promise you she's not around. She was always adamant that she'd never be around when . . . well, when she shouldn't be around. And if she was about to stop by, she'd have disappeared in a flash. She's wanted us to be together."

"Oh?"

She turned, leaning up on his chest. "I'm not sure what her real reasoning is. But she's always been extremely practical. She'd be fine with me sleeping with you. You're a cop, and I'm safe when I'm with you. So, there would be no old-fashioned values going there."

"She's a smart woman . . . uh, ghost," he said.

"She was always smart and funny and out-there. She took me to Europe when I was young. She was involved in my life. And don't get me wrong, my folks are great, and they taught me and gave me all good things. But Granny K was a major part of my life."

"Maybe that's why —"

"I see her?"

"I think it's more than that," Ryder said. "Though, I don't know. I've met plenty of Krewe members who knew from the time they were very young they could see the dead. Most went through several years of therapy because of it. Some came from families where it wasn't so strange. With me . . . it's new. It's all new. It's just been months, but I'm a fast learner. They definitely help." He frowned suddenly, holding her shoulders. "We have to find Granny K tomorrow. We're going to need her help."

"With what?"

"We're not going to get anything from the museum. We have a footprint, so we'll know the trespasser's shoe size and maybe what brand but little else. And the police have been looking for the jacket and hat the man who attacked Kimball was wearing. They haven't found anything yet, but maybe she can ask around. I'm sure she has friends everywhere in the French Quarter."

"She was walking around there today. Maybe she's already been on the case."

She was serious, and so was he. But it was night, and there were agents out on the street watching over the houses. Kimball was under police guard at the hotel, as was his family.

And Ryder was here, naked, and so was she, and they'd made love once . . .

"Tomorrow is another day," he told her.

She smiled and kissed him again.

191

And if they were to only have that night, well, he was damned sure going to make it count.

CHAPTER SEVEN

They slept late. Which was all right, Sienna thought. She woke wondering at first if she'd gone stark raving mad or been alone so long she'd started having vividly sexual dreams, but he was lying beside her, then he smiled and reached for her.

They'd managed to laugh together with all else. And somehow, it was really good.

But when he reached for her, all she could think about was the way she had doubted such love scenes in movies and shows. She felt like she was breathing fire.

He frowned when she pulled away, and she knew he was wondering if she had regretted any of her actions.

No.

She realized she loved seeing him in her bed, loved the bronze of his flesh against her sheets, the rakish fall of his hair on her pillow, and even the concern in his eyes.

"Teeth!" she said. "Sorry! I must brush

193

my teeth!"

She fled to the bathroom. He was right behind her.

"Got an extra toothbrush? I mean, if we're going to be minty fresh . . ."

She smiled and reached into the little cupboard beneath the sink. They stood side by side, brushing their teeth.

"Ah, so much better," he said. He looked at the shower, and then looked at her with a question in his eyes. She smiled. The water came on. They stepped beneath it.

Their kisses were minty fresh.

And when her lips traveled over his flesh, it was slick, clean.

They only played so long there. A bit of soap on the floor sent her flying against him, pushing him against the tile of the shower. They caught each other and sank to the floor, Ryder banging his head against one of the faucets, saying, "Ouch!"

Laughing, they struggled to get up, found towels, and made love in the daylight.

It was Sunday, normally a lazy day, except Ryder groaned softly and then stood. "We need to find Granny K. I think we should get dressed first."

"Good call. But what do we want her to do?"

"Bring me to friends. Are you going into work?"

"Well, I like to stop by, at least."

He nodded. "I'll get you there. I'm going to call Fin and have him stay there with you. I want to see if Granny K will come with me down to Canal Street and then into the French Quarter. I want to join the search for the jacket and hat that I'm sure Kimball's attacker dumped somewhere."

Sienna hopped up. She hesitated and then asked him, "You'll come back to the museum after?"

"You bet."

They both hopped back into the shower — separately — and dressed. Ready to leave her room, Ryder turned back to her.

"Do you like me at all?"

"Well, you're not repulsive."

He smiled. "You already said I would do. I mean . . ."

"I like you. We need to get moving."

They headed down to the kitchen. Granny K was seated at the dining-room table. "I pushed the button!" she said proudly. "Coffee is ready!"

"Granny K, thanks for brewing the coffee, but —" Sienna began.

"Oh, good lord!" the old woman said. "If you two had come running down the stairs

195

stark naked, I would have shown myself out quickly. Ryder! Young man, I am delighted to see you here."

"And I'm delighted to see you. I was hoping to find you," Ryder told her.

"I heard about the incident at the museum last night. And I knew you were here," Granny K said.

"Someone told you?" Sienna asked.

Her grandmother shook her head. "I knew Detective Stapleton wouldn't leave you. I had no idea what you'd be doing — and I don't want to know — but I knew he wouldn't leave you."

"Granny —"

"Leave it. So, Detective, you were hoping to see me?"

"I need your help," Ryder told her.

"I am ready and willing!" Granny K said.

"I'll get the coffee," Sienna murmured. "And I have some power bars. I guess that will do for breakfast for now . . . I'm starving. Maybe two power bars."

"All that activity!" Granny K said.

"Hey, now!" Sienna snapped.

Her grandmother's ghost just shrugged.

"Now, Detective, tell me how I can help."

Ryder told her about the attack on Kimball and the man who had managed to escape. He'd been stopped by the streetcar between Bourbon and Royal Streets. The man could have fled down Bourbon or Chartres, or maybe even Decatur Street. Then, of course, he could have headed toward Rampart Street — or the river. But he needed to find someone who might have seen the man, seen him throw away the jacket and the hat.

"I was with friends in the French Quarter yesterday," Granny K said. "But we were toward Esplanade on Bourbon, seeing a few ghosts, specters, remnants, or whatever we are near Lafitte's. There are a few charming rascals who still enjoy hanging around that area. But my friends have friends. We can see who is in that area. We are seeing Sienna safely to work first, right? Although, the museum . . . Should she be going there? Maybe you should take a leave, Sienna."

"That wouldn't solve anything," Sienna said.

"We will drive Sienna to work," Ryder said.

"But will she be safe there?" Granny K asked. "After last night . . ."

"If I know my boss, the security system and the cameras are, I'm sure, going through a top-notch redo right now," Sienna assured her.

"I'm sending a friend. A man I've worked

with, someone from the Krewe," Ryder said. "Sienna will be with Fin until we're with her again."

"I'll be safe," Sienna said.

"And we're set. We should get moving," Ryder said.

When they stepped out, there was a man waiting for them. Ryder quickly introduced them. "Sienna, Granny K, this is Special Agent Finley Stirling, one of the finest investigators I've ever gotten to work with. Fin, this is Sienna and Granny K."

"You see me, dear?" Granny K asked.

"I do. And it's lovely to meet you," Finley Stirling assured her politely.

Sienna assumed Ryder had to have called the man while she was in the shower; she didn't think he'd been watching over the street the night before. He looked freshly showered, but he hadn't dressed in a suit. In jeans and a denim jacket, he looked casual enough to be hanging out at a museum on a Sunday.

Finley was a tall, well-built man, and like Ryder, he had an air of competence and authority about him.

"Special Agent Stirling." Sienna nodded toward him.

"Fin, just Fin, please," he told her.

"Fin!" Granny K said. "Well, you are a

hottie, too, sir! Oh, dear, I suppose that wasn't appropriate. Oh, wait. I'm dead. I don't have to be appropriate."

"No, you don't, and I'm just going to accept the compliment," Fin told her. He looked at Ryder and then at Granny K. "Have you met, in your wanderings, a young woman named Kathryn Anne McNeil?"

"Well, yes, I have," Granny K said. "Lovely woman! She was quite the independent in her day. She had family money and did as she pleased. She spent time with Jean Lafitte and Andrew Jackson. Fascinating!"

"She was very helpful on our last case," Fin told Ryder. "If Granny K can find her, Kathryn knows everyone in the French Quarter."

"You mean everyone dead in the French Quarter," Granny K said, grinning.

Well, Sienna was glad her grandmother seemed to have her sense of humor in death as she had in life.

"We'll look for Kathryn first, then," Ryder said. "Then we can meet up after."

Sunday morning wasn't particularly busy. People were out, headed to church, but even so, a Sunday morning was a lazy time in the city when there were no festivals going on. They took Ryder's car, and the ride to the museum was quick.

As they neared it, Sienna asked, "Hey, how do I introduce Fin?"

"Truthfully," Ryder told her. "It won't hurt if it becomes known there's a federal agent on the property."

Sienna couldn't see Fin Stirling's gun, but she was certain he carried one, probably like Ryder, tucked in a holster in the waistband at the back of his jeans, covered by his jacket.

"Well, we're here," she said, hopping out of the car before Ryder could come around to open the door for her.

Fin stepped out as well.

"We'll see you when we see you," he said.

Ryder nodded to him and drove away.

Sienna looked at Fin, who grinned and told her, "You have a pretty amazing grandmother."

"I . . . Thank you. This is all a little . . . well, amazing to me. It's so . . . natural. And ordinary," she said.

"What? Oh, us chatting with your grandmother?" he asked her. "It isn't easy for anyone, because it's not something that's normally part of the human experience. And I'm assuming that's why those of us who can do it, well, we come together. It's why the Krewe is so special. And why Ryder belongs with us."

"You were working a case with him before?"

"Just a few months back. And he worked with my colleague on the Axeman's Protégé before that." He smiled. "So, welcome to being one of us!"

"I'm not a cop or an agent."

"Don't have to be! I'm married to an actress."

"Who sees the dead?"

"Yep. Should we head inside?"

"We should. I'm sorry, I have some work to finish up in my office, but . . ."

"I will never be more than a few feet away from you," he told her, then pulled out his phone. "And not to worry. I have pages and pages of information to sift through."

She smiled. They went in. Clara greeted them, happy to meet Fin and wide-eyed to learn he was an FBI agent.

"They promised there would be cops around all day but, Special Agent Stirling, I'm happy as heck you'll be here with us. We're opening in a few minutes. Morrie is going to give all the tours. But Artie won't be on the floor. He'll be busy trying to trace all the computer machinations that went on, along with a fellow from the police, and there will be men working from Byron's security company, beefing up alarms and —

oh! Dr. Lightfoot went out and bought a retired police dog last night. His name is Ruff. Maybe it's from the idea of *rough and ready.* I don't know. You may want to meet him."

They thanked her. And while Sienna did have work she wanted to finish up, she asked Fin, "Do you mind if we meet Ruff first?"

"I'd love to," he assured her. "And see the tableaux."

"This way, then," she said, and they headed toward the back. Fin took in everything as they passed through the hallways. She paused as they came to the split between the wax tableaux and the children's play area.

"The person who came after you was down this way?" Fin asked.

"Yes."

"May we?" He smiled. "I do carry a big gun."

"Of course."

Fin admired the historical figures. They came to Murderers' Row. "Madame La-Laurie! Some say she was so bitter because she'd been run out of the islands by a revolution. Others say she was just as sick as possible and cruel as a demon. Or that she made it to Paris and died there, while still others believe she came back and lived out her days on the other side of Lake Pontchartrain."

"And what do you think?" she asked him.

"I haven't a clue! Except I don't care about her past. The behavior she and her husband exhibited was despicable."

"Agreed," Sienna said.

"The Axeman," Fin noted.

"And a copycat in recent history."

"Like I said before, Ryder worked the case, hard as anyone, even when our unit was put in charge," Fin said. He looked at her. "Then he also worked the recent Display murders with us."

"And that's why he's joining the Krewe?"

"He discovered he sees the dead and we don't think he's crazy because of it. He learned about his ability through the Krewe and the recent cases here."

"I'm originally from Terrebonne Parish," she said. "I heard about the events that happened around that movie being filmed."

He nodded. "Ryder became more than a little involved. Anyway, he'll be an amazing addition. The man is dedicated to the truth. Not just justice, but the truth."

She couldn't help but think about the night before. And she realized she was a heck of a liar: she was *liking* him more and more as the hours went by.

And she wasn't sure that made her happy. If this was a passing thing brought about by proximity — and possibly the fact that neither one of them had much of a life other than working, these days — then she'd really have no life other than work.

"Yes, he's quite a detective," she said.

They'd reached the vampire tableau.

She paused. Morrie and Artie had set it all straight. Light was beaming in from outside and from the display lights now burning brightly.

The tableau was made up of wax figures, nothing more.

"Interesting. Well planned," Fin said.

"Maybe. Maybe it was just some jerk kid or even adult. And maybe the cameras just went on the fritz because . . . because things go on the fritz. I mean, technology is wonderful when it works. Sometimes it doesn't."

"You still want to deny there might be danger in this for you?"

She remembered the sound of rustling, when the figure had jumped off the tableau dais and come after her — and then the attacker ran past Lightfoot to disappear over the fence.

She remembered her imagined whisper,

204

born out of paranoia. *She knows . . .*

She hadn't mentioned the whisper to Ryder or Fin, because it might have only been in her mind. And besides, it couldn't have referred to her.

She didn't know a damned thing.

"Oh, hell, no!" Sienna assured him. "Not at all! I'm glad you're here and glad that, when you're not, Ryder is so . . . dedicated."

And has associates who can cover for him so he can be with me, she thought.

"All right, so right out this door," she continued, "are the animals, the petting-zoo beasts, the rescues. A few birds, our little bear cub . . . and Dr. Lightfoot and his new guard dog."

She hurried ahead of him. When she opened the door, she saw Jared in one of his lab coats on one of the small stages where he gave talks about domestic and wild animals with his new acquisition, Ruff.

It was a beautiful dog. Ruff was a big shepherd, but he was seated obediently. Lightfoot was giving a little speech to a group of children who had gathered around, talking about the training that allowed such an animal to behave perfectly but to protect and defend as well.

Sienna and Fin waited, watching as Lightfoot, down on his knees, allowed the children to greet the dog. Ruff allowed himself to be petted and hugged.

Seeing Sienna and Fin, the vet stood and offered them a smile. They approached the small stage, and Sienna quickly introduced Fin and then congratulated Lightfoot on the dog. "May I?" she asked.

"Ruff, friends," Lightfoot said.

Ruff barked happily. Sienna and Fin pet the dog.

"He's great, isn't he? I spent half the night with the retired cop who owned him. He's a brilliant creature, already knows me, obeys my commands," Lightfoot said. "Screw modern technology! Now I'll really know if someone is acting up around here."

"He's beautiful," Sienna commented.

"A great asset," Fin said.

They talked a few minutes, then Sienna remembered she really did have a few things she'd like to get done.

They left the animal section of the museum and headed back through.

Sienna didn't even glance at tableaux; it might be a while before she could enjoy them again.

When they reached her office, Fin assured her he'd be fine in a chair, going through all the information he had on the case.

"Well, thankfully, we have a big dog here

now. Nothing can happen with Ruff around," Sienna said optimistically, sitting behind her desk.

Fin was quiet.

"What?"

"The thing about a guard dog . . . Well, you saw Ruff. He's really well trained."

"Right."

Fin was still quiet.

"So . . ."

"Well, we just have to hope this isn't an inside job in any way. Because if Lightfoot tells Ruff the people here are friends, well, to Ruff, no matter what, they'll be friends."

"It isn't an inside job," Sienna said.

He nodded.

She realized he simply wasn't going to argue with her. He thought someone at the museum might be involved in some way. How exactly she couldn't begin to fathom.

But if he thought someone there might be guilty . . .

Then Ryder did, too.

Ryder had become accustomed to either ignoring the dead, pretending he was talking on the phone, or nodding or shaking his head when a spirit started speaking with him in public.

It was part of the talent he was still learning.

And being out with Granny K put his talent to the test. She knew everyone, and in his walk with her, he felt as if he had jumped into a macabre Mardi Gras celebration.

He saw every mode of dress from every decade, from bustles to bell-bottoms, and hair styles from wigs and pompadours to mullets and shags and everything in between. Granny K knew everyone, but first she wanted to make her way to Lafitte's because Kathryn Anne McNeil was often there, sitting in the courtyard area, meeting with old friends.

Ryder wondered if he looked like a robot gone amok as they walked. Granny K stopped frequently, and each time, she asked ghosts if they'd been around Canal Street and seen the runner and the incident in which a boy had almost been hit by the trolley.

No one had.

As Granny K had suspected, they found Kathryn at Lafitte's.

The spirits greeted as ghosts, almost melding into one another, or perhaps actually doing so before breaking apart.

Kathryn knew Ryder; they hadn't met formally, but she had seen him with Fin.

She listened gravely and shook her head.

She had been a beautiful woman, slim and gracious and almost regal in her early-nineteenth-century gown and updo. He thought she and Granny K — despite the centuries between them — had hit it off easily because they were both determined that gender and mores were not more important than right and wrong, and that their thoughts and opinions were valuable.

Kick-ass women of any century, he thought.

Kathryn was thoughtful and amused as he realized he'd be sitting at a table by himself — according to what most people would see — talking to himself.

But he had his phone and was wearing earbuds, and he just smiled at them both.

Kathryn smiled, then grew serious.

"So difficult with this one . . . Fires and corpses burned and tossed into the river! I mean, one hears, but not in the sense we did when the Axeman imitator was out there, or the horrible murders when the victims were *displayed.* Sadly, those doing the killing were out there. This case you're trying to solve seems far more . . . subtle, but also devious. I wasn't in that area yesterday, but I have a friend, Millie, who often is. You can find her with Jacques Le-Blanc, a charming fellow who often sailed with Lafitte. You can't miss him — he has a bandanna and is most obviously a buccaneer. If you take a stroll down that way, I'm sure you'll find them."

Ryder quickly finished the food he'd ordered, and he and Granny K started toward Canal Street.

They found Jacques — easily recognizable, as Kathryn had said — and Millie, who had apparently lived in the early days of the twentieth century and passed away in the 1920s. At least, that's what Ryder assumed, based on her style of dress and the little cap that perched upon her short-cut hair. The pair were admiring a motorcycle parked in front of a hotel on Canal.

"Aye," Jacques said, when questioned by Granny K. "We saw the incident." He looked at Ryder. "Fine running and fantastic leap, sir! The boy owes you his life."

"Well, thank you, but I did lose the man I was chasing. Did you see which way he went, by any chance?"

"Ah, well," Jacques muttered, looking at Millie. "We were watching out for the lad, poor wee thing."

"But," Millie said excitedly, "he didn't pass out toward Bourbon, so I'd say he went down Royal Street."

"Rue Royale," Jacques said. "Yes, quite

210

possibly!"

Ryder thanked them. A man passing by who skirted around them thought the thank-you was for him, which was fine, because he had stepped around. He smiled at Ryder; Ryder smiled back.

He made a point of adjusting an earbud and told Granny K, "Down Royal."

Of course, the problem was he knew the patrol officers in the area would have been thorough; they'd have checked out any garbage bins carefully with gloved hands. And they'd found nothing, according to Captain Troy.

"Where else?" he wondered aloud.

"I'm sure you'll think of something, dear," Granny K told him.

He stood and looked down Royal. He knew the French Quarter. He'd known it all his life. He closed his eyes briefly to think.

And then he started walking quickly.

There was a deli, a great fast-food place, just a few blocks in. It was small, privately owned, and had only a few employees. There was a large waste container right by the door.

He doubted it was emptied daily.

He reached the deli, burst in, and forgetting he was in plainclothes, he headed straight for the bin, pulling on a pair of gloves and ripping off the lid.

"Sir!" a young clerk called out, running over to him.

"Oh, sorry. NOPD," he explained quickly, scrambling for his ID. "I need —"

"No, please, go ahead," she said. "Just . . ." Her voice trailed.

"I promise I won't leave a mess," he told her.

"Ah, yes! A man raised right!" Granny K said with approval.

The clerk smiled awkwardly and stood back. "You know, I'm sorry, customers don't like seeing . . . icky garbage."

"I'll be quick," he said.

He was, and it didn't take much.

Of course, the jacket and hat were covered in garbage, and he didn't have a big-enough evidence bag to hold them, something he should have thought of. But the clerk brought him a clean garbage bag. He noted the hat was for a large head and the jacket was size large as well.

He made sure any garbage that had spilled over went back in the bin.

He didn't have to pretend he was on the phone this time as he called Captain Troy.

A patrol car would swing by, and the items would be brought to the lab immediately.

He had no idea of how compromised they might be by the garbage, but there might be something, a hair, a trace of DNA, something.

And then he had to hope the person was in the system.

Although a small success, it seemed worth celebrating.

The patrol car came, and the items were on their way to the lab. He remembered Granny K was beside him.

"How did you know?" she asked.

"I didn't. I hoped."

"But you were right. And right out of the gate!" she said.

"Sometimes we get lucky. And I had help. Thank you."

She smiled. "I like being here for good reason," she told him. "But I swear to you, dear boy, I am not around when I shouldn't be. You will continue staying with Sienna, won't you?"

"That's going to be up to Sienna."

"I think she'll want you to."

"Not because you pressure her," he said.

"Hm. I'm not thinking that at all, Detective!" she said indignantly. "Anyway, I have a date tonight with friends, so you'd best be on the alert!"

He smiled as they made their way back to

the car. He felt good. He had to believe they were going to get somewhere, because there was little else going well.

Tomorrow, they'd hope for answers. He was due to meet with Betsy Mahoney, the doctor's widow, again. She had been, as expected, tearful and grieving. She wanted to help, but her mind was scattered. She didn't want to be away from her children now, but she hadn't wanted them to come to New Orleans . . . or to the morgue. She had tried to talk to him, but she'd been distracted. She had agreed, however, to meet with him again.

She was desperate and eager for them to catch her husband's killer.

For tonight, they were all on watch.

Because this killer would strike again. And while Kimball was under protection, a known target, they didn't know who else might be in the path of a monster with an agenda.

It was late in the afternoon when Ryder returned.

The day at the museum had been uneventful, Sienna and Fin assured Ryder.

He told them they had found the items he'd been searching for, and Granny K had been extremely helpful.

214

She'd also been determined to be off when they returned to the museum.

She had plans for the evening, as she'd told him.

Fin suggested Ryder meet Ruff before they left for the day, so they went out back again, and this time, Sienna forced herself to stare at the tableaux as they passed, cementing in her mind the fact that the characters were wax figures and nothing more.

Ryder had a way with dogs. Once Dr. Lightfoot said it was okay, Ruff was all over Ryder, and the detective seemed to enjoy the attention.

"I'd love to have a dog," he admitted, down on his knees, playing with the shepherd. "But I'm never home, so I figure it would be cruel."

"Well, I'm not leaving this guy for a while!" Lightfoot assured them. "Lori has offered to cover for me. She says she's not afraid now — not that she was before — but she admitted even with the beefed-up security, she feels better with Ruff here. But I'm not leaving this guy yet."

"What about our little bear cub?" Sienna asked.

"They love each other," Lightfoot said, "which is good. I don't think our little guy

215

is going back in the wild. The trap that left him half-dead caused a problem with one of his legs. He'll walk okay, but he'll never be able to run."

They chatted a few more minutes and then left.

They headed back to Sienna's house in Ryder's car. Fin left them after they arrived, assuring him the houses on the block were being watched.

So far, nothing.

The Kimball property was now flattened earth — with a big black spot where the house had once stood.

Ryder wanted to check on the Craton family, so once they were in the main entrance, he stepped to the right to tap at their residence door.

Sienna was sure someone looked through the peephole before opening the door. Judy Craton seemed wary and worried.

But the woman smiled as she opened the door, greeting Ryder with pleasure. "Hey! And thank you. I received calls from Captain Troy and someone named Jackson Crow with the bureau, both assuring me people were and would be watching over us. I'm so grateful. I have to admit, I wasn't sure about Whitney helping with a sketch, but I don't know if I'd have been able to say I was scared just because . . . that could have happened to anyone. But I sleep at night, thanks to you."

"You're welcome, but please — it's really Crow and Troy who run the operations. Anyway, we just wanted to make sure everything is fine here."

"Yes, all fine. Oh, we just finished dinner. I made a massive lasagna. Plenty left. May I get you some?" Judy asked.

Ryder looked at Sienna. She shrugged.

Judy turned away to call her husband. As she did, Ryder said softly to Sienna, "You weren't planning to whip up something incredible for a meal, were you?"

"No. Were you?"

"Nope. Lasagna sounds great."

Ronald came to the door, urging them to come on in. Then Whitney and Noah, shier, came out. But in a few minutes, Ryder was helping Noah make a few adjustments to a block castle, and Whitney was solemnly telling Sienna about her new favorite book, *All Creatures Great and Small* by James Herriot.

"The author was a veterinarian. Just like Dr. Lightfoot! I asked Mom if we could figure out how to meet him, and she told me that he passed away a long time ago. I was so sad," Whitney told her.

"I bet he was wonderful. You can come

back and see Dr. Lightfoot anytime. In fact, he just got a great new animal, a personal pet, a German shepherd named Ruff."

"Oh, wow! Can we go and see him?" Whitney asked her mother.

"Maybe next weekend," Judy said.

"How are things at the museum?" Ronald asked, and Ryder glanced at Sienna. They both knew he wasn't talking about the museum but the case.

"I heard there was a break-in," Judy said.

"May have just been a kid," Sienna said. "Nothing was stolen or damaged."

She stared at Ryder, not wanting him to scare her housemates with any remotely possible association to the house next door being burned to the ground.

"I'm sure next weekend will be great," Ryder said. "Sienna and I can make sure we're there, too."

That made the kids happy. They went to take their baths then, as ordered by their mother.

When they were gone, Ronald asked flatly, "So nothing on the firebug?"

"We're following leads."

"So horrible! Anything on the homeless man?" Judy asked.

"Well, he was apparently seen by a lot of people. He was around for several days but hasn't been seen since the fire. We're still hoping something will break from the sketch. And as I said, we are following leads. I'm sure you understand I'm not at liberty to discuss them."

The two nodded gravely. They talked a few minutes more as Sienna and Ryder finished up their meals. They both thanked Judy and assured her it was delicious.

Then they bid them good-night and headed across the hall.

Once in her own half of the house, Sienna leaned against the door and looked at Ryder.

"You're staying?" she asked.

"Am I invited?"

She wondered if they were both against being the one to admit that yes, it would be good if he stayed.

"I invited you the night before last."

"Ah, but that was before last night," he said.

"You know, you can really be annoying," she told him.

He laughed. "But come on, seriously, you must like me a little better . . . maybe? Quite frankly, until we had the lovely dinner invitation, I was going to close and lock the door, look at you with Valentino eyes, and ask if you wanted to fool around and then make dinner, or make dinner and then fool around."

"Valentino? Fool around?"

"Hey! *Valentino* . . . It's an expression. Yes, from a long-dead movie star. Fool around . . . Well, I'm trying to be polite and charming and not terribly graphic."

She was definitely liking him more and more.

She kept her back to the door but checked the bolt, then walked across the room to him.

"What a pity," she said softly, stopping less than an inch away.

He arched a brow. "A pity?"

"I was thinking about being just about as graphic as possible."

He smiled. She was in his arms. His mouth was hot and moist, and she had been anticipating their time alone together, she realized, and, well, they did say anticipation was . . . seductive.

Their clothing wound up all over the parlor. She thought they might wind up right there on the sofa she had first offered him as a bed.

But he was great at sweeping her off her feet.

"I like magic," he said to her softly. "The sofa . . ."

"Hard on a tall guy?" She couldn't help

grinning. "A hard, tall guy?"

"Something like that," he said.

"Hm. You know what?"

"What?"

"I can walk. I'm excellent at maneuvering this stairway."

"But this is fun. Romantic, right?"

"Not if you pop my head against the wall."

He groaned. She laughed. And in a minute, they were in her bed, and his mouth covered hers, and his lips swept over her flesh, and she felt the surge of reality over anticipation.

Seduced, enraptured, twisting in his arms, writhing, touching, caressing . . .

Later, they lay together, breathing. Just breathing. And she could wonder what it would be like if this ended, and he was just . . .

Gone.

It had to end, of course. She wasn't at all convinced as he was that everything was related, but if someone was trying to kill Martin Kimball, they had to find that someone.

And she wanted that; she wanted it desperately. The Kimball family were good people, the kids were young, and the truth had to be discovered . . .

"Hey," Ryder said softly.

"Mm?" Sienna replied.

"Do you almost-kind-of like me yet?"

She rolled to lean up on his chest and study his face.

"Yes. Almost-kind-of," she said seriously.

"And I'll still . . . do?"

"In a pinch."

"Ouch," he said. Then he sighed, turning on her.

"What?"

"Man, I'm going to try harder. My reputation, you know!"

They both started to laugh.

And the night was wonderful, and sleep, when it came, divine.

CHAPTER EIGHT

Ryder had an appointment to meet with Betsy Mahoney at the station at ten.

That meant he had time that morning.

They slept late, until eight, finally rose, and found Granny K was not down in the parlor.

"We could have run down the stairs naked," Ryder teased.

"Probably best we didn't, anyway," Sienna said. "And I remembered to set the timer, so the coffee will be brewcd."

And it was. But even as he took his first sip, Ryder's phone rang. It was Captain Troy.

He moved out into the parlor to answer the call while Sienna was wiping down the kitchen counter.

"We got a hit right away," the captain told him. "There werc fingerprints on the jacket — it was pleather, or fake leather, whatever the proper term is for that type of material.

We sent the prints out, and they traced back to a Terrence Berger —"

"Terry Berger!" Ryder said.

"You know him?" Troy asked.

"Can't say I know him. I've met him. He was at the gallery showing I went to the other night. He was living in the same area when the McTavish house went up in Terrebonne Parish ten years ago. He runs bayou tours and a shrimp boat there," Ryder said. "I didn't speak with him long. He said he was in the city because of Freddie Harrison, who was having a showing at a gallery owned by Thayer Boudreaux, another man who had lived in the area. Thayer was just a high-school kid back then, but now he has an art gallery on Royal." Ryder was puzzled. "What could the old shrimper gain from killing McTavish or going after Kimball?"

"The info just came in. I figured you'd want to be on the lookout for him. We've got a trace on credit cards to find out where he's staying in the city."

"He may not still be here," Ryder said. "Damn, he didn't mention anything about where he was staying."

"Think Sienna might know?"

"I can ask her. She can also check with Lori Markham, a Harrison cousin, and

Thayer Boudreaux or even Freddie. One of them might know."

"I'm looking at the files and info you've emailed me regarding that last house explosion. I have the names of everyone on the street or in the immediate vicinity. The Harrison children were just kids at the time. I don't see how —"

"The parents weren't kids," Ryder said. "And they came in for their son's show. See what you can get me. We have cops on the street looking for him, right?"

"We do. His picture is out. I included your FBI associates in an APB, too. Of course, I assumed if we found him, you wanted first crack at him. We'd hold him, let him get nervous, until you got here. But nothing yet. Checking what we can."

"Just give me ten minutes. I'll ask Sienna, and if she doesn't know and we don't get anything soon on our own, I'll have her try her friends."

When he ended the call, he saw she had come out to the parlor, too, and was looking at him.

"Okay. What?" she asked suspiciously.

"They traced a fingerprint on the jacket discarded by the man who went after Kimball. It belonged to Terry Berger," he told her.

She frowned. "Terry Berger? Are they sure? There must be a mistake. Why would a shrimper want to kill a man I doubt he even knows?"

"I'm going to need to find that out," Ryder said quietly. "We have to find him. Do you know where he was staying?"

"I doubt he stayed in NOLA. Even if he left the gallery showing late, he would have driven home. It's about ninety minutes. Terry always seemed to be a gruff old guy, even when I was young, but he liked home. He didn't like the city. I was surprised to see he had come in for the show, but he was always friendly with his neighbors."

"I think he did stay in the city, because it would have been a long drive in and out."

"Maybe he owned the jacket and donated it to charity," Sienna suggested.

There were, Ryder knew, often other explanations for what seemed obvious. But he had to find the man, even if it led to finding another explanation.

"Sienna, it's all we've got. Maybe Terry did give the jacket away. If so, we need to find who he gave it to or where he donated it."

She stared at him, but not with the hostility she might have at one time.

"Terry lives a simple life. He loves his

226

boats and the bayou. He's got a little wooden house, down the street from where I grew up."

"Does your family still own the home?"

"Yes. My parents are there." She inhaled. "And I . . ."

She broke off.

"Yes?" Ryder pressed.

"I talk to them every few days. But I haven't talked to them since the Kimball house burned, and I guess they didn't read about it. They'd have hounded me if they knew an arson had taken place next door to where I'm living," she admitted.

He nodded, then glanced at his phone. Troy hadn't called back yet.

"Could you take a few hours this morning?" he asked her.

"Yes, I put in far more than forty hours. I just need to let Clara know I won't be in until the afternoon. But why?"

"If you don't mind, I'd like you to come to the station with me. We can see if they've found anything else."

She looked at him and smiled slowly. "Is my guardian off today?"

"Pardon?"

"Fin. Is he busy, off duty?"

"Oh, no. He's working. And agents will be guarding your neighbors."

"I . . . Okay. I can just call Thayer and ask if he knows if Terry did decide to stay in the city. He probably went out with Thayer and Freddie and the Harrison family after the show. He *might* have stayed here. And if so, one of them would know."

"Let's see what else they might have."

"Okay. I'll just call Clara."

She did, and as they left her house, the neighborhood was quiet.

Sienna was quiet, too, as he drove. Then she said, "I really need to just bring my car home if we're going to be doing this."

"Yep. Good plan."

She seemed to be looking out the window, looking for something, as they drove.

"What is it?" he asked her.

She inhaled and exhaled.

And looked truly unhappy.

"Sienna?"

"The sketch of the so-called homeless man hanging around the neighborhood," she said softly.

"What about it?"

She winced and then admitted, "Something about it bothered me. You can't read much from it because the man had so much hair and so many whiskers, but there was something in the eyes that gnawed at me."

"And you know what it is?"

She looked at him and nodded. "I think . . ."

"What?"

"The homeless man might have been Terry Berger."

It just didn't gel.

Sienna couldn't believe Terry Berger had planned on burning down the McTavish home and killing that family ten years ago, gone on to Atlanta to kill Mr. McTavish via a hit-and-run, and come into NOLA to attempt to kill Martin Kimball.

What she had said was true: Terry loved the bayou. He loved the isolation and the sound of the birds. He loved what he did because he did it alone. Even taking tourists on bayou trips was at his discretion and when he chose to do so. He was a good guide. He knew every tree and bird and creature prowling the waterways.

Officers looked at her curiously as she entered the police station with Ryder, who greeted all with waves or nods as he came in.

He was heading to his captain's office, she quickly realized.

She followed him in. A man she judged to be in his mid-to late fifties stood, watching as she and Ryder entered.

229

He offered her his hand. "Miss Murray, I presume?"

"Yes, sir."

"I'm Captain Troy. Please, take a seat."

She did, taking one of the two chairs in front of his desk. When she was seated, Ryder and Captain Troy did the same. She couldn't help but notice his given name, Ebenezer, on the plaque on his desk.

An unusual name, certainly. She'd only ever heard it used before in Dickens's *A Christmas Carol.* An unusual name for a parent to have given a child, she thought.

Ryder was staring hard at the captain.

"Nothing," Troy told him.

"Well, then, I guess it is time for Sienna to find out if anyone knows anything, but she doubted he would have stayed here in the city. But if he did go out with the Harrison family and Thayer Boudreaux after the show, it was an hour and a half drive home — and he was back quickly if, indeed, he was the man about to attack Kimball," Ryder said.

Sienna realized both men were staring at her. She hesitated.

She couldn't believe it, and yet, she couldn't deny it. Because the sketch the police artist had drawn from the descriptions given by Whitney and Grace had shown her those eyes that were somehow familiar . . .

And now known.

She couldn't imagine Terry Berger pretending to be a homeless man in her neighborhood, either.

"What do you want me to do?" she asked, looking from the captain to Ryder.

Ryder leaned toward her. "We need you to be casual. Talk about something else — art, friends, or old times. Then you could say you were surprised about Terry Berger being there."

"Who did you want me to call?" she asked.

"Lori Markham. She didn't go out with her cousins, but she might know what was going on with them," Ryder told her. "And you can call her with some excuse about work, so it will be the most natural."

"What if she doesn't know anything?"

"We'll go from there," Ryder said.

He and the captain were both looking at her.

She sat in silence.

"On your cell phone," Ryder said.

"Oh, yes, of course," Sienna murmured, pulling her phone from her shoulder bag. She looked at them both as she dialed.

Lori answered cheerfully. "Hey, where are you? Taking a morning off?"

231

"Oh, I'm coming in. You know me. But I thought I would call and see if everything is all right. I guess I'm nervous after the other night."

"Everything is fine. Byron had the security company come in and go over everything again. Dr. Lightfoot just did his monthly checkup on our birds of prey, and . . . I have twenty little kids in the petting zoo with their doting parents watching. A few of them asked me if I could make sure our hand sanitizer was at least seventy-five percent alcohol, and I assured them it was."

Sienna laughed softly, hoping the sound was natural. "I'm glad all's well," she said. "Hey, it was really nice to get out the other night. I mean, wow! Definitely a few surprises. I can't believe even Terry Berger came in for the show. He never leaves home. And he hates the city. He must have liked us kids more than we suspected if he came out for Freddie's show."

It was Lori's turn to laugh. "He was always keeping an eye on us, remember? He'd warn us he'd call our parents if we acted up. And I know he called my aunt and uncle a few times. And Thayer! Well, he was such a high-school hunk, he was always getting into trouble. I think Terry picked him up from school once when Thayer's folks

232

were working. He was really always a nice old guy. Just gruff."

"Oh, I didn't mean he wasn't nice. He's just such a homebody. I still can't imagine him staying in the city."

"I don't think he did stay. I guess they weren't done until two or three in the morning, but I think Terry still drove home. I heard Thayer ask him where he was staying and if he needed anything, and Terry said he didn't need a thing, and he wasn't worried about time — he was going home."

"I guess the late drive was nothing for him. I do remember he liked the middle of the night for being out on the bayou," Sienna said. "Anyway, I don't want to keep you from twenty little munchkins. I'll be in soon. Just being lazy."

"You are entitled to have days off, you know."

"Yep. Though, Byron has managed to make us all feel like the museum is home as much as home is, so . . . See you in a bit!"

"I'll be here, making sure these little guys don't pull any tails."

She ended the call.

"As far as Thayer and the Harrison family knew, Terry Berger wasn't staying here. He didn't care how late they were out. He was going to drive home."

She saw the captain and Ryder exchange a glance.

"Do you want —" Troy began.

"No, I'll go myself, after I see Mrs. Mahoney," Ryder said. "Excuse me, I'll be right back. I have an appointment. Captain, I'm not going to keep Mrs. Mahoney long. I just want to see if there is anything she's thought about that might help in any way. I should just be a few minutes. Then, Sienna, I'll get you to work."

She didn't get a chance to protest or ask what she was supposed to be doing. He left Captain Troy's office before she could.

She was left to look at Captain Troy, silent.

"I saw you looking at my name plaque," he said.

"I . . . Yes. Your name is unusual," she said. "My mother is a huge fan of Charles Dickens. Were you named after Scrooge?"

"Well, here's the story. Dickens traveled to Scotland where he saw a gravestone for a man named Ebenezer Lennox Scroggie. Scroggie was identified there on his marker as a *meal* man, but Dickens saw *mean* man. Now, the Scots have sometimes had a reputation for being frugal — cheap. But that's not what was meant by the tombstone. Scroggie had been a corn merchant and he was known to be generous to those in need. But no matter, the cheapskate Ebenezer Scrooge came into being, and the man beneath the gravestone gained a very strange immortality." He leaned closer to her across his desk. "Guess what?" he asked her.

"What?"

"I'm not cheap, and I wish to hell I was more frugal. But sometimes, being Ebenezer helps keep people in line because the imagination will always take us further than any reality."

She smiled. "Great story," she told him.

He smiled. "I didn't distract you, huh?"

She laughed. "You're the captain! You don't have to distract me."

He shrugged. "This is a serious situation. I admit, even I was wondering about Ryder's direction — until Kimball was attacked on the street. It's an important case. I don't want anything else in my city burning up. I don't want anything else anywhere burning up. And it's highly possible Dr. Mahoney's murder is associated . . . He was headed here, then was murdered and burned. That's a firebug. And we don't want one, nor do we care to inflict one on anyone else."

"I still don't see it. A firebug ten years ago, waiting and attempting to kill again?"

"*Killing* again," Troy said. "And Ryder,

well, he's always had an instinct. I'm going to miss the hell out of him, but I understand. And I like his unit. He made a call and brought down people. Helps tons when we're all still struggling with city budgets after last year." He hesitated. "I know they'll send him back if he's needed."

"I guess it's what he wants and needs to do," Sienna said. She still felt awkward, sitting there. "Captain, there's probably a place you could perch me while Ryder is . . . speaking with Mrs. Mahoney."

"You're welcome here, and in fact, I'd like you to tell me a story," he said. "First, if you don't mind, go back. Ten years. To the long-ago fire."

"I . . ."

"Please."

She was sure the incident was on record, so she didn't lie, she just altered her own perception a bit, telling him she believed they had mistakenly estimated the time of her grandmother's death, and it had been her grandmother who had told her to go.

Then he wanted to know how she'd managed to rush to the Kimball house in the nick of time.

That time, she lied. But not really: she had smelled gas. After Granny K had wakened her. But it wasn't a lie, it was just an

236

omission.

He listened and kept her talking. He asked questions, offered suggestions, and was altogether thoughtful and courteous. She could easily understand how the man had risen to his rank. And she'd never think of the name Ebenezer in the same way again.

Betsy Mahoney reached Ryder's office just a minute after he slid in himself. He greeted her at the door, and before anything else, taking her hands, asked her how she was faring.

"I feel lost. They won't release my husband's body yet. But the police department here has been wonderful. And the medical examiner and everyone at the morgue . . ." Her voice hitched. "I never thought I'd see a morgue. I mean, yes, I knew we'd die one day. But it would be natural, and if Lester went first, he'd be in a hospital or at home. We have already paid for our funerals and plots there, because he never wanted the children left to . . . to need to struggle in any way to pay for funerals."

"You'll still get to take him home," Ryder promised her.

"So many people loved him!" she said. "I know funerals are for the living, but he saved so many lives and prolonged others.

237

Not just by keeping people on machines. He gave them quality of life, too."

"I didn't know him, but I'm so sorry. His loss is truly tragic. And I know you must feel lost and you're suffering, and I'm so sorry to ask you to talk, but . . ."

"I know," she said. She looked at him with wide eyes. "That was it, Detective Stapleton. He liked to play craps. And only now and then. He didn't bet the mortgage or the household money. Twice a year, maybe. He liked to come here, and he liked to go to Las Vegas. We usually took two trips alone each year, one to each place. But as I told you, we couldn't both leave. And look what it's brought! Maybe, if I had come with him, he'd still be alive. And I wouldn't be away from the kids now."

"Please, don't think that way. Maybe, if you'd come with him, you might have been killed, too, and then you wouldn't be going home to your children. I believe the person who did this has little or no conscience, and that killing anyone who's in the way would be nothing more than collateral damage."

She nodded, trying to smile.

"He had no enemies, you told me," Ryder said.

She shook her head. "I'm not just making that up. He cared about everyone. He was loved in private practice and at the hospital. He worked wonders with kidney patients. Sometimes, his patients needed transplants. Many got them, and some, of course, didn't, but there was never anyone who blamed my husband for lack of effort."

"You don't believe there's anyone out there who believed he failed them?"

She shook her head. "He kept people living longer than anyone else projected. He worked with a new dialysis machine. It's under trials right now, and I know he was saying there were people working around the clock to see if any improvements could be made. And any medical device in trials —"

"You don't think anyone killed him because they believe an experimental machine killed a loved one, do you?"

"There hasn't been a failure yet," she said.

"Did he work with others?"

"I know he had meetings at the hospital where he worked and with other nephrologists. But from what we've gathered so far, everyone was for it."

Never was everyone for everything, Ryder thought, but he didn't argue the point.

"You can call the hospital, of course."

He nodded. He wouldn't call the hospital himself. He'd have the best person at the

Krewe call the hospital. They could do that while he headed out to Terrebonne Parish.

"Detective, I've been thinking. And I'll keep thinking. My sister has been able to come out here to be with me. She's waiting for me. If —"

"No, it's fine. I appreciate you coming back in."

She smiled weakly. "It's easy — when the police are watching out for you," she said.

"Still. Thank you."

She nodded and left. He put a call through to Jackson Crow, who promised to have Angela start investigating the hospital and new dialysis machine as quickly as possible.

Then he headed back to Captain Troy's office. He looked through the window before stepping in: it seemed Troy and Sienna were doing just fine.

He smiled, wondering if Troy had started out with the story of his name.

Then he stepped in.

"She's doing all right. Her sister has arrived in the city. I let her go. She'll call me if she can think of anything else. Sienna, let me get you to work."

"You'll keep in touch," Troy said. It wasn't a question.

Ryder nodded gravely.

They were out of the office and in the car

before Sienna looked at him and said, "You're not taking me to work."

"It's all right. Fin is already there. He's been out with Lightfoot and the animals, getting to know Clara, Morrie, Artie, Lori — and Lightfoot."

She shook her head. "You're going to Terrebonne Parish."

"Yes."

"Then so am I."

"You just told Lori you were coming in to work."

"And Lori just told me everyone deserves a day off."

"You said you were going in. Sienna, I don't think you want to go with me. I'm going to be calling the sheriff there and . . ." He hesitated and pulled the car over to the side. He could just call the local authorities, but he wanted to search for the man himself.

Local people might not be so keen on apprehending the man.

"I don't think you want to be with me," he told her. "You don't want to believe he did anything wrong. I'm sorry. He is wanted as a person of interest in an attempted-murder investigation. And arson."

"He might listen to me when he won't listen to you."

"You're a civilian. I can't risk having you

on something like this."

"What?" she demanded indignantly, staring at him. "You dragged me into all this!"

She had a point. He sat silently and then pulled out his phone and asked Fin to meet them at Sienna's house.

She was pleased at first. Triumphant? She called in and spoke with Clara this time, saying that if everything was running smoothly, she was going to take the whole day off.

Everything, according to Clara, was moving along just fine.

It wasn't until they were in front of her house waiting for Fin to arrive that Sienna suddenly said, "Oh!"

"Oh?"

She let out a long breath. "If we're going to Terrebonne Parish, to Terry Berger's place, we'll go right by my parents' house."

"Is there a problem with your parents?" he asked her.

"No, not at all. I adore them. But I didn't tell them about the fire being next door. My mom texted about how awful the fire was, but she didn't realize how close it was. I didn't tell her or my dad anything because I didn't want them to be worried and start trying to make me come home." She winced, looked at him, and admitted, "I think they might see it as more than a co-incidence, too, and try to talk me into coming back where they believe I'd be safe."

He was quiet. "Well, you can pretend we're not just down the street from your parents."

She smiled ruefully. "What? You're not going to say I should go home for a while?"

"Hell, no. I can watch you here. If I'm right, Terrebonne Parish is where it all started."

Fin had arrived. He didn't park with any kind of subterfuge but rolled his car in front of Sienna's house, exited quickly, and slid into the back seat.

"So," he said, "no one admitted to the man staying with them in the city, huh?"

"I told Ryder that Terry Berger didn't like staying in the city. He likes his home. He likes his shrimp boat. He's right on the bayou. He doesn't care when he sleeps, but he does care about where he sleeps. Honestly, I don't think the man has ever been out of the state of Louisiana," Sienna explained.

"Okay, then, you're driving. I don't mean to be rude, but I'm probably going to be dozing off."

"Doze away," Ryder told him.

He wasn't surprised: they'd all learned to

sleep when they could. And he was grateful to Fin. The man was an experienced agent who had done basic surveillance and witness protection for him, never saying a word but respecting Ryder as lead on this case. Then again, Ryder had respected the work of the FBI agents who had led the other cases they had worked together.

Fin wasn't the only one who dozed off. Sienna had her head leaned against the window at first, watching the scenery as they drove. But soon, her eyes were closed, and she was sleeping, too.

They both woke up about twenty minutes out. The two of them engaged in conversation, Fin explaining he'd very recently married, and yes, his wife saw the dead. She was a working actress. Their assistant director, Adam Harrison, was rich and had been a philanthropist and had been engaged in getting the right law enforcement to the right place and situation several years before he had become part of the bureau himself and formed the Krewe of Hunters under Jackson Crow.

Adam owned a theater not far from Krewe headquarters. And there were plenty of films going on in the DC, Maryland, and Northern Virginia regions.

Then Sienna fell silent. They were in an

area where the houses were half a mile apart, horses roamed in paddocks, and it seemed that most yards also offered gardens with not just flowers but fruits and vegetables as well.

"One turn and we're on my street. We'll pass my house, and Terry Berger's place is just down about a mile, on the opposite side, right on the bayou," she said.

Glancing at her quickly, Ryder saw she appeared to be tense.

Then she smiled at him and seemed to relax.

"Neither car is there. Of course, they're both at work! And up ahead, there on your left, that's Terry Berger's place. He's right on the water there. The bayou runs on that side of the street down this block."

They drew up in the yard. As she exited the car, Sienna walked around to the side looking to the back.

"He should be here. His boat is at the dock."

They walked up a path of broken stones through overgrown grass and weeds. The house was two stories, of wood construction, and in need of paint.

Ryder tapped at the door. They waited. "No answer."

Fin stepped to the door. "Special Agent

Fin Stirling, Mr. Berger. Sorry to bother you, but we do have a few questions for you."

Still there was no answer.

Aggravated, Ryder knocked on the door again, this time with force.

The door creaked open, but there was no one there.

Ryder looked at Fin. Fin shrugged and said, "Not locked, and we could be worried about the man. Legal entry," he said.

They all stepped into the house. The ground floor seemed to be one big room encompassing a kitchen, a table and some chairs, and a sofa. A stairway led up to the second floor.

Again, Ryder glanced at Fin, and they both nodded. Ryder left Fin with Sienna as he hurried up the stairs.

The second floor offered a room in each direction. He went left first and discovered Terry Berger's bedroom. The bed was unmade. Clothing hung out of drawers. There was a small closet that yielded a collection of rubber boots, shirts, and rain jackets.

He left the bedroom. There was a bathroom in the center of the hall. Berger wasn't much of a housekeeper. Dirt crusted the floor, and the sink held a thin gray film.

He headed to the next room, which he thought might have been a second bedroom that had been turned into an office. There was a simple table in the middle along with a plain chair. A computer and printer sat on the table along with a messy pile of folders.

And a calendar. Ryder dug in his pocket for a pair of gloves and opened the calendar. Flipping through, he saw that dates were marked for bayou tours and for shrimping. Some were marked having to do with appointments in the city, and one was a notation about crawfish and catfish.

He searched for the week before the fire at the Kimball house.

There were strange entries. *Nothing afternoon, learning* on one day and *Nothing afternoon, watch day — must buy gas first* on another.

Gas? Enough for the drive into New Orleans to pretend to be a homeless man and watch the comings and goings at the Kimball house? Or to use as an accelerant?

He flipped to the date of the show for Freddie Harrison at Thayer Boudreaux's gallery. The note there read, *Gallery show. Screw it. Coming home.*

He looked at the next day. *Action.*

He closed the diary and left it. When they caught Terry Berger, he wasn't going to be told Ryder had conducted an illegal search and seizure. As it was, they were fine: they had entered because the door had been left open, and they had been worried about the health and well-being of Mr. Berger.

He left the room, and heading back down, he touched the banister.

He felt something sticky and was glad his hand was still gloved. But he looked at his hand immediately. The substance was a brownish-crimson color.

Blood.

"Fin!"

Fin came running up the stairs. He saw Sienna was at the base of the stairs, looking up as Fin joined him.

Fin didn't touch the banister. He looked at Ryder.

"Anything upstairs?" Fin asked.

"Not that I saw," Ryder told him. "He might have been hit right here and dragged down and out. Anything below?"

"Uneaten food on the table," Fin said.

"The boat," Ryder murmured.

They both hurried down the stairs. Sienna backed away, looking at them.

"Terry might be hurt," Ryder said. "We're going to check the boat."

There was a back door, and they hurried out across the lawn to the dock.

What effort Terry Berger hadn't put into his house, he had put into his boat. She was fiberglass, forty feet, with well-tended nets and a clean canvas over the helm.

"Mr. Berger!" Fin called as they headed down the dock. The boat was securely tied. He called out again, and there was still no answer.

"It's Ryder Stapleton, Mr. Berger!" he shouted. "Coming aboard to see if you're all right!"

He leaped onto the deck.

And right into a pile of pooling blood. Fin was at his side, shouting for Sienna to wait.

She didn't wait. She was hopping onto the deck as he spoke.

"Oh, lord!" she whispered, and Ryder knew she realized what they were standing in was blood.

He strode quickly to the cabin and helm.

And there, he found Terry Berger.

The man had a small gash on the top of his head. Ryder was certainly not a medical doctor, but he didn't think the blow to the head had killed the man.

Rather, it was the slash across his throat.

He lay on his back by the helm, eyes open, staring blankly, and glazed. Blood had soaked his shirt, his pants, and the floor. He still held a straight razor in his right hand.

"Stop her!" he cried to Fin, knowing Sienna would try to follow him.

This time, Fin managed to block Sienna's path, even as he pulled out his phone to call for the local authorities.

Ryder backed away the best he could so as not to disturb evidence. They needed a crime-scene unit and a medical examiner.

"Suicide?" Fin said quietly to him as they stood at the opening to the cabin.

"Yeah. He whacked himself on the head before coming down here to slit his own throat. You think?"

"Someone tried to make it look like suicide," Fin said.

"I guess he's supposed to look guilty. Well, not *look* guilty. I believe he was our homeless man and he did attack Martin Kimball. But not on his own."

"He's supposed to look guilty of it all," Fin said. "Razor in his hand — had to commit suicide because the police were closing in."

"He was working for someone," Ryder said. "And that someone decided to get rid of him when he might have been arrested . . . and forced to talk."

"Sorry end," Fin said. "Then again, he was ready to stab Martin Kimball to death. And he was down the street years ago when

250

the McTavish house was set ablaze."

"Which, in my mind, narrows down the suspects," Ryder said softly.

They could hear sirens. Sienna was standing on the deck, almost frozen in place.

He reached for her hand, hopping onto the dock and helping her over.

"Terry is dead," she said.

"Yes."

"But . . . he was guilty of all this?" she asked.

She sounded confused. Because Terry didn't seem like a man who might come up with a strange and twisted agenda that targeted certain men and their families.

"He was guilty, yes, but . . ."

"He was a puppet and someone else was pulling the strings?" she asked. "And that *someone* must be someone I know?"

He was saved from answering her.

Police cars and the medical examiner had arrived, and he stepped back toward the front with Fin, ready to explain why they had come — and what they had found.

A dead man.

CHAPTER NINE

Law enforcement had gathered on the scene. But they were in a city and a parish, with police and a sheriff — and their little group consisted of a federal agent and a NOLA cop.

Sienna recognized the sheriff when he arrived. The position had been held by Lawrence Patterson when the McTavish house had burned to the ground, and he still held it.

He arched his brows at seeing her, but she was standing back with Ryder.

Fin had apparently worked with Captain Wayne Tremont before. Tremont liked Fin, was glad to meet Ryder, and was courteous to Sienna.

"This is hard to believe," Sheriff Patterson said.

It was strange. She had thought of him as an older man before, and now she realized he was about forty-five and had been young for a sheriff when the McTavish house had burned.

"Sienna," he said at last. "You do manage to be around for some of our most startling occasions."

She smiled weakly, not sure how to answer, but she didn't need to worry.

"We brought her along with us specifically because she knew Terry Berger and the area, Sheriff," Fin said.

"We weren't expecting to find . . . what we found," Ryder said.

"But you're NOPD," Patterson said.

"Ryder is a consultant with my unit, as well as a detective with the NOPD," Fin said. "Sheriff, you must be concerned about this. We have Berger's fingerprints on evidence from a knife attack on the man whose house was burned to the ground in NOLA."

"Yes, I understand you've worked in this area before, Special Agent Stirling," Patterson said. "Just remember, we're Terrebonne Parish out here."

"We always strive to respect local jurisdiction, Sheriff," Fin assured him.

"Fin is a fine agent," Captain Tremont said to the sheriff.

Tremont had snow-white hair and a worn and serious face. Sienna had never met him, but her small neighborhood was on the

253

outskirts of Houma, which was larger than some of the cities in the parish, but still small — very small — in comparison to New Orleans.

The medical examiner was in the boat doing his preliminary examination of Terry Berger. A crime-scene unit was working in the house and waiting for the ME's clearance to investigate on the boat.

"So, we heard about the fire in New Orleans," Patterson said, staring at Sienna. "And speculated on the similarities to what happened here. I understand you were involved in getting the family out, Sienna. Did your dead grandmother warn you again?"

His question was voiced lightly, as if in jest. She could still hear the mockery.

"Actually, Sheriff, it was my nose," she said sweetly. "Gas — hell of a smell."

"Ah," he said. "Still. Interesting that you were right there for both."

"And thank God, right? Hey, I heard about that fire ten years ago," Captain Tremont said. "You saved a baby — a whole family!"

Ryder looked at Sheriff Patterson with his jaw set. Sienna realized he was indignant for her and about to rise to her defense as well.

"My parents' house is just down the street. If I'm not needed, I believe I'll head down that way," she said.

"Ryder and I can handle anything needed for the reports. I think that would be fine," Fin said, staring at Patterson.

The sheriff was silent.

"I'll see Sienna to her folks' house," Ryder said, "and be right back."

He took her by the arm, and they started walking. She didn't look back.

"Ass!" Ryder exclaimed when they were out of earshot.

She had to smile. "Hey, I think you were suspicious of me at first."

"This guy has been sheriff a long time?"

"He was a hell of a lot nicer ten years ago," she said. "I think my parents are casual friends with him. Back then, he just thought I needed therapy. And in a way, I can't blame him. Fire and a dead man. And here I am again."

They quickly reached the house she had grown up in. It was a long walk, but they were both emotional and taking long strides.

But as they neared the house, Sienna's footsteps slowed.

"They're home!"

"That's good. I wasn't happy about leaving you alone. Please tell me there is an alarm system on the house?"

She nodded. "They installed one after the McTavish house went up."

"Good."

She had a key, of course. Her parents had always insisted she keep a key, that her childhood house would be her home all her life.

But she hesitated; she wasn't coming alone. She tapped on the door.

Her father swung it open. At first, he gave her a beaming — though confused — smile. Then he looked anxious, and she knew he would have heard sirens in the neighborhood and maybe even seen all the vehicles down by Terry Berger's house.

"Dad, I'm fine," she said quickly.

"Oh!" he said exhaling sharply.

"Hugh, who is it?" her mother called, but then she, too, came to the door.

"Sienna! Oh, but the sirens —"

"I'm fine," she repeated.

Then they both stared at Ryder.

He quickly offered his hand to her father. "How do you do, Mr. Murray? I'm Ryder Stapleton, NOPD. An associate of mine and I needed to take a ride out here, and Sienna wanted to come. To see you, of course."

"Nice! I'm Marlena, and this is my husband, Hugh," her mother said to Ryder, quickly adding to Sienna, "Oh, sweetheart, that's great, but . . ."

Her mother's voice trailed.

Sienna loved her mom and dad. They were wonderful parents, and while her father liked his space and solitude, he was a passionate believer in equal rights, justice, freedom of religion, and much more. Her mother echoed him. He worked for an advertising agency, and she had been a reporter who early on had embraced the concept of mass communication and gone into website design, working for a major firm. They kept in shape and still loved long walks together, biking, and other physical activity.

They weren't fond of the big city — New Orleans — but loved the area they lived in.

"What is going on? Is everything okay?" her dad asked. He looked at Sienna.

"I'll explain," Sienna promised.

"I'm afraid I must get back," Ryder said.

"Is Terry all right? I mean, he's a crusty old crab, but he is a neighbor," Marlena said. "Yes, in our area, our homes are a bit apart, but we drove by a great deal of activity, and we're worried. Naturally."

"I'm afraid that Terry is dead," Ryder told them.

"Oh, no! Poor old fellow. No family, no

real friends . . . just neighbors, really," Hugh said. "Did he have a heart attack?"

Ryder glanced at Sienna.

She looked at her father. "No, Dad. I'll explain everything. But Ryder needs to get back."

Her father looked concerned, but he nodded. "Of course. Come on in, sweetheart."

"I'll be back as soon as possible," Ryder said.

She watched with her parents as he walked away. Then she felt them both staring at her.

"Um, should we go in?" she suggested.

"Yes, of course," her mom said. "Come into the kitchen. I just put a casserole in the oven. We can have some lemonade while we wait for it to bake."

"And you can tell us what exactly is going on," her father said.

Maybe it was time she did. She'd leave out the bit about Granny K — they hadn't believed her the first time, and they wouldn't believe her now and would probably insist she get more therapy.

But she was going to tell them about the fires and that Ryder was a detective, and that Fin, who they would meet, was with the FBI — and that what had happened ten years ago was catching up with them all now.

258

■ ■ ■

The autopsy on Terry Berger would not be performed until the next day.

The medical examiner pointed out that the razor was found in Terry's right hand and the slash went from the left of his throat to the right, suggesting that, yes, he could have pulled the blade himself. But Fin and Ryder emphasized the bloody smudge on the banister and the concussion on Terry's head.

Ryder couldn't help speculating on how unlikely it was that Terry had used a blunt object on himself before heading out to his boat to commit suicide.

Sheriff Patterson argued if a murder had taken place, the murderer could have tossed the body into the bayou and it might well have been heavily decomposed and compromised before it had ever been found.

"If Terry Berger was guilty of torching houses and attempted murder —" Patterson began.

"And possibly a hit-and-run murder in Atlanta," Fin put in.

"A hit-and-run murder?" Patterson asked. "I knew about McTavish, of course. We all thought it was sad the man died in the street after his family survived that fire. But that was an unrelated accident . . ."

"Unless he was hit on purpose," Ryder said.

"There was no suggestion of such a thing at the time," Patterson said. "I mean, it wasn't our jurisdiction, but we read about it."

"We'll find out if Terry Berger was in Atlanta at the time," Fin said, shrugging.

Patterson looked at him. "If so, then I'm going to assume you'll believe him guilty. And if you're right, well, it's completely possible he did decide to kill himself. It's beyond me why Berger would have done all this, but maybe the guilt and remorse were too much. The two can do a hell of a number on a person."

"Well, his guilt and remorse were a long time coming," Captain Tremont said.

"I'll want to be at the autopsy," Fin said.

Patterson looked as if he would argue: to him, it was a local suicide, and his officer should be handling it.

But he didn't fight Fin. He told Captain Tremont to make sure the paperwork was thorough.

"Well, I guess I'll be seeing you again then, Special Agent Stirling — and you, too, Detective Stapleton."

Ryder was silent, and the sheriff said, "Consultant, right?"

"Sir, I am, but I may be back in NOLA. My jurisdiction now," he said politely.

Patterson nodded grimly and then left.

The body was gone. Crime-scene investigators continued to work.

But Fin and Ryder were free to go, getting in the car to drive down the street.

"So, this is going to be fun," Fin said.

Ryder shrugged. "Fun. Hm . . . Well, interesting."

"Have you met her parents?" Fin asked.

Ryder looked at him quizzically. Fin shrugged with a wry smile. "Okay. Sorry. Shouldn't have asked, I guess."

They reached Sienna's house, and Fin stepped forward to knock on the door. Sienna answered it, but as Ryder had expected, her parents were right behind her.

Introductions went around again since Marlena and Hugh Murray had met Ryder but not Fin.

They all headed to the kitchen. Dinner was ready, Marlena told them, and they all worked together to set the food out.

"We always overdo it when we get to have Sienna home!" Marlena said. "And that works — leftovers for the following days. But it will be nice to have people sit down

261

and enjoy a dinner that won't leave leftovers. I mean, hopefully!"

"Wonderful. And thank you," Fin said.

"Our pleasure!" Marlena assured him.

The three members of the Murray family were good at working together: plates went down, and casserole dishes followed, and then glasses and a large pitcher of sweet summer tea.

"So," Hugh said, looking at Fin, "what's it like being in a little place like this?"

"Well," Fin told him, "I grew up right in downtown Houma, so frankly, it feels just like coming home."

"Ah. Ryder — or Detective Stapleton. What about you?"

"The heart of New Orleans," Ryder told him.

Hugh passed around a casserole dish that held a sweet-potato concoction that proved to be delicious.

"We'd heard about the fire in New Orleans," Marlena said, casting her daughter a reproachful glance. "Interesting, but my daughter never mentioned it was right next door to where she was living!"

"I didn't want you to worry," Sienna said wearily.

"And yet here you are, with an FBI agent and a NOLA detective when a neighbor is found dead," Hugh said. "And, oh, yes, I'm forgetting. The detective came to see you because you were the one who saved the family in NOLA, too."

"I could smell gas," Sienna said. "Mom, Dad, really —"

"You didn't smell gas a decade ago," Hugh reminded her.

"Hugh," Marlena warned.

Ryder had no idea as to how Sienna wanted to handle the questions her parents were asking. He was determined to sit silent and follow her lead.

But Sienna suddenly seemed to explode with energy, though she was still and her voice was level and calm when she spoke. "Well, you know, I told you ten years ago Granny K warned me, and you two just thought I needed therapy. But here you go. Granny K warned me again. Yes, some spirits remain. Thanks to her, I see many, and I don't need therapy, and I'm really sorry if you don't believe me."

"Sienna!" Hugh said, frowning, his tone worried.

"My son can be such a jerk."

Ryder hadn't realized Granny K was there, but she was standing at the kitchen entry, shaking her head.

"Oh, sweetheart," Marlena began. But she

broke off, troubled.

"Sienna, seriously, you could wind up in real trouble, real danger," Hugh said, then turned to his wife. "Marlena, what is wrong with you?"

Marlena was shivering.

"Cold," she said. "It's suddenly cold in here."

"Because," Sienna said flatly, "Granny K is here."

"My mother is here? Sienna, that's cruel," Hugh said. "I loved my mother, dearly, you know that, and for you to act as if . . ."

He suddenly turned on Fin and Ryder. "Are you encouraging this nonsense?"

"Frankly —" Ryder began, but he fell silent. Hugh's expression had changed completely.

Granny K had come to stand behind her son, placing her hands on his shoulders, speaking to him softly.

"You're a good man, a bright man. I was always proud of you as a boy, and I'm very proud of the man you became. But open your mind, son. There are always going to be things one person sees and not the other, and things one senses in life — and death — and others do not. Listen to your daughter."

Hugh was so silent Ryder wondered if he

had heard his mother's words.

But he hadn't. He had simply felt her presence, whether he realized it or not.

"She's here. Now?" he asked, his tone stilted.

"Yes," Sienna told him.

"Why can't I hear her? She was my mother."

"I don't know," Sienna told him softly.

"What did she say?"

"She's proud of you, but you need to understand that others might see and hear what you do not," Sienna told him.

"You can actually see and hear her?" Hugh paused, looking at his wife. "You don't just feel cold like your mother?"

"Yes," Sienna said softly.

Hugh stared at Ryder and then Fin.

"Good lord! You see and hear dead people, too?"

Ryder let out a long breath. "Yes."

Granny K spoke up. "Tell my dear son that while I know he puts in and cooks, his wife prepared a lovely meal, and none of you are eating it! Oh, I loved Marlena's sweet-potato casserole!"

Sienna smiled.

"What?" Hugh asked.

"Granny K is upset that we're not eating. She knows you cook and that you pitch in, but Mom made a great meal and we're not eating it. By the way, Mom, she really loved your sweet-potato casserole."

Marlena smiled weakly.

Hugh frowned for a minute, and then, to Ryder's amazement, he laughed.

"This isn't possible. It can't be. But if it is, Granny K looks out for you!"

"Yes," Sienna said.

He shook his head. "Eat, please. I have a million questions. I mean, can you see every dead person? Wait — eat while you answer me! I can imagine my mother haunting me." He laughed again. "Oh, Mom," he said to the air, "you haunt Sienna. That's brilliant." He waited a minute and looked at his daughter. "Did she say anything?"

"She's too busy laughing. Hey, come on, let's eat!"

They ate, but Hugh and Marlena asked questions throughout the meal.

Ryder, Fin, and Sienna all answered. No, not everyone became a ghost. No, ghosts didn't really know what happened next. Yes, there was usually a reason they stayed, no, not always because they were cheated out of life, and no, none of them had all the answers. Hugh addressed his mother several times, waiting for one of the others to repeat her answer.

The meal ended; the dishes were done.

Ryder knew it was time he spoke to the group about the day.

"We managed to avoid any media. Please, no one say anything. No one in New Orleans will know we were out here, that we were the ones to find Terry Berger's body. It could be very important as we try to put all the pieces together. The Terrebonne authorities found the body of a man who was suspected in the arson that occurred in New Orleans."

"Because you think there was someone else involved?" Hugh asked.

"Yes," Ryder said flatly, and at his side, Fin nodded seriously.

"You should just stay here with us, Sienna," Hugh said to his daughter.

"She could be in greater danger here," Fin warned. "We have her street covered in the city, and her place of work."

It was time to head back, especially for Fin, who would attend the autopsy in the morning. Ryder said he hadn't determined what he was going to do yet, but if Sienna was staying in the city, so was he.

"But all three of you could just stay here!" Marlena said.

"Mom, stop, please," Sienna begged. "I love you, but I'm being protected by two amazing agencies that are actively working these crimes."

"You'll call every day?" Marlena begged.

"I will," Sienna promised her. They thanked her and Hugh again, then left. Granny K was going to ride with them. She'd had to hitch a ride out to Terrebonne Parish, and that had been a pain.

Right when they were leaving, Hugh Murray caught Ryder at the door.

"I don't know exactly what is going on. But I saw the way my daughter looks at you, and I've seen the way you look back. I'm assuming there's something more going on there."

"Mr. Murray," he began, "I —"

"I don't care. I don't care if it's for now or forever. For now, no matter what the hell is going on, you stay with my daughter, and you keep her safe. Do you understand me?"

"I will keep her safe," Ryder promised, and he added quietly, "I swear to you, I would give my life at any given moment to protect her."

Hugh made a sniffing sound. "I watched you and listened to you tonight. You're a good cop. Protect and Serve. You'd probably give your life in the line of duty for anyone. But this is dead serious. You keep her safe."

"I will," Ryder promised.

"Is my mother really a ghost, and you people actually talk to her?" he asked.

Ryder nodded.

"She's going with you?"

"Yes, she is."

Hugh gazed at him. "Tell her how much I love her. She was a smart, caring, and wonderful woman, and I appreciate every moment I had with her."

"I'll do that," Ryder promised. He pulled out a card and handed it to Hugh. "In case you want to check in on how things are going."

Hugh nodded. "I will keep this." He paused. Sienna had already hugged her parents and said goodbye. Looking at his daughter, he smiled suddenly. "And tell her to call us and check in so we know she's all right. Make sure she knows she needs to do it, or we'll be calling you."

Ryder smiled and nodded, shook the man's hand, and headed toward the car.

Granny K was in the back already, with Sienna beside her. Fin was in the driver's seat.

He crawled in shotgun and waved again to Hugh, where he stood on the porch.

"What was that all about?" Sienna asked.

Ryder turned to look at Granny K.

"He wanted you to know what a great parent and person you were, and he wanted me to tell you that he loves you."

Granny K smiled. "I raised a good boy!" she said.

"And?" Sienna asked suspiciously.

"He told me to keep you safe," Ryder said. "And that you have to call them more often."

Sienna muttered beneath her breath, groaning, but then she sat forward, pointing to a house they were passing. "That's the Harrison house, and there, on the bayou side again, that's where Thayer grew up. And ahead is where the McTavish house once stood."

Ryder noted the proximity of the homes. The place where Terry Berger had lived, the Harrison home, and where football hero Thayer Boudreaux had grown up.

They were silent and thoughtful as they drove from the outskirts of Terrebonne Parish.

Then he spoke, thinking aloud. "You were a kid. Thayer was eighteen, but that's still a kid. And the Harrison children were all kids."

"They couldn't have been involved," Sienna whispered.

"They couldn't have done it alone, certainly," Ryder said.

"Let's hope we find something out through investigating Terry Berger's death. We'll get some rest and sharpen up for tomorrow, huh?" Fin suggested.

"I'm quite fine, actually," Granny K assured him. "I think I shall see what nightlife there is up and moving, roam the French Quarter a bit, see who I find and what they've been up to!"

Ryder glanced back at her. "You would have made a great detective, Granny K."

She laughed softly.

"I'll want to go about with you again sometime," Ryder told her. "If I may."

"Oh, my dear boy! You may go about with me anywhere at any time."

They dropped her in the French Quarter.

Sienna's Garden District was quiet when they returned. But Ryder saw a gray sedan parked on the street and glanced at Fin, who nodded: the area was still being guarded.

Fin left them, and they made their way through the main door to Sienna's half of the house.

She seemed awkward as they entered her apartment.

"Is something wrong?" he asked her.

She shook her head. "No . . . Yes. Terry

271

Berger is dead. He was kind of an old icon when I was growing up. I never knew him well, but he was always there. He was the last person you'd suspect of wanting to do harm to others. He just wanted to be left alone. I heard he was even a grumpy tour guide in the bayou, albeit a knowledgeable one. Why would he have wanted to hurt the McTavish family? And go after the Kimball family and kill that doctor?"

"To me, it's the work connection. But we're having a hard time going through all the red tape because tech development is so guarded. There's so much money in it," Ryder said.

"But —"

"That's it!" Ryder said, more to himself than to her.

"What's it?"

"Money. Somehow, it's money. And Terry Berger must have needed money. After the pandemic, a lot of people have still needed more than what they have to get by. Someone hired Terry. I don't know if he was the one to set the fire all those years ago. But I do believe he was the supposedly homeless man on the street, and he watched the Kimball family and their house and figured out just how and when to get in. He set that fire. And he failed to kill the man, so he had to attack him on the street. But he didn't act alone, and I don't believe he was the one to plan everything."

"Then, who?" she wondered. "Like we said, my friends were just kids back then, remember?"

"But not kids now."

She sighed.

"Would you do something for me?"

"What?"

"Go back over the past."

"I swear to you, I've told you everything about the other night."

"Not the other night. Lie on the sofa and close your eyes and tell me everything you remember."

She looked at him a bit skeptically, but shrugged, sighed, and leaned back.

"All the way back," he said.

She sat up and stared at him. "What? Are you hypnotizing me?"

"No. I can't hypnotize anyone. But if you close your eyes and remember, well, sometimes it can tell us something."

"Fine."

She lay back again.

"Granny K was dying. You were watching her. But she told you that you had to go and help Mrs. McTavish and the baby."

"Yes." Sienna took a breath. "Granny was

born in Scotland but came to the United States when she was young, and her accent only seemed to come out when she was upset. I remember her urging me to leave by saying, 'The wee bairn is 'neath the stairs,' and when I started to protest again, she said, 'I've had a fantastic go of it, and I'm quite fine with me fate. Go save that baby!' "

"And so you went."

Sienna nodded. "I was worried about her, worried my parents were going to be angry. But I went because she was so insistent."

"What did you see as you ran?"

"You saw the neighborhood today. The McTavish house was down the road, houses on the bayou on one side, not on the other, and a long, curving road. I saw Terry Berger coming out of his house, out the front door, looking down the road. And Thayer Boudreaux was in front of his house as well, and the door was still ajar, so I guess he was just coming out. They both looked confused. And concerned. And then I passed the Harrison house — the whole family was out in the front. They were having a picnic. They all just looked startled and confused."

"And then?" Ryder pressed softly.

"I got there. Eleanor was on the floor by

the stairs. I imagine she'd been running for the door when she realized she had to get out. There was a well under the stairway, and the baby had rolled out of her arms and into that area. I got the baby and Eleanor and dragged them both out. Then, of course, there was so much smoke . . . I don't really know what happened. I wound up in the hospital for the smoke inhalation. My parents were there. They thought I was taking my grandmother's death hard or the smoke had made me crazy. I remember them talking to Sheriff Patterson and him saying they needed to be gentle with me and maybe even humor me, if I remember right."

"Interesting," he murmured.

"I've told you all this," she said.

"Yes, but after today, I can almost see you running. Both Mr. and Mrs. Harrison were in the front yard?"

"Yes."

"And you saw Terry Berger?"

"Yes."

"So he could have set that fire," Ryder murmured.

Sienna sat up. "Yes, but we're still at a place where anyone could have set the fire. The house was almost a mile from mine. It was burning when I got there."

275

"And then you were in the hospital, and Sheriff Patterson was there, too."

She frowned. "Ryder, he's been sheriff a long time. I can't imagine he could be guilty of anything. Well, except for being a dick at times."

"That's true. But no, I'm not accusing the sheriff of being the brains behind it all."

"Maybe it was all just Terry Berger. Maybe he had a grudge against people who work in the computer field or with software."

"Money, medicine," Ryder muttered.

"And what does that mean?"

"There's big money in tech and in medicine. Anyway, I say we give it up for tonight." He stood, catching her hand. Then he gave her a twisted smile. "After all, I have your dad's permission to stay close — as long as I keep you safe."

"Oh!" She gave him a good swat on the arm. "Don't bring up my dad!"

"I can fix it, I promise," he assured her.

She took off, running for the stairs. She beat him to the second-floor landing, but he caught her there, sweeping her up into his arms.

"I can't romantically carry you up the stairway if you run off on me."

"I walk extremely well."

"I may be just *You'll do,* but you are the

picture of grace and beauty. The green of your eyes, the silk of your hair . . ."

"The jut of your gun."

"Maybe that's not my gun."

She laughed and lowered her face and kissed him as he held her. They kept laughing as he stumbled backward a second, found his footing, and made it into the bedroom.

He could joke about the gun.

But he also wanted it within easy reach, so as they fell together, he grabbed it and the little holster from his waistband and saw it was carefully set on the table where he could grab it at a second's notice.

"Hm, so it was the gun," she teased.

"Oh, cruel," he said.

"Maybe reality is better," she told him.

"I shall strive to rise above myself, to be better than *You'll do, in a pinch!* I shall ever endeavor to —"

"Oh, dear lord!" Sienna said laughing. "You're the worst poet ever. Thankfully, you are rising to the occasion and faring better than *You'll do* so far."

Her lips locked with his. She shoved him, rolling with him, pushing up against him, and finding his mouth with hers while they both struggled with their clothing, kissing bared sections of flesh, and then both just whispering words of wonder and encouragement.

Coming together again and again, being with her was even more comfortable, and still, every second seemed new, and holding her, touching her, knowing her was sweeter, more erotic and exotic. And it might have been then, that night, that he realized just how much he was coming to care for her.

Not even in the heat of sex. After. When he felt her curled in his arms, when he realized he wanted to sleep like that every night, wake with her every morning. But he couldn't be honest yet. He wasn't ready to voice his real feelings.

"You are staying all night, right?" she whispered to him.

"Hey, I wouldn't go back on my word to your dad, right?"

She slugged him in the shoulder again.

He rolled and pinned her. "I'm staying the night," he said softly. "As long as you'll let me."

She smiled, saying nothing. But her arms wound around his neck, and they kissed, tenderly, and held one another.

CHAPTER TEN

It was early in the morning, and Granny K was not in the kitchen when they came down.

Ryder was on the phone with Fin as Sienna poured coffee and searched her calendar for any meetings or appointments during the day. She saw she had made special arrangements for a group of librarians who were coming in for a tour. They had a convention in town, but they had specifically wanted to come to the Oddities Museum.

When Ryder was off the phone, she asked, "Are you going back to Terrebonne Parish for the autopsy?"

He shook his head. "Fin is going to handle it. Angela — Special Agent Angela Hawkins, at Krewe headquarters — is working on finding out if Terry Berger was in Atlanta when McTavish was struck and killed. She's also seeing if there is a connection with anyone else. It's important I'm here in the city today. I have to go through files, which I can do with my phone, sifting through everything I've been compiling regarding the three victims, so . . ."

"You don't want to leave me in the city unless you're also here," she said, smiling.

He shrugged. "Fin should be back by noon or one. I think, once he's here, I'll take a walk with Granny K. Assuming I can find her."

"You think someone might know more?" Sienna asked.

"Someone out there knows something," he said. "Ready to go to work?"

She was.

As usual, they both paused when they left her house, looking up and down the quiet street.

Ryder nodded toward a sedan, and she knew he saw the undercover officers who were watching the neighborhood.

She was glad the houses were being guarded. She wasn't sure it was necessary anymore, assuming the so-called homeless man had been Terry Berger.

They were almost at the car when Judy Craton came hurrying out, calling to them.

"Detective, Sienna — is it true? Are we okay now?" she asked anxiously. She was out of breath as she reached them. "We saw on the news that a man named Terry Berger was found dead last night by police in Terrebonne Parish, and that he was the man NOLA police suspected of burning down the Kimball house. I've been worried sick about Whitney, and I'm hoping she's safe now. I know you have people around, Detective, but I've still been so worried. And Grace will be relieved, too! So, is it true?"

"I do believe Terry Berger was the supposed homeless man Whitney saw, and he was probably the one who set fire to the Kimball house, yes," Ryder told her. "And we do have people watching you. I think Whitney is safe, and we'll see to it that Grace knows as well —"

"Oh! I've already been on the phone with her. Of course, we've all seen the news. I'm grateful if Whitney and Grace were able to help."

"They did help," Sienna assured her.

"Like I said, I think they're both safe, but we'll spend a few days making sure," Ryder told her.

"Thank you," Judy murmured. She backed away and waved. "I didn't mean to keep you!"

"Not a problem at all. And thank you," Ryder said.

Sienna smiled. Judy went into the house, and they continued to the car. When they reached it, Sienna paused, looking at Ryder.

"Whitney and Grace really are safe now, right? It won't matter they gave police the description for the sketch that went out, because Terry Berger is dead, and he was the main suspect as far as the public are concerned."

"I honestly believe they should be safe now."

"That's good. But, I'm still confused. Say Terry Berger set both fires and went after McTavish in Atlanta and then tried to attack Martin Kimball here. What about the doctor found in the river? What would Terry have against a kidney specialist from North Carolina?"

"Exactly," Ryder said.

"Ryder, I understand your gut feeling, I really do, but maybe . . . maybe Terry did just go mad. Maybe there is no conspiracy."

"Maybe," he said pleasantly. "Then again, maybe I'm right. And if so, and we don't discover the truth, Martin Kimball will be vulnerable, and there might be others out there in danger, too."

"So you're going to find whatever it is that ties them together." He smiled and opened the car door for her.

"I am," he said.

She nodded.

And there was no question: he was coming in with her to work.

Clara greeted Ryder happily, telling him she was very glad he was there and had friends watching over them when he couldn't.

Ryder assured her they were all happy to look over the museum.

They headed through the entry to the main hall and the entrance to Sienna's office. But once there she told him, "I always go through and check on Dr. Lightfoot and the animals before starting out on anything else."

"Okay."

She smiled. "You're coming with me?"

He nodded.

Determined, she barely glanced at a single wax figure as they made their way out back.

The museum had just officially opened for the day. No visitors had made it to the back yet, but Jared Lightfoot was out, his new pet, Ruff, at his side, as he made quick examinations of the creatures in the petting zoo.

Ruff barked and wagged his tail, warning his new master the pair was there.

"Morning!" Jared called out, smiling as he

walked to the double gates that led out of the area. "I'm just checking the eyes on our guys like I do each morning. Bright eyes usually mean a healthy creature. How are you two? Sienna, you're okay, right? You weren't ill yesterday, were you?"

"No, thank you, I'm fine. I just took the day off."

"Did you hear?" Lightfoot asked anxiously then. "Wait, you must have heard," he said, looking at Ryder. "It's all over the news. A man named Terry Berger was found dead on his boat out in Terrebonne Parish — suicide! Go figure. He was suspected of having set the fire by your house, Sienna."

"Yes, we know, thank you," Ryder said.

Sienna realized he didn't want to advertise the fact they'd discovered Terry Berger's body.

Or even that they'd been out of New Orleans, in Terrebonne Parish, the day before.

No one else knew, or suspected, anything other than the Kimball house had fallen prey to arson. They didn't know Ryder had stopped Terry Berger from sliding a knife into Martin.

They didn't know the police suspected a man from North Carolina pulled out of the river as charred remains might have been a victim of the same killer.

Or that whoever had slipped into the museum and hidden among the wax figures might be associated in any way.

No one knew.

Unless someone did. Someone who had paid Terry Berger and was perhaps the master puppeteer?

"Well, it's sad all around, but if he was guilty and died by suicide, I guess it's better than him trying to kill someone else, right?"

Sienna nodded. "Anyway, everything is good out here, right? Happy, peppy animals, bear cub coming along fine, and, of course, Ruff!"

She bent down to give the dog a good scratch.

"All is well. Lori had a doctor's appointment or something, but she'll be along soon."

Sienna thanked him, and they went back in.

This time, she made a point of stopping among the tableaux that depicted some of the most heinous deeds to have taken place in the city.

The vampire brothers were set as they should be. Victims lay on the floor, waiting to be drained of their blood.

The Axeman of New Orleans held his

weapon, likewise frozen in the setting. Madame LaLaurie simply looked out with her furious and indignant glare.

"Wax figures can be amazingly lifelike," Ryder said.

She looked at him.

"Especially when the tables are turned," he continued. "Usually, a wax figure represents flesh and blood. But flesh and blood can try to appear to be wax. And it's good you know these scenes, Sienna. I've made a point to study them, too."

She shook her head. "I'm not afraid of the wax figures anymore. And we don't even know the person in here wasn't just some jerk playing games. Byron revised the entire security system with the cameras, making sure the system can't be hacked and closed down again. And we have cops outside and inside most of the time," she reminded him.

"Anything can be hacked," he said, "and anyone can be taken by surprise. Anyway, we can head to your office. I have some reading to do."

She wondered if it was going to be possible to concentrate on her own work with him sitting in her office.

He moved the chair that usually sat in front of her desk to the back wall so that he was facing the door.

And he was quiet, deeply involved in whatever it was he was reading on his phone. Looking over the calendar, Sienna discovered she could focus, taking the notes from various meetings and compiling them into the proper invitations and letters and adding pictures to her work.

But she didn't forget he was there.

She realized his presence allowed her to work without worrying about who might be coming through her door.

A two-pronged deal, she thought. She was coming to like him being around far too much, at home, in bed, anywhere, and there was nothing wrong with feeling safe. Except she had never liked guns. There were just so many accidental deaths due to guns, and it really only had one purpose: to kill. She'd grown up around hunters, but she wasn't fond of the concept of killing for sport, though to be fair, her neighbors had only ever shot what they intended to eat.

She preferred to support local grocery stores.

But she turned to Ryder, interrupting his reading. "Hey."

He looked up. "Hey?"

"Would you take me to a gun range?"

He didn't smile, and he offered no comment.

They both went back to work.

Ryder received a call from Fin around eleven.

The agent was already on his way back. The autopsy had been performed first thing that morning, and Fin had gleaned all that he could.

Ryder was aware Sienna watched him as he listened to Fin.

"I don't believe the man died by suicide. Results were inconclusive, according to the ME, but when you put all the finds together, to me there was no way the man did that to himself. The concussion and bleeding could have been caused by a fall. The injury to the head did not kill him, the cut across his throat did. The ME said that while it was *possible* Terry Berger could have banged his head and made it down the stairs, it wasn't *probable*. But he couldn't rule out that Berger might have fallen, even tried to kill himself with a fall and failed. The blade had been wiped down. Only Berger's fingerprints were on it. In my mind, he was taken by surprise, whacked on the head, and dragged out to the boat and cut. Whoever killed him then wiped the razor clean and

288

put it in Terry's hand, making sure he put it in the right hand for the man to have carried out the deed. Based on all you've told me, Terry Berger just doesn't fit the profile for a man who would be out to kill computer-software techs and a doctor. Or dress up like a homeless man to scope out a residence before setting it on fire."

"Thanks. Angela sent me all kinds of information. I'm going through it now. There is no record of Terry Berger having been in Atlanta on the day McTavish was killed in the hit-and-run incident. But there's also nothing to suggest he wasn't. We know he didn't like hotels. He left New Orleans right after Freddie's show at Thayer's gallery. The drive to Atlanta from Terrebonne Parish is eight to nine hours, so he could have easily struck the man in the street and headed straight home, since apparently there were no witnesses to what happened. McTavish was hit on a side street at night and not discovered until another man was leaving a restaurant to pick up his car where it was parked. I've been reading more about our victims and everyone in the neighborhood and can talk about that when you're back."

"McTavish and Kimball worked with

computers, but Mahoney was a doctor," Fin mused.

"But there could be a connection, and I think there is. Kimball is working on medical programming. We haven't yet found a way to get information on his private high-tech work, but I believe he is working on something that might revolutionize something in medicine, which would connect him to Mahoney. If they can improve kidney care in any way, that would be a massive discovery. Mahoney was a nephrologist."

"You're onto something. But what about McTavish?"

Ryder glanced over at Sienna and admitted, "His work, from what I've read, had to do with money movement, possibly a system that would work well with stock-market exchanges." He hesitated. "Angela is still working on the movements of others."

"Which may or may not mean anything. If there is a puppet master controlling all this, his pockets may run deep."

"Right. Did you see Patterson today?"

"The good sheriff? Oh, yes, he was there. He's impatient with the whole thing. Says Terry Berger never was a normal guy and that what happened in Terrebonne Parish was a long time ago and can't have anything to do with whatever problems you're having in New Orleans. Anyway, I'm on my way. All is quiet there?"

Ryder nodded. "I'll see if we can head out for a bite now and meet you at the café. With any luck, Granny K will find us there." He and Fin ended the call.

"You want to go out now?"

"Can you?"

"Sure. You're looking for my grandmother again to scour the city for any dead who might be helpful?" Sienna asked.

"I am."

"And leaving Fin with me."

He nodded, thinking she was going to argue with him.

"Okay," she said.

They both stood and headed for the door. Before they reached it, there was a tap on it.

Sienna opened the door. Artie was standing there.

"Ah, hey! And, hey there, Detective Stapleton. I heard you were here."

"Hi, Artie," Ryder said.

"You were heading out," Artie said. "I'm sorry, but wow. Did you hear about last night?" he asked Sienna. Then he looked at Ryder. "Dumb question, I guess, but Terry Berger was found dead! We just saw him at the show, and now they're saying he might have torched that house next to yours. Are you okay, Sienna?"

She nodded. "I knew Terry, of course. Not well. It's sad," she said simply.

"Well, if he was trying to kill people, it's still sad, but at least he's not a danger to anyone anymore. Anyway, I wanted to ask you for some help this afternoon. Morrie has a dentist's appointment at three, and we have two groups scheduled. Can you take one of them through? If not, Lori can come in, but Jared will have to handle the petting zoo, and he's much nicer to animals than he is to kids."

"I'll be fine taking a group through at three," Sienna assured him. "We're just running out for a few minutes to grab something now. Brunch, I guess. But I'll be back."

"With law enforcement!" Artie said, grinning at Ryder.

"Oh, yes. She'll be with law enforcement," Ryder said.

Artie looked confused.

"Huh. If Terry Berger is dead . . ."

"We don't know if the man had anything to do with what happened here, Artie," Ryder said.

"Oh, well, yeah, of course . . . Okay, thanks, and get going!" Artie said.

He headed off down the hall, and Ryder

and Sienna paused in the lobby to tell Clara where they were going.

She was accepting a credit-card payment from a woman with two children in tow and just smiled and waved.

"I'm hungry, so this will work well," Sienna said. She glanced at him, a curious smile on her face. "You think Granny K will find us?"

"I do."

"So she's around, even when she isn't around?"

He laughed. "I don't think she spies on you. I think she does hover close a lot of the time. Then again, she is a social butterfly among the spirit world."

They reached the restaurant and ordered. Soon after their food arrived, Granny K did, too.

"What is on the agenda today?" she asked.

"Fin is going to meet us here and hang with Sienna at work. I thought you and I might prowl around a bit and see what we can find out."

"The French Quarter again?" Granny K asked.

"I was thinking of maybe seeing who might be around. We're not far from Saint Louis No. 1, and I don't know if you have friends who might wander around cemeteries at times."

Granny K was thoughtful, and then she brightened. "Thomas Gaspard. He's not buried or interred there, but he lived in the Tremé area and still loves to come to the coffee shops and just wander. His family owned a large piece of property and had a few carriages and horses before he was killed in the service. Desert Storm. He left behind a son who works with Thomas's dad now, and he loves to see how well they work together."

Sienna looked at Ryder strangely.

"I thought you were prowling the French Quarter again?"

"Well, we may. Granny K and I do all right together, but a nice walk along some of the open spaces and more neighborly little places around here might be nice."

Sienna groaned. "What do you think you're going to find?" she asked.

"I don't know."

"It's fine with me," Granny K said. "Oh, and there he be, that lovely young Fin!"

Fin came in and greeted them all, taking the chair next to Granny K.

"Welcome, young sir!" she said.

"Granny K, you are such a flirt!" Sienna said. It didn't bother the old woman a bit.

"Ah, well, I may be dead, but I still have

me ghostly eyes! Indeed, welcome, you very handsome young man!" she told Fin.

Fin grinned and thanked her.

"He's pretty cute, too, don't you think?" Fin teased, indicating Ryder.

"Indeed, a lovely lad, if ever I've seen one!" Granny K said.

Sienna sounded as if she was choking for a minute.

"What, dear?" her grandmother asked. "I adored your grandfather, and I do believe we'll meet again. But here I am, in the spirit, and my spirit does have eyes, me lass! Forgive me, Ryder. You're a lovely man, in ever so many ways. I used the term *lad* loosely!"

Ryder chuckled and thanked Granny K as well.

He noted that he, Sienna, and Fin were exceptionally good at pretending it was just them in conversation while politely including Granny K as well. The tables were well-spaced at the restaurant, but others around them only saw a group of three just chatting and laughing.

"Sienna, do I have time to order food?" Fin asked.

"Sure. I'm pretty caught up. I have a group at three, but I seriously doubt it will take you that long to order and eat!" Sienna told him.

"No, not at all," Fin promised. He glanced at Ryder.

"Anything else?" Ryder asked him.

"No, just that Angela is working on Terry Berger's books, trying to fathom where certain deposits might have originated. She's still searching with a forensic accountant. I don't have much, other than knowing there were deposits."

"Large amounts?" Ryder asked.

Fin nodded. He glanced at Sienna. "Ten thousand in cash, most of it about ten years ago but also deposited in increments that came to the total."

"You're saying, then, that Terry was paid for setting fire to the McTavish house — ten thousand dollars in cash?" she asked.

"I'm saying he mysteriously deposited ten thousand dollars in cash ten years ago. And the situation suggests that, yes, he might have been paid to burn down the house."

"But he didn't kill McTavish in the fire."

"No."

"So, why was he still paid?"

"Maybe he finished the job," Ryder said quietly. "We don't know that he was in Atlanta, but we don't know that he wasn't."

"He owed a huge sum on his boat at the time," Fin explained, then fell silent. Their waiter had returned to the table, cheerful and ready to take Fin's order.

After he'd placed it, Ryder stood. "Granny K, shall we?"

"Indeed. Such a pleasure, being with you all. Ah! Had I lived a bit later, I might well have longed to be a detective." She grew serious. "Work that saves lives. Well, this lovely lad — man — and I are off."

She loosely linked an arm with Ryder's. He smiled and nodded to Sienna and Fin, and as she said, they were off.

"What exactly are we trying to find out about?" Granny K asked.

"Okay, I believe someone has been pulling the strings for a long time. McTavish was in computers, and his work had to do with software that aids in banking, the stock market, and other financial interests. But Dr. Mahoney and Martin Kimball are both in medicine, in a way. The more I think about it, the more I'm convinced Kimball's work has to do with software that would manage a medical device that might revolutionize dialysis or other treatment for kidney disease."

"And what would that have to do with banking?"

"Maybe not so much banking, but maybe the stock market."

"Who would kill a man and his wife and babe for money?" she wondered.

"I'm sorry to say, money is often the motive for murder."

"Well, why hide in the museum?"

He didn't want to answer her. The truth was he was afraid the puppet master — whoever it was that had given a ten-thousand-dollar cash deposit to Terry Berger — might be worried about Sienna.

She had stopped him twice.

And perhaps he blamed her for a third time, since her interruption had saved Kimball's life at the fire, bringing in the police involvement that had led Ryder to be watching Kimball when Berger had nearly attacked him in the street.

"He doesn't know I'm the one who told Sienna to save people, and the mastermind behind this is frightened of Sienna," Granny K answered her own question.

"I don't know. Maybe."

She sniffed. "Leave your car where it is. You're young and healthy, you can walk! We have to get back there into Tremé where the big properties are with the horses and carriages and oh! There's a man who owns an adorable llama!"

They walked. There were long stretches where they didn't see anyone — living or

298

dead. They passed pleasant residential areas and came to the larger lots of land.

He didn't see the man at first, but Granny K did. She pointed him out saying, "Ah, there he is. Thomas Gaspard. Leaning on the fence, watching the old mare in the field. She's thirty or so, grand old lady! She was young when Thomas was alive."

"Thomas!" Granny K called his name. The ghost moved away from the fence, smiling and waving as he saw her, and then frowning when he saw Ryder.

"Lovely lady!" Thomas said, still frowning. "But . . . are you trying to haunt this fellow?"

"How do you do, Mr. Gaspard. I'm Ryder Stapleton, with the NOPD."

Thomas had been in his midthirties when he'd died, Ryder thought. He had close-cropped brown hair and eyes to match and had stood a lanky six feet or so in life. He looked at Ryder, still confused, and then at Granny K.

"I'd heard about such people, but . . . this guy can really see me?"

"Yes, I see you and hear you," Ryder said. "I admit, I'm new to this talent or craft —"

"Gift or curse," Granny K supplied dryly.

"But I had help discovering I could see those who chose to be seen, and sometimes,

I hope, lend a helping hand."

"Ah, son, that's nice. I bear no ill will to others. War is always horrible and ugly, and it is what claimed me, but I am a happy spirit, sir, watching over those who stayed behind and carry on my legacy. Adore my son and grandson, and love my horses, too!"

"That's so lovely, and so much like me! I had but one son, and that one son had a beautiful, kind, and giving daughter, and I watch over her!" Granny K said. "As does Detective Stapleton here. Ryder to his friends."

"I'm happy to be a friend," Thomas Gaspard said.

"Thank you," Ryder told him.

"So what is it that I can do for you?" Gaspard asked. "I don't think this lovely lady brought you by just to shoot the breeze."

Ryder smiled. "You're not far from the Oddities Museum. I'm curious as to whether you'd noted unusual behavior among any of the employees, or guests for that matter."

"I did hear there was some commotion over there the other night," Gaspard said. "I love going by. That's one place that takes the care of their animals very seriously. An on-site vet! I like that. And I like that Dr.

Lightfoot. I was, in fact, trying to read one of his last pieces in a magazine, but you know it's difficult to read when you're leaning over someone's shoulder and they decide to close the magazine!"

"Lightfoot wrote a piece for a magazine?"

"Oh, yeah. It was excellent. He agreed that certain animals shouldn't be kept in captivity, but that those who condemned all animal rescues and venues were fearfully wrong. It was well written, from what I saw. He suggested that instead of looking at sea parks and dolphin habitats, the do-gooders should be stopping all the medical and cosmetic testing and experimentation being done on animals. I tend to agree."

The beautiful mare Granny K had pointed out trotted over to the fence, and Thomas stroked the animal's nose.

The horse knew he was there, sensed his spectral touch, and loved it.

"Have you seen any of the others behave strangely?" Ryder asked. "I suppose the ones you see the most are Dr. Lightfoot and maybe Lori Markham. Do you see the docents, Morrie and Artie, or the receptionist, Clara, or the owner, Byron Mitchell?"

"Oh, I've seen the owner. Rolls up now and then in a car that, I must admit, I hitched a ride in once. Nice!"

"You jumped into Byron Mitchell's car?" Ryder asked. "Did he know you were there at all?"

Gaspard laughed. "He told his chauffeur to turn the air-conditioning down. But that's all."

"And how was riding with him? Did you learn anything about him?"

"Good things," Gaspard said. "When he spoke to his chauffeur, he was polite, used *please* and *thank you*. Talked to him just like a friend. I think he might be one of the rare good rich dudes. Not that all wealthy people are bad, but some get to thinking money makes them better. They stopped for food while I was in the car, and Mitchell reminded the chauffeur to make sure he tipped, even for takeout, because restaurant people worked hard. I liked the guy. I was impressed with him."

"Great. Sienna likes him, too."

"Sienna is Granny K's granddaughter. She's all right. Someone did a good job raising that child."

"Why, thank you, sir!" the old woman said. "Well, mostly her parents. Good people, too!"

"Sienna comes out every morning to check on Dr. Lightfoot and Lori. She's always concerned, nice, and gentle. Lori's good — but she can be impatient, with the kids and the animals. Oh, nothing cruel. She's just short sometimes. I see the older lady, Clara, and she's just smiley and pleasant. Don't see so much of those docents you were talking about, Artie and Morrie. They just don't come out back often. Well, I do see them now and then, but just to stop to talk to Lori or the doc. It's not a big place. And I'm sad to say I wasn't around when the commotion went on, though I heard there was talk the culprit disappeared over the fence and through some of the yards back here. Guess it won't happen that way again. That is one beautiful dog the doc went out and got for himself."

"Ruff is great," Ryder agreed. The only problem with Ruff was he had been taught to trust everyone working at the museum.

But could Lightfoot be in on it? Was his passion against animal testing something that could cause him to kill?

He had a hard time seeing Lightfoot paying someone to burn down a house, murder them with a vehicle, or go after them with a knife.

Especially setting blaze to a house with children in it.

Nothing was impossible. Killers could be charming in their day-to-day lives.

303

"Anything odd about people who come to the museum?" Ryder asked. "And please don't tell me that *It's New Orleans.*"

Gaspard laughed at that. "I guess most people don't know just how much normal there is here! But I don't really see people going in the front. I see them when they're in the back, in Dr. Lightfoot's territory. I see a couple of guys come to see Lori now and then or to help the vet. One is a pretty big fellow, and I think she calls him Thane — no, *Thayer.* He's got a way with the creatures and the strength to pick them up. A few other guys come by, and an older couple. He's tall and has tons of gray hair, and she's . . . cute, but plump, you know, a little square. Oh, I think they surprised Lori once. She was angry when she saw them."

"An older couple?" Ryder said. Lori Markham was Joel and Mary Harrison's niece. She had opted not to go out with her family after the gallery showing. "And he was tall, and, as you said, with plenty of gray hair, and the woman was short . . . and plump?"

"Yeah," Gaspard said. "The museum can be busy. I see all kinds of people there. I couldn't begin to describe them all."

"That's okay. Thank you. I'm going to find that article you were talking about, the one

304

written by Dr. Lightfoot."

"Hey, if you find it, maybe you could let me read over your shoulder, since I didn't get to finish it."

Ryder smiled at the man.

"I guess we should be getting back," Ryder said. "I appreciate your help, really. And I'm happy to let you read the article. We can meet at a coffee shop, and you can tell me when to turn the pages."

"That would be great."

They left Thomas, stroking the horse he had loved in life and still did in death.

Animals, it seemed, did sense much more than people.

"Did you get what you wanted?" Granny K asked as they headed back, walking to the museum rather than the coffee shop.

"I don't know what I want. But I am more interested in the Harrison family and Lori Markham and . . ."

"Dr. Lightfoot," she said.

He grimaced. "I like the man. But we never know what drives another person. He does have a passion for animals."

As they neared the museum, Granny K said, "You just make sure nothing happens to Sienna, do you hear me?"

"I only leave her when I know she's being

watched by someone I'd entrust my own life to."

"Don't you ever let me see anything different!" she warned.

"Good lord, no," he promised. "Trust me. I'd never want you haunting me with malice until the end of my days."

"With malice?"

"Right."

"You don't mind me haunting you?"

He grinned. "Haunts are some of my favorite people. Let's walk. I have to start doing more research — and finding out just how far the Krewe of Hunters can push."

CHAPTER ELEVEN

Sienna was glad to take on the group that arrived at three.

They were high-school juniors, and they were a good crowd, interested in the many exhibits under the banner of How Things Work, but even as they explored the hands-on electrical, water-driven, and mathematical exhibits, they whispered about getting to the wax gallery and Murderers' Row.

That was fine.

Her group was from one of the local high schools, and the majority had grown up in New Orleans or nearby Metairie or Gretna. They knew the local stories, some factual and some legend.

All of the tableaux, except for two, represented true killers and events that had taken place in or near the city.

The two that weren't based on real crimes were a display dedicated to the Rougarou

— Louisiana's particular creature in the line of wolfmen — and one that was dedicated with gratitude to the brilliance of novelist Anne Rice, who had surely increased tourism in New Orleans with her fantastic characters, often set in known places or areas.

Personally, Sienna loved everything written by Rice, and she had been appreciative that Byron included the tableau that paid the author homage.

The young people stopped to admire the Vampire Lestat.

"You've read the book?" Sienna asked one of the girls who stared at the scene with love in her eyes, after Sienna had told the group Anne Rice had once lived in New Orleans. Her book had made the city and its history intriguing to so many people.

"I saw the movie," the girl said dreamily.

"Tom Cruise was yummy," another said.

One of the boys scoffed. "He's an old dude now."

The girl, whose name was Trixie if Sienna remembered right, turned to him, smiling, and said, "You should look so good as an old dude, Corey."

The group laughed.

"Isn't Brad Pitt even older?" one of the boys said, but he was teasing, and his tone

308

was light.

"Again," Trixie said. "However old the guy may be, you should look so good at that age."

The whole group laughed good-naturedly.

Sienna went on to describe the real incidents that had occurred.

"So Minnie Wallace poisoned her husband, like thirty years older than her, and inherited his money, and got off in court because people claimed he was taking rat poison for his health?" Corey asked.

"They found arsenic, and there is some arsenic in all of us, but yes, most people now certainly believe she was guilty," Sienna said. "Her second husband died, and that was deemed a natural death as well, and in the end — she wasn't in New Orleans then, mind you — the fellow she was with died of cyanide poisoning. But she was in Europe, and he was in Chicago, so she couldn't be found guilty, though many believed she had been poisoning him and had an accomplice or had left poisoned food."

"But she never went to prison and wasn't executed?" Trixie asked.

"No. She died in San Diego in 1957 at the grand old age of eighty-eight."

"So you can get away with murder," Trixie said sadly.

"Sure. People do all the time," another girl muttered.

"And these guys, the vampire brothers, they really drank blood?" Corey asked.

"Yes, but they were caught," Sienna assured him.

"And the Axeman," Corey muttered. "No one ever knew who he was, but we had a new one, and that mystery was solved, right? I'll bet Minnie Wallace wouldn't have gotten away with all the killing if she'd been doing it now."

Fin had been standing at the back of the group, just observing and listening, all the while.

So far, it seemed the kids must've assumed he was a backup museum employee.

As the kids walked around the hall, exploring the exhibits before heading out to the rescue yard, Fin came up to her.

"I talked to Byron Mitchell, and he tells me he's been assured by his security company that the cameras can't be hacked again."

"I hope that's true," she said.

"We can hope. We just don't entirely trust everything," he said. He was staring at the Axeman exhibit.

"You worked the recent case?" she asked him.

"I was background on it, yes. And Ryder caught a lot of it," he said quietly.

She noted some of the kids watching her, whispering and giggling.

Trixie finally approached Sienna and Fin, looking at Fin curiously. "You're some kind of a cop, aren't you?" She giggled. "My mom said there would be cops here. Because some guy was in the museum, playing around in here."

"I'm not a cop," Fin told her. He didn't supply that he was with the federal government.

But Ryder returned, heading to her and Fin.

Granny K wasn't with him.

"Ah!" Trixie said as he joined them. "He's a cop."

"I am," Ryder told her.

"I thought he was the cop," she said, pointing at Fin.

"Oh no, he's much bigger than a cop. He's FBI," Ryder told her.

"Oh!" Trixie said, running off to join her friends.

"Well, her mother will be glad to know she was safe here," Sienna said, looking at Ryder, waiting for him to say something.

"Sorry. Should I have lied?" Ryder asked her.

311

She shook her head. "No, they'll behave. They haven't been a bad group."

"Any success?" Fin asked Ryder.

"More questions, but we can look for answers. We can get started as soon as Sienna can leave," he said, indicating the presence of the teenagers.

"Let me get them outside so they can have some time with the animals. I think they all have to be back on their bus by five thirty," Sienna said.

She headed to the back door to the animal area and called out, "Dr. Lightfoot is waiting for us. He's going to show you all of our rescue animals, including a cub and some of the birds of prey we're watching over, and then there's the petting zoo!"

"Murderers are cooler," someone muttered.

Maybe it was good that both Fin and Ryder were there. While some of the teens seemed to want to linger, they glanced at the two men and headed for the back.

Dr. Lightfoot and Lori were waiting. Lori stuck to the background while Jared led them to the enclosure with the bear cub, explaining his injuries and how he might not make it back in the wild. Then he gave them a lecture on the birds of prey and explained again how one of their hawks would never be able to make a flight of more than a few feet and that he would stay at the museum, while another had a foot that was mending just fine, and he would be released back into the wild.

Ruff had been in Dr. Lightfoot's apartment, but when he finished with the birds, he introduced the dog to the group, one by one, explaining the dog had been a police canine, beautifully trained. Ruff had spent time sniffing out drugs and as a cadaver dog. He had even been used to sniff out COVID-19.

The kids loved Ruff.

But everyone loved Ruff, Sienna thought.

And as long as he had been introduced and Dr. Lightfoot was not under attack, Ruff loved everyone.

Sienna knew that was something that worried Ryder.

But that was because he still thought someone here might be involved — which still made no sense to Sienna. Her friends here had been young ten years ago, certainly not old enough to be masterminding criminal activity. Except for Clara, Jared, and Byron. But Byron was always giving money away, not looking to make more. And Clara was . . . Clara. Sweet and focused on her family when she wasn't at work. And all

Jared cared about was his animals.

Lightfoot was finishing with his show on how well Ruff had been trained.

Lori then took over, but for teens — this group at any rate — the petting animals just weren't that exciting.

"Darrel already smells like a goat!" one teased.

Sienna watched Lori struggle with the kids and went in to help, but she noted Ryder stayed back to talk to Dr. Lightfoot. She edged as near as she could to hear what they were saying.

Lightfoot was happy. She realized Ryder had asked him about articles he had written.

"You want to read my work? That's great!" Lightfoot said. "Where did you hear about that, anyway? I never even told the guys at the museum."

"I'm not sure. We were talking to someone. Remember, Fin?" Ryder said.

"Yeah, I remember us talking about wanting to read articles if the doc here had written anything, but . . ."

"I think it was a lady at a place on Magazine Street. I'm not sure," Ryder said.

"I'm proudest of the piece I wrote for *Animals Adored,*" Lightfoot said. He sighed. "So much was said that was so horrible about animals being held in places like this. But I should know because I'm a vet. Some of the places that have been attacked have saved all kinds of creatures. Down in Florida, such institutions have people on call to rescue manatees and all kinds of sea creatures. Mind you, what I wrote is an opinion piece, but I'd love it if you read it and gave me your thoughts."

"Will do," Ryder assured him.

The kids were laughing. They had initially thought the petting area was only for little kids, but they were all having a good time. Trixie laughed as one of the baby goats pushed her around, wanting more of the feed Lori had handed out.

She escaped and stood by Sienna, looking at her. "Boy, have you got a cool job!"

"It's pretty great," she said, then smiled awkwardly.

"And the view's not bad, either. Those cops are hot!" Trixie said. "I can't wait to be out of high school. These guys are all so . . . juvenile."

She proved her point by indicating Corey and Darrel.

Corey was following Darrel around, as if he would offer him some of the feed.

In Sienna's mind, Darrel was doing okay. He just rolled his eyes and went with the

315

teasing, turning and pretending to butt Cory.

Soon enough, the bus will come!

She did like children — little ones and teens. But she was curious as to what was going on, why Ryder was suddenly so interested in Dr. Lightfoot.

Jared? She couldn't believe he was involved.

No matter what kind of an article he had written.

Eventually, five thirty rolled around, and the teens all returned to their bus. Sienna told Lori and Dr. Lightfoot she was leaving for the day and, with Ryder and Fin, returned to her office to gather her bag and head out for the night.

As soon as they were in the car, she turned on Ryder.

"What are you doing? Dr. Lightfoot? Do you think he's guilty because he wrote an article?"

Ryder was driving, and he didn't look her way. "I want to read what he wrote."

"He thinks people need to lay off rescue places that save animals," she said.

Fin cleared his throat. "Sometimes, the way to find a guilty party is to clear all those around the guilty party."

She shook her head. "He's made of kind-

316

ness! Sure, he likes animals better than people, but he wouldn't hurt anyone."

"Sienna, I agree Dr. Lightfoot seems to be a wonderful person. The more we find out, the better equipped we are to clear him. I just want to get my hands on some of his articles," Ryder said. He looked at Fin. "Has Angela been able to speak to any of the CEOs?"

"She and Adam are working on it," Fin said.

Sienna let out a sound of exasperation. "What?"

"I believe McTavish was attacked and later killed because he was working on breakthrough technology. I believe Dr. Mahoney was killed for the same reason, and they will keep at Kimball until they get him. We need to know what their technology had in common."

"Money," Fin told her. "You know we believe Terry Berger was working just for the money. Maybe at first he thought it wouldn't be hands-on. He'd just burn a house down. It was hard going, keeping up his boat, his business, and his home. But then McTavish got away. Someone — if not Terry — managed to kill him with an automobile. Then Dr. Mahoney came for a bit of gambling, wound up taken, killed, and burned. The burning suggests Terry did the deed himself."

"Don't you see?" Ryder asked her. "The more people we can clear, the easier it will be to see the truth of the matter. We're trying to see if Adam Harrison can manage to get someone in the tech industry to talk to us. And of course, I want to get my hands on that article and find out more about Jared Lightfoot."

"Not just him. Byron Mitchell is a man with money. We'll be checking on him, too. And frankly, anyone else around both at the time McTavish was killed and now."

"Well, it's still early. I know where we can get a copy of the article," Sienna interjected.

"You do? I figured we'd be on a difficult hunt for an old article," Ryder said.

"The bookstore near me. Better than a library. They keep everything by local writers and artists handy."

Ryder and Fin looked at one another. "Sounds good. Bookstore, dinner, and you can head home."

The article was easily available at the bookstore, just as Sienna had thought. But it was while they were there that Granny K found them. Sienna saw Ryder greeted her warmly and asked her to tell someone named Thomas Gaspard he'd found the

318

article, and they could make arrangements for Thomas to read Dr. Lightfoot's words in their entirety.

"Who is Thomas Gaspard?" Sienna asked him.

"One of Granny K's friends."

"Of course. What was I thinking?" she said.

They paid for the article and headed to a small Italian restaurant off Canal near Sienna's place. Both Ryder and Fin knew the owner, and Sienna was surprised she didn't. The food was delicious, and the owner and his daughter great fun, and it was nice to just talk about the ordinary things in life, like pasta, for a while.

After dinner, Fin and Granny K saw them into Sienna's place and then moved on together.

It was still just eight thirty when they returned and Ryder tapped on her housemates' door. Judy Craton answered, smiling as she saw him, assuring him everything was fine.

When they entered Sienna's side of the house, Ryder went through it all, top to bottom, checking windows, looking in closets, and even under the bed.

"You have people watching the house, Judy said all was fine, and . . . still?" she asked him when he came back down the stairs from his second-floor search.

"I promised to keep you safe," he said.

She laughed. "You know, I've been out of college several years on my own. I love my dad, but I don't need him watching over me forever."

He laughed. "I made a promise."

They both smiled. She realized there had been a lot of tension between them during the day, and it had just slipped away.

"So, what do you want to do? I know you're anxious to get to the article."

"Don't you love reading in bed?" he asked her.

"Long day," she told him. "I played with the goats and sheep and the minihorses today, not to mention received a lot of love from Ruff. I'm hopping in the shower."

He nodded, and she assumed he was going to join her.

He did, but not until she'd been in there for a while, and when he did, she started to laugh.

"What?" he queried.

"You started to read the article. Oh, how quickly passion fades!"

"I'll show you faded passion," he threatened playfully.

He grabbed the bottle of liquid soap and

displayed an ability for incredibly seductive foreplay and then sweet emotion as he caught her in a long, lingering kiss as the water thundered down to rinse them off.

And then towel-dried but still sweetly damp, he showed her passion.

Later they lay and laughed together, and she was the one to crawl up and retrieve his article and hand it to him, adjusting herself up on his shoulder so that they could read together.

The article featured a picture of Dr. Lightfoot holding an injured falcon and treating the bird's wing. The first part explained his background, his degrees, and his work in various places before he had taken on a full-time position with the Oddities Museum.

Then he wrote clearly about the rescue efforts and successes with many institutions that had been maligned through the past years, pointing out many specific cases.

He then went on a tirade — well written and convincing, but a tirade, nonetheless — against big businesses and even the medical profession for using animals to test products, including those that were hazardous or deadly to the creatures. While human lives were beyond value, so were those of all God's creatures, and there were alternatives to much animal testing, albeit more expensive.

"Well?" Sienna asked, knowing she and Ryder had both finished reading.

"He can write."

She was quiet, and he asked, "You didn't know about this? He didn't run into the museum with the magazine to show everyone?"

"No."

"That's interesting. One would think he'd have been proud of it."

"Well, he is proud of it. He was thrilled when he knew you had heard about it," Sienna pointed out.

"True."

"So, you want to eliminate people. Does this make Jared look innocent or guilty?"

"It makes him interesting," Ryder said.

She let out a sigh of frustration and turned her back to him while he set the article next to his gun and holster on the bedside table and turned off the reading lamp.

He didn't press her. But later, during the night, she turned to him or he pulled her back into his arms. She was never sure which.

It didn't matter.

It was a good way to sleep.

■ ■ ■ ■

"I have done everything I can to check financials on Dr. Jared Lightfoot," Angela told Ryder over the phone. "He has always made a decent income as a vet, but he is far from rich. He accepted a pay cut to come work for Byron Mitchell at the Oddities Museum, but he does better there because he has no overhead and no personal expenses except for his own food. There are no massive amounts going into or out of his checking or savings accounts in the past twenty years."

Fin had met Ryder and Sienna at her house, and they had come into the museum together. As usual, they'd started by checking in with Clara, then heading to Sienna's office, and then out to see Jared.

Ryder had left Fin to accompany Sienna as he had taken the call with Angela from Krewe headquarters, standing by the petting zoo where he could talk easily without question of anyone else listening in.

"What about Byron Mitchell?" Ryder asked. He liked the man, admired what he had read about him, but he was in the vicinity and certainly had the funds to finance murder if he so desired.

"Finding his money is like a bazillion-piece jigsaw puzzle," Angela said, "but we're working on it."

"We know Terry Berger did deposit cash in the amount of ten thousand dollars. Over a bit of time, but still . . . ten thousand. How did he explain it to the bank? Or did he? Aren't questions asked?"

"It wasn't deposited all at once. The amount was deposited in bits, and that way, there wasn't paperwork involved," Angela told him.

"What about now?"

"Nothing huge in the last couple of weeks or even months. If he'd been paid by anyone, he hadn't gotten around to depositing the money yet."

"Okay, thank you. Keep up on Byron Mitchell and the others, too, please."

"Some of this is difficult. As I said, Byron's finances, well, if he's a killer, he's the most giving killer I've ever seen. He has a magic touch with the stock market, but he's given away millions upon millions. He's fair to his employees, and he doesn't micromanage. Our forensic accountant told me he breaks even with the museum and makes a little — he's savvy enough not to lose money, even for a tax break — but it's a pet project that's important to him. He's given to cancer research, to underprivileged children, to hospitals, you name it. Every cause, he's there."

"He sounds almost too good to be true. Where did his money come from?"

"Family money, but he has made it work."

"Okay, please stick with all that. And also the Harrison family, the Boudreaux family, Artie Salinger, Morrie Nielsen, and Clara Benitez. Oh, and Lori Markham. I know Sienna has a point. Half of these people were young when the McTavish house was set ablaze. But they were still in both cities when both things happened. And I'm still hoping to find out if anyone was in Atlanta."

"Credit cards aren't giving us anything. We're still trying," Angela assured him.

"I'm curious on this, too. At the time of the McTavish blaze, Thayer Boudreaux was a senior in high school. I believe people thought he would go pro football, but he wound up owning an art gallery. That might make his financials interesting, and with Freddie being an artist, his would be interesting, too."

"We'll keep digging on all fronts," Angela said.

"Of course. And thanks."

He had barely ended the call when he saw his phone was ringing again. It was Captain

Troy, and he answered it quickly.

Troy wanted to discuss the death of Terry Berger. He also wanted Ryder to come in and speak with a group of officers and keep everyone apprised of the facts that the case wasn't closed and that Martin Kimball and his family remained in danger.

"News travels fast these days. Reports of Berger's death — be it suicide or murder — have people believing this case is over. You don't think it is, and we need to get everyone on board, clear the noise from all the different news agencies."

"I'll come in," he promised.

"I'll set you up with our folks in an hour. I talked to the man who will be your new supervisor, Jackson Crow. He assured me he has people down there, watching where we can't always be, and where we're growing thin on staffing resources."

"Thanks. I'll be there, ready."

As he ended that call, Fin came to stand by him at the petting-zoo paddock.

"That was Captain Troy. I have to head in to speak to the troops. I hate leaving. I know there's something going on here," Ryder said, frustrated. "I mean here at the museum. Where's Sienna? Did she head back to her office?" he added anxiously.

"You know if she had, I'd be gone, too,"

Fin assured him.

Fin pointed across the paddock over the open area between Dr. Lightfoot's apartment and the bird sanctuary and rescue cages.

Sienna was taking pictures of Dr. Lightfoot as he put Ruff through his paces.

"I read the article," Fin told him, as they both watched. "It doesn't clear the man because he was certainly down on anyone involved in animal research. He did mention medical research, but we know McTavish had nothing to do with that."

"And his financials don't suggest any big money coming in or out," Ryder said.

His phone rang, and he glanced at the number. He had made sure to have the phone numbers of anyone he'd spoken with in his caller ID.

He was surprised to see the number come up for Grace Wooldridge.

"Grace," he said, answering the phone. "Are you all right?"

"I am, sir, thanks to you," she said.

"No, ma'am. The FBI has kept agents watching the house, as have the police department."

"Well, I'm sure that's why we're safe. But then that awful man is dead, right? The person who set fire to the Kimball house?"

327

"We believe the man who set the fire was, indeed, the homeless man you described," Ryder told her.

"Yes, well, this is probably silly, then, but I think there was a disturbance in my backyard last night. It might have been cats — well, part of it was cats, I heard them yowling — but I think there was someone back there, too. Who knows? A neighborhood teen trying to get back to their own home without being seen, or maybe even a poor down-and-outer seeking garbage or throwaway items or food? But I have to admit, even with that awful man dead, it unnerved me."

"Grace, what makes you think someone was back there if you heard cats?" Ryder asked her. "Were your grandkids out in the yard?"

"No, they're out of town for a few days. I'm alone here. Last night, as I said, I heard the cats yowling and thought nothing of it. But when I went out this morning, well, I'm not a tracker or anything, but there are broken branches and scuffs on the fence that leads to the Kimball place. Of course, that's all flattened now, and we do know one of the kids down the street used to sneak through the backyards to get to his house. His father would watch for him on the street, but he could slip through the back door and pretend he'd been home. And it might be something like that, but the agents watch the front — all three properties. Maybe they missed something?"

"We'll check it out, Grace," he assured her.

"Thank you," she said. But she wasn't finished; she was waiting.

"Is there something else, Grace?" he asked.

"No. It's just . . . When are you coming? Soon?" she asked him.

Fin was watching Ryder.

"I have a meeting at the precinct, but I will come as soon as I've finished there. Meantime, I'll call my captain back, get some officers to sit right out in front," he said.

She gushed out her thanks, calling him *sweetie* and *honey* a few times.

He wasn't offended. Grace was the best of Southern hospitality. She didn't seem to have a mean bone in her body, and her words were always used in the way she'd been taught to be caring and polite to others, whether she knew them well or not.

He ended the call and looked at Fin.

"I'm here," Fin assured him. "But I did want to let you know, Lightfoot said Byron called him and told him the security system was going to be down for a few days. He put new tech in on top of old, and apparently, for the cameras to work the way Byron Mitchell wants, the entire system has to be redone. They've already had some snags — the old wiring wasn't listening to the new commands, and the cameras weren't working in all locations."

"So this place is wide-open," Ryder said.

"Don't worry, I won't leave her," Fin said. "This is your case, Ryder. Get in and lay it out for the PD officers and get over to see Grace after."

Ryder appreciated the fact his friend — soon to be coworker — understood he was determined to investigate this himself, without casting any doubt or aspersions on the abilities of others.

"I'll head out," Ryder said. "Let Sienna know where I'm off to."

"Will do," Fin confirmed.

Ryder called Captain Troy back as he headed to his car, asking that a patrol car be sent to Grace Wooldridge's house, and Troy stated it would happen.

Then he headed to the precinct.

He met Captain Troy in the large conference room before the others began to trickle in.

"Martin Kimball called in, hoping he and his family could move about freely again. The media are saying Terry Berger was an arsonist. We haven't officially tied the murder of Dr. Mahoney in with the fire at the Kimball house, nor can we say with certainty the same person started the fire years ago that threatened the McTavish family, nor a vehicular homicide in Atlanta. Terry Berger was, by all evidence, most likely the man who set the Kimball house on fire, and the man you prevented from attacking Martin. End of it, to some people, so I deem it wise for you to explain to our officers out in the field where you see there's more going on. Help them see, and tell them what they need to be looking out for."

Ryder wished he knew.

"Right," he said to Troy.

Within a few minutes the room was full, and Captain Troy spoke first before turning it over to Ryder.

Ryder enumerated the events he suspected to be associated. He reiterated that he sincerely believed Martin Kimball remained in danger.

And acknowledged they had no leads on the murder of Dr. Lester Mahoney. The doctor had headed for New Orleans on a break, was stabbed and burned almost

331

beyond identification, then thrown in the river.

"But we know Terry Berger attacked Martin Kimball. Isn't he probably also our firebug?" an officer said. "Doesn't that also suggest he set the fire and burned the doctor from out of state?"

"I believe he might have committed the murder and burned the body, yes," Ryder said. "But as is often the case, we're also trying to follow the money. From our investigation, there's nothing to suggest Terry Berger knew Martin Kimball or anyone in his family. We know he posed as a homeless man to observe the neighborhood and the Kimball family. We also know ten years ago, after a similar fire in Terrebonne Parish, Terry Berger mysteriously made a quick series of cash deposits that totaled ten thousand dollars. That suggests murder for hire. The fire ten years ago was also accelerated with a mixture of ethyl ether and gasoline. The owner, a man named McTavish, should have been home at the time but was not. He was later killed in Atlanta, in a hit-and-run, as you have been made aware. We are keeping the case open. We still worry for neighbors around the Kimball property, and for Kimball himself. I know you have been diligent in watching him, and I do believe that has kept him safe and working. I believe he and Mr. McTavish and Dr. Mahoney all fell under attack for the same reason, though we have not ascertained what that is. We are watching the Oddities Museum, as you know, because of a break-in. That may be associated with the fact that one of the employees was instrumental in getting Mr. Kimball out of his house. We do have federal agents working with us on this, and I appreciate everyone considering our investigation still open, continuing due diligence, and reporting anything that might be associated with these attacks and murders to me or Captain Troy immediately."

He was done. He was glad to see the officers in the room were talking among one another as they broke up the meeting, nodding, considering his words — and not pegging him as a conspiracy theorist.

"That was good," Troy told him. "I didn't drag you in here to interfere. A good detective needs everyone at his back."

"I agree. You got a car out to watch over Grace Wooldridge?"

"You doubt me?" Troy asked him.

Ryder smiled. "No, sir. But I'm heading out there now. I want to see just what scared her. She's a pretty tough woman — a steel magnolia, if you will."

He was still standing with Captain Troy when they were approached by Tim Busby, the plainclothes cop Troy had assigned to watch the museum a few times.

Today, Tim was wearing an old Rolling Stones T-shirt, one that caricatured Mick Jagger's mouth and tongue, sold at concerts throughout the years.

Tim often reminded Ryder of Shaggy from the *Scooby-Doo* series of comics and shows. He wore his hair a little long and a little unkempt and had the shape and form of the character. Though thin, Tim was wire-muscled.

He nodded to Captain Troy and told Ryder, "I just wanted you to know I'm on it. I'm headed over to the museum now to take over from Ben Larkin. And I wanted to assure you we're both taking this seriously and —" he paused, looking at Captain Troy, then he shrugged and continued "— not a laid-back babysitting assignment."

"Thanks, Tim," Ryder told him. "I appreciate that."

Tim nodded and headed out.

"Go," Troy told Ryder. "But keep in touch on this."

"Yes, sir."

Ryder spoke briefly to a few other officers as he left the building. In his car, the traffic

334

chafed him, even though it wasn't bad.

Driving, he saw Tim was ahead of him, turning off toward the museum while Ryder headed for the Garden District. He wanted to go to the museum himself. Or rather, go to Sienna.

But Fin was there. Fin would call him if there was anything out of the ordinary.

He reached Grace's house. Troy was true to his word: there was a patrol car parked directly in front.

Ryder waved to the officers and headed to the door.

Grace was there, watching, and ready to let him in.

"Detective Stapleton, please, come in. Thank you, thank you!" she said.

He stepped into the house, surprised she seemed more agitated than she had been on the phone.

"What is it? Has something else happened?"

"Well, yes! I got up my courage and went outside. There is an old wooden fence around my yard, you know — it's only a little scorched from the fire. But I went back there and looked over the fence and, Detective Stapleton, what I saw was . . . dead! Bloodied and brutally slashed!"

335

CHAPTER TWELVE

Sienna saw Ryder leave, and she saw Fin remained leaning against the fence watching her.

While Ryder hadn't said it clearly, she knew Dr. Lightfoot's anger with those people testing products — even medicines — on animals made him appear suspicious. She didn't know what Dr. Mahoney, found in the river, might have had to do with animal testing. He was a nephrologist. He didn't test medicines; he used them after testing had been completed. But he did use the newest treatments available, and maybe . . .

No. She couldn't fathom it.

After she'd taken some pictures and some video, she sat on one of the picnic tables between Jared's apartment and the rescue shelter, hoping that he would join her.

He did.

"I read your article," she told him.

"And what do you think? Am I wrong? There are things I do understand — amusement venues have sometimes practiced cruelty. And they should be punished. But certainly not those who are saving lives. I have friends who work in different areas of animal care and rescue who were threatened — as in death threats — when some of the videos came out about the cruelty of holding animals. I'm telling you, if you want to stop cruelty to animals, you should stop the way some people treat their dogs. Infuriates me! Idiots who leave a dog in a boiling car in summer or who tie one up in a yard when it's below freezing. Anyway, I took a lot of grief over what I wrote, but I stand by every word I've said. There are animals out there who wouldn't make it if they were set free. And sometimes their numbers have been so decimated in the wild, the only reason they still exist is that some have been kept in zoos." He smiled suddenly. "Don't get me started on trophy hunters!"

"Well, I think a lot of that is being banned."

"Not enough, and legislation changes constantly. The only way we stop it is to keep protesting and hope other countries do the same. But anyway, what did you think?"

"You know I love that Byron Mitchell has the rescue shelter, and that he has you on full-time. I thought your article was great. Passionate and well written."

Lightfoot beamed. "I am so glad! What did Mr. Detective-Turning-FBI think?"

"Ryder?"

"Yes, I heard he's leaving the police force. He was staying on to investigate the case of arson that took place next door to you."

"I didn't know he had announced it anywhere," Sienna said.

"I don't think it was announced. I don't know, would it be announced? Anyway, Byron knew he was planning on leaving. I'm surprised he and his FBI friend came in today."

"Oh, I imagine they're hanging around a while longer. Especially since Byron has said the security system will be down a few days."

"Well, he tried to put in new technology over the old and it just didn't work. He wants cameras in every room and out here, and screens set up for Clara, you, and me. He's thinking about hiring security guards, too. I told him I feel a lot better now that I have Ruff. That dog knows when someone is near, and he knows if it's someone who belongs."

"Ruff is amazing. I mean, we have strangers in here all day long and they aren't *friends*," she said.

"I tell him it's work time and that people are allowed," Lightfoot said, smiling. "At night I let him know he needs to tell me if anyone is around. This dog was so well trained, and you're right, he's amazing. He is a people pup. I haven't had him long at all, and I'm so attached to him it's almost pathetic."

The dog was with them, sitting attentively at his feet. His ears pricked up, and Sienna turned to see that Fin was joining them.

"Special Agent Stirling!" Lightfoot said in greeting.

Fin smiled and sat. "You know what this place needs?" Fin asked.

"What's that?" the vet asked.

"A coffee shop," Fin told them, glancing at his watch.

"We'll go get something soon," Sienna promised.

"I can make you a cup of coffee," Lightfoot offered.

"Thanks. But I was just whining. I had coffee. I still have a place here in the city —"

"In New Orleans?" Lightfoot asked.

"Yes, in New Orleans," Fin said. "I had

339

plenty of coffee this morning. I was just thinking Byron Mitchell might consider opening a café."

"He should. We can suggest it," Lightfoot said.

"Well, I should leave you be and get back to my office," Sienna said, rising. "I'm there if you need anything. Except we may be out to brunch or lunch or something in a bit."

Lightfoot laughed and watched them go. He looked relaxed and easygoing.

He was happy, Sienna thought. Animals were his passion. He lived right on the property, and he had total authority over the animals. Byron hadn't wanted to micromanage the place. He trusted Lightfoot — the way he trusted her.

And the others . . .

Artie and Lori were young. Morrie and Clara . . .

No. Clara was like Mother Goose, or Mother Goose and Mary Poppins all rolled into one.

Fin smiled at Lightfoot, gave Ruff a pat on the head, and followed Sienna. But when they were walking back inside, he stopped in the Murderers' Row area of the wax figures.

Sienna stopped, too, looking at him. He was surveying the way the tableaux had been set up. They were all on two raised platforms, one on either side of the hall that led to the back exit. They weren't very high, and the scenes all had velvet cords that roped them off from the aisle as deterrents to those who might want to touch.

In the history aisle, only Andrew Jackson and Lafitte had models that stood on the floor, ready for photo ops. They were the newest of the wax editions, well crafted, and yet . . . they, too, needed frequent maintenance.

"Is something bothering you?" she asked Fin.

He smiled at her.

"Something, but I'm not sure what. You think whoever was in here popped up from that last tableau, on that side? The vampire brothers?"

She nodded.

"Easy enough. There are, what? The two brothers, two living victims in the scene, and four that appear to have been drained out?"

"I don't think the person popped out from there. I know that he did."

Fin nodded.

"Well, if the back wasn't locked and Dr. Lightfoot was in his apartment, someone who had hidden behind one of the enclosures might have slipped in that way. Or . . ."

"Or?"

He shrugged. "Whoever it was, they were in here already."

"We're a small museum, and we've never had trouble before," Sienna told him. "Clara makes announcements about closing, and Artie and Morrie make a sweep. But someone could have been in here, I suppose." She shrugged and said ruefully, "I guess we expect people to behave properly when they're in an establishment, and for the most part, they do."

He nodded. "Most of the time, people behave properly. Most of the time."

"And when they don't, they steal, destroy, rape, and murder?" she asked quietly.

"And sometimes just cause mischief," he told her. "Anyway, let's get you to your office, and we'll both get to work. And then we can go to lunch!"

She nodded. Of course she had veered instantly to the truly evil: they were standing in the Murderers' Row section of the wax museum.

She found herself thinking again about the trespasser who had jumped down from an exhibit, and she couldn't help wondering if she had imagined the whisper.

She knows . . .

She had to have imagined it. People didn't whisper to themselves. Or perhaps the person had been a real mischief-maker and was acting out as a ghoul or the like.

She just didn't know. And she wasn't adding fuel to the fire when they probably had just been the victims of a teenager enchanted with the grisly display.

It was broad daylight. The museum would soon be busy. The sun was shining gloriously.

There was no reason to be afraid, and she had assured herself she was going to get tougher, stronger, with the courage to know the difference between being a little spooked and discerning real danger.

But she was glad to be back in her office.

And yet, as she read through letters from those seeking to have events at the museum, she found that her mind wasn't on her work.

Her mind was back in Murderers' Row.

And she was seeing each of the figures, each of the tableaux, and wondering what Fin had seen as he had stared at them as well.

"Slashed? Dead? Grace, a person?" Ryder asked, trying to keep his voice low and not grab the woman by the shoulders.

There were cops right outside!

343

"Rats," Grace said.

"Rats? You don't mean —"

"I mean rodents! But . . . they were slashed. More than one of them. They're lying just on the other side of the fence."

Ryder let out a slow breath. "Rodents were viciously killed?"

She nodded somberly.

"Okay. Let's go. Show me."

She nodded and walked him through the house to the back door.

It was a pretty yard with several of the live oaks and magnolias common to the area scattered by the wood fence.

Grace barely stood as tall as the fence, but she showed him how, by gripping the fence and standing on her toes, she could see over it.

Ryder walked over to where she stood and looked over. While the side of the fence and the similar trees that backed the Kimball property were scorched, one giant magnolia stood at the corner of the two yards just the other side of the fence. It was difficult to see the blood against some of the burn marks on the tree, but at the foot of it were three rats — or the pieces of what he guessed were three rats.

As Grace had said, the creatures had met a brutal and bloody end.

He pulled on a pair of gloves and got a solid grip on the woodfence and hoisted himself over to the Kimball property on the other side, hunkering down to look at the dead rats. They had obviously been done in by someone with a sharp blade, either a knife with a honed edge or a razor. Whoever had done the killing must have moved with the speed of lightning, trapping the creatures against the thick growth of the tree trunk before doing them in.

"Well?" Grace asked nervously through the fence.

"They are dead," he said dryly. "And, yes, someone had to have been out here."

"No suicide there," Grace stated with a humph.

"No, no major rat-suicide pact," he agreed.

"I'll be just across the yard."

The ground was soft, having been disturbed by the wrecking crews and bulldozers that had cleared away the last of the burned rubble. He couldn't discern footprints, just scuff marks here and there. But even those stopped midway across the yard.

Whoever had been there, they hadn't made it all the way across.

And they hadn't been in Sienna's yard.

Why? Had they seen the police? Or did

someone realize that, whatever their intent, it wasn't worth it when a police officer was sleeping in the house — with a gun?

He walked back across the yard and leaped over the fence, not wanting to touch more himself. He didn't know if even the best crime-scene investigators could get anything from the site, the fence, or the dead rats. But he thought about the way he had seen Terry Berger, so close to driving a knife into Martin Kimball.

And Dr. Lester Mahoney, head bashed in before being burned and thrown in the river.

Someone besides Terry Berger was running around with a knife.

And maybe, just maybe, he could get something.

He landed next to Grace Wooldridge. She looked at him anxiously.

"I'm calling someone in," he assured her.

He silently cursed himself.

He'd been sleeping in the house right next door to the Kimball property. He hadn't heard anything. But why would anyone come through the Wooldridge yard and into the burned-out Kimball yard if not to reach the house where the Craton family and Sienna lived?

Had their intention been to come through but they'd been waylaid? Maybe a patrol

346

car or the agents on duty through the night had made themselves known?

Or possibly, the company hired to clear the rubble might have had someone back out, someone who really hated rats?

"I'm scared," Grace told him.

"Is there somewhere you can go?" he asked her. "Family in the area?"

Grace sighed. "It's just that this house has been in my family for years. It's all I have. Sometimes I still can't believe it's mine . . ."

"Grace, if someone breaks in with whatever weapon they used on the rats, what are you going to do? Hold up the walls? I promise you that your life is more valuable to your family than any material possession. But I don't believe your house or your life is in danger. What I do fear is there might still be someone out there who doesn't care what collateral damage falls along the way of achieving whatever it is they want. We have cops *and* agents watching the neighborhood. But I'd feel better if you were somewhere safe."

She listened grimly and almost smiled, then nodded.

"The kids did want me to come," she told him.

"Where are they? We'll get you safely to them."

Her smiled deepened. "One of those places people with kids like to go when they want their kids to have a good time . . . Disney!"

"Great. We'll get you on a plane. Go pack. I'm going to make a few phone calls."

She looked at him with uncertainty and then smiled again and headed for the stairs.

When she was gone, he thought about his position — awkward, given the timing. He was still NOPD.

He hesitated and called Captain Troy first, explaining the situation. Troy would first call everyone involved with putting out the fire and clearing and razing the remnants of the home.

However, Ryder had never seen anyone involved with such efforts that carried the kind of weapon used to do the rats in — or anyone involved in working at ground level who had that kind of hate for or fear of rats.

"It's unlikely we can get anything," Troy told him. "But you never know."

He explained he wanted Mrs. Wooldridge out of the house, and Troy promised the officers in front could get her to the airport. Troy would arrange for her ticket.

"What about the house?"

"I'll have Special Agent Fin Stirling take up residence here for a few days," Ryder told him.

"Well, that's a relief. Off my payroll!" Troy said. "You know, you're one expensive detective, Stapleton. But I'm still going to miss the hell out you."

Ryder smiled and said, "Captain, I'll miss you and the force, too."

Grace Wooldridge was an exceptional woman, Ryder decided. She reminded him of Granny K: she knew how to move when she wanted, and she tended to move forward.

She was back down the stairs in just a matter of minutes, a bag packed.

"I want to put an agent in your house," he told her. "With your permission."

"Oh, a police officer?"

"No, a good friend I've worked with before. An agent named Fin Stirling. He's been on this with me, watching the neighborhood and being where I can't be."

"If he's a friend of yours, sweetie, he is welcome here. Let me give you the spare keys."

She went to the kitchen and came back, telling him the set included keys for the front door, the back door, and her son's Jeep. She didn't want to take them apart because she was notorious for losing keys if they weren't banded together.

"This is fine," he assured her. "And thank you."

"Oh, and please tell the agent he is more than welcome to have anything in the kitchen. Anything at all — groceries are items that can be replaced. And there is delicious — if I do say so myself — gumbo in the clear plastic container in the fridge."

"That sounds wonderful. I'm sure he'll enthusiastically accept your offer."

His phone rang. It was Troy.

The officers parked on the street in front of her house would be taking her to the airport and seeing her through to security. She had a reservation on a plane to Orlando that was due to leave in just three hours.

Ryder thanked Troy and told Grace, asking her then, "Someone will meet you?"

"Oh, yes, the family is picking me up at the airport!" Grace said. "I just have to give them my flight info, and they'll be there for me."

"That's great. I'm going to lock up for now, check that back door, and we'll lock the front together," Ryder said.

They went through the house, Grace pointing out the remote control for the television and the best area for seamless internet access.

When they stepped out the front door,

she paused, turned back, and impulsively gave him a hug. "Thank you, sir, for taking the time to care about an elderly woman who others might have just ignored or waved off."

"Hey, you helped us," he assured her. "Enjoy your family!"

He waved to the officers. One of them hopped out to take Grace's bag and open the back door for her.

"Hey! I'm in a cop car, and I'm not even going to jail!" she called to him.

He smiled and waved back.

But he didn't leave. The crime-scene people were on their way.

Dead rats were dead rats.

But he thought he just might want necropsies done on them.

By one man in particular, who cared about all creatures — great and small.

Dr. Jared Lightfoot.

CHAPTER THIRTEEN

"Mind waiting longer on lunch?" Fin asked Sienna.

She looked up from her computer. She'd managed to concentrate long enough to go through her photos and decide which she was using for the next month's newsletter.

Time had gone by more quickly than she had expected once she'd gotten herself to focus on work.

"I had forgotten lunch, but I thought you were in a hurry to get out," she told Fin.

"If we give it a few more minutes, Ryder will join us."

She glanced at the time on her computer screen. It was, in fact, way past time for lunch: nearly two thirty.

"When is he coming back?"

"He's here."

"Here?"

"Yes, he went straight out to see Dr. Light-foot."

"Oh? Why?"

Fin seemed to hesitate.

"I'm sure he won't be long," he said.

"Fin? Let's go find him. Maybe we can hurry him along. I'm hungry now myself. I had no idea it had gotten so late."

"I don't think you want to join him and Lightfoot right now."

Sienna stared at him and frowned. "Is he . . . arresting Lightfoot? Does he think he has evidence against the man because of an article?"

"No, no, nothing like that," Fin assured her.

"Then?"

"Necropsy," he said.

"I'm sorry . . . necropsy? Ryder has Dr. Lightfoot doing a necropsy?"

"Um, three necropsies, actually. On rats."

"Rats?" Sienna said blankly.

Fin sighed. "He went out to see Grace Wooldridge because she was frightened, heard noises last night, thinking it might be cats or kids cutting through the yard, but she wanted Ryder to come out. Anyway, someone was cutting through the yards. And that someone sliced up three rats."

Sienna stood. "Let's go."

"It's not going to be pretty, Sienna —"

"I can deal."

353

She headed out quickly, and Fin followed her.

For once, she didn't pause to study the tableaux in Murderers' Row; she was set on haste. And yet, even wanting to get where she was going, she felt an odd pull to the section.

There was something nagging at her about it. She didn't understand what it was.

But for the moment, she was heading straight to Dr. Lightfoot's surgery.

It was attached to his apartment but had a separate entrance from the outside. The door wasn't locked. Sienna usually knocked anyway, but she didn't that afternoon.

Ryder was there, standing by the stainless-steel surgery table. Ryder saw her and Fin enter, but the vet appeared to be oblivious to newcomers: he was focused on the tiny animal parts lying on the table.

Then he noticed them.

"Disinfectant, gloves . . . I'll be scrubbing this whole place down, not that it's a guarantee these guys have anything, but they are black rats, sometimes called ship rats or roof rats. They're common in sub-tropical climates, like those found here, and their numbers were running wild in the streets in NOLA after Hurricane Katrina and a few other storms, as well as when

COVID-19 was at its height," Lightfoot said, shaking as he studied the dead creatures. "We have many around here and must watch population control. Still, so inhumane! Someone went to town on these guys. They like to eat fruit, leaves, insects — and they love pet food when people leave it out. Most of the world fears rats, and yes, they do carry diseases, all the way back to the Black Plague. But they're also incredibly smart creatures. And like all things, they have a place in the world." He looked up at them and shrugged sheepishly.

"What I really need to know, Dr. Lightfoot, is what kind of instrument was used to kill them. A straight razor or a knife?" Ryder asked.

"A knife, but a very sharp one," the vet said. "Judging from the wounds, I'm going to say it was a knife that was six to eight inches long."

Sienna had to admit, while rats weren't her favorite creatures by far, the bloody pieces of the little animals on the table were sad and gruesome, especially the heads with little faces that seemed to stare at her.

"It looks as if the weapon was wielded with great anger. Not a shock, I guess. Many people are out-and-out terrified of rats," Lightfoot said. He looked at Ryder. "Was there a reason you brought these to me?" he asked.

"You're the best."

"You're investigating the murder of rats now, Detective?"

"I'm afraid the person who wielded the knife might use it on a person," Ryder said flatly. "Thank you. It was rather outside the description of my position to bring these poor guys to you, but I do know you're the best."

"No problem," Lightfoot said. "I'll do blood tests to make sure they're not carrying anything, and I will swab this place down like nobody's business, and you need to do the same."

"Right. Thank you," Ryder told him.

Lightfoot suddenly seemed more aware of Sienna and Fin, standing a few feet back.

"Ah, Sienna! You're white, dear girl," Lightfoot said.

"Well, I guess those little guys have my sympathy, too," she said.

"We should get going. We haven't been out of the museum yet," Fin told Ryder.

"Ah, yes, we should get out," Ryder said.

"Disinfectant at the sink right there!" the vet said.

"Thanks," Ryder told him.

"And Detective, what would you have me

do with the remains?"

"Dispose of them properly. I believe there's an animal cremation service —"

"Yes, we've had to use it, sadly," Lightfoot said. Then he smiled. "Luckily, so far it's just because one of our goats lived far beyond the expected life span. Most of the time, dead rats are left to rot or be flushed down a toilet, but I won't have that here."

"That's great that you've only lost one, very old animal," Ryder said. "And thank you again."

"You think someone is still out there?" Dr. Lightfoot said.

"We leave room for all possibilities," Ryder told him.

"Hey, lunch — almost dinner!" Fin said lightly.

They finally left the surgery and headed back through the museum to Sienna's office for her to pick up her shoulder bag. Ryder and Fin waited in the hall while she stepped in.

There, she felt an odd sensation again. She wasn't sure what it was. Nothing seemed to be out of place; it was just . . . off.

Her computer seemed to have moved half an inch. She left her bag by the wall, and it also seemed to be in a just-slightly different place.

Her drawers and computer were closed. She had a password for the latter, and she'd never shared it.

She gave herself a mental shake. She was seeing wax figures move and imagining people going through her office. It was daytime; the museum was open, and there were customers milling about in all the halls, enjoying everything the museum had to offer.

She headed out of her office and quickly rejoined Ryder and Fin without saying anything.

"Same place?" Fin asked.

"Well, it's close, and it's late, and I thought we should stop back in before calling it quits for the day," Ryder said.

"What?" Sienna demanded. "You want to see if Dr. Lightfoot decides to have a bonfire with the rats himself?"

Ryder didn't respond to her sarcasm but turned to Fin.

"I volunteered you to stay at the Wooldridge house tonight. I've sent Grace off to meet up with her family in Orlando."

It was a statement, but there was a question to it.

"That will be fine," Fin told him.

"Aren't you married?" Sienna asked him.

"She's doing a show in DC," Fin said. "We are newlyweds, so being apart isn't much fun, but I respect her work, and she respects mine. We met here not long ago."

Sienna looked at him. "You're married to Avalon Morgan?"

Sienna had seen the actress in a few productions. She was good. And of course, it made sense. Ryder and Fin had both worked the recent Display murders case, and she had read that Avalon Morgan was one of the lead players in the film.

She'd heard, too, the film would be coming out, dedicated to those who had been "lost to human monsters."

"Yes, I am married to Avalon. We met just a few months ago, but we married really quickly because we knew we wanted to be together."

"Wow," Sienna said. "Congratulations!"

"Thanks. I'm sure you'd like her very much."

"I'm sure I would," Sienna agreed, and then she remembered she needed answers and turned on Ryder. "Okay, what the hell happened today? Why did you bring Dr. Lightfoot dead rats?"

"We're almost at the café. Let's wait until we're seated, preferably at a quiet back table," Ryder said.

She fell silent until they reached the restaurant. They were way late for lunch and too early for dinner: it was easy to get a table at the back of the restaurant.

"Ryder?" she said, as soon as they had ordered.

"First, though I count no one out yet, I feel Dr. Lightfoot is just what he seems, a dedicated animal lover and a peaceful one, aware the pen can be mightier than the sword."

"So?" Sienna pressed.

"In one sense, he was probably the one person who wouldn't think I was crazy for wanting to know how the rats were killed," Ryder said.

"You really needed to know that?" she asked suspiciously. "I felt sorry for them, but you do realize people kill rats all the time, right? That gangster movies are full of people calling one another *dirty rats*?"

"I do." Ryder looked over at Fin. "You told her where I was, right?"

"Yep, precinct and then Grace's house."

"Okay, so . . . you think Grace murdered rats and we need to watch her?" Sienna asked.

"No, but I did want to know exactly what the creatures were killed with. They weren't crushed, and they weren't torn apart by a cat. Someone with a knife tore into them with real passion."

"And it wasn't Terry Berger," Fin said gently.

"Grace heard noises. Cats, she thought, and there were cats playing back there. But someone had also been leaping the fences and traveling through the backyards. Grace's and the Kimball property. They didn't come as far as your yard."

"Kids," Sienna said. "Kids sneaking home think their parents won't realize they blew their curfews if they come in through their back doors."

"Maybe," Ryder said.

"But that's one violent kid with a big knife if he did that to rats," Fin said. He looked at Ryder, and she thought he was wondering if he should go on or not.

Because she was there.

"Not to be rude but, please, just speak. I think you two have at least decided I'm not guilty, nor will I say anything to others," Sienna said.

"Angela got back to me with the financials," Fin told him.

"And?"

"The Harrison family and the Boudreaux family have a number of stocks." He paused for just a second. "And so do Sienna's parents and," he added, "Sheriff Patterson."

"Oh, my God!" Sienna exploded. "You think my parents —"

"No," Fin said.

She stared at Ryder.

"No," he said firmly.

"Well, why not? They were in the neighborhood!"

"Sienna, your folks haven't even been into NOLA to see where you're living now," Ryder said.

"How do you know that? I never told you that —"

"They didn't know you lived right next door to the house that burned to the ground," Ryder said quietly.

She was silent, looking from Fin to Ryder.

"So, they're just off the hook? You're looking for someone who paid Terry Berger to do the things he was doing. My folks could have done that from Terrebonne Parish without knowing exactly where I was living."

"True," Fin said.

"But we'd know," Ryder told her.

"Oh?"

Ryder and Fin looked at one another.

"They checked your parents' financial statements. They never paid out big sums or made large deposits. Everything they've done can be traced. They're an open book."

"Wait — you can get into records like that?"

"We can see certain . . . things," Fin said vaguely. "In the case of Terry Berger, we were investigating a death. We don't go against the Constitution, ever, not at the Krewe. But there are many venues that are public forums that can be investigated."

Sienna shook her head. "I guess I should be glad. So —"

"Byron Mitchell, Boudreaux, the Harrison clan, Artie, Morrie . . . even Clara," Ryder told her.

"Clara!"

Ryder shrugged. "Not likely, but she plays the stock market."

"And that makes her —"

"No. It just means she's had large sums of money at various times during the past years," Ryder said. "Sienna, believe me, we're not after your friends or your coworkers, but we're finding out more all the time. There is huge money in medicine, sad as that may be. Brian McTavish was working on software that would have helped prevent insider trading, creating a wider playing field for the average person, and I believe it matters to them because there might be several companies working on something specific, and it's important to our killer because he's invested — somewhere. But it's tough to decipher because this kind of tech and breakthroughs in this kind of medicine are kept in-house and carefully guarded. Several things are coming up in medicine, and much is run by computer programs. I believe it is the reason for all these arsons and deaths."

"It's that complicated and far-reaching?" Sienna said, frowning. She winced. "Ryder, it almost sounds like a crazy conspiracy theory!"

"Sienna, I've gone over this in my mind dozens of times."

She thought he was going to say more. And she thought their food arrived at a convenient time to let him rethink his words.

When he spoke again, she was sure it wasn't what he'd been intending to say.

"We've searched through so much paperwork. We know someone was paying Terry Berger. We don't even know Terry Berger committed all the crimes. We just know he received a large sum of cash he deposited carefully so the amount wouldn't be flagged when the McTavish house went up years ago. We know he was in New Orleans when the Kimball house burned. We know he watched the neighborhood, and we know he attacked Kimball on the street. With a knife. But someone else has a knife, someone watching the neighborhood still — someone who doesn't like rats."

"Well, that could be a large portion of the world," Sienna said. "And still, you think this is all over money, when they were willing to pay out ten thousand dollars to Terry to get the McTavish house burned?"

Fin stepped into the conversation. "It is highly likely Terry Berger himself went to Atlanta to manage the hit-and-run. He would have done all the driving without staying anywhere, since he hated not staying in his home. He probably pulled off on the way there and back to take little catnaps in rest areas."

"But what about Dr. Mahoney?"

"We don't know," Ryder said.

"All right," Fin said, reaching across the table to take Sienna's hand. "We're not afraid anymore for Grace or little Whitney because they could recognize Terry Berger, and whoever is behind this killed Terry, so they aren't any kind of a threat anymore. We are still worried about you. You called it on them twice. They don't know why. Someone was in the museum when you were there — and that someone might have thought you were alone."

They all sat in silence for what seemed like too long.

"Hey! It's early, we've just eaten . . . Want to run down to Royal Street and see some art?" Ryder suggested.

Sienna groaned. "You think Freddie did all this in between caricatures?"

Ryder grinned. "I honestly like the pieces he did of certain Saints players. And yes, why not see how he's doing? And maybe Thayer will be in."

Sienna groaned softly and shook her head. But it was fine. Why not?

They finished the meal and walked back to the museum first. People who had come early were leaving, but as they checked with Clara and walked down the halls, there were still groups in the various areas. Artie and Morrie were both finishing up with groups out back, they discovered, and Dr. Lightfoot was happily talking to four teens about birds of prey.

"All looks well," Sienna said.

The place appeared to be running like clockwork.

As they reentered the building, Sienna found once again she didn't want to look at the figures in the wax museum, and she wondered just what it was that was bothering her about them.

And she believed Ryder and Fin both studied the area with more than casual observation as well, walking slowly through it.

In her office, she checked her email and decided to put a call through to Byron.

He answered quickly, she thought. First ring.

"Sienna!" he said. "Is everything all right?"

"Everything is fine. I was checking in with you."

"I'm sorry. I should have talked to you first about the security system. But Dr. Lightfoot was so upset about our after-hours guest. He's a good man and takes the lives of every one of our animals to heart. I hope I didn't fail to refer to you. I don't know what I'd do without you."

"No, no, it's fine. Byron, you own the museum. We do your bidding, remember?"

He laughed softly. "I'm the idea man on this. You're the totally essential one."

"Not at all. No one here needs management. They're all great. And all is well, just checking in."

"I missed seeing you the other night when I made Lightfoot leave. But I'll be back in again soon, I promise."

"I'm always happy to see you," she told him.

They ended the call, and she was ready to leave for the day. She joined Ryder and Fin in the hall, and again, she felt certain they had been talking about things they didn't want to say in front of her. But both smiled at her when she emerged.

"Ready?" Ryder asked.

"I am."

They bid Clara good-night and headed to the car, driving to the French Quarter, finding a nice spot near Esplanade where they could park.

"You really like Freddie's art?" Sienna asked Ryder.

"I really do. Don't you?"

"Yes, I think he's very talented. Are you seriously considering buying a piece, or are we just — hm, how did you put it? — getting to know Freddie and Thayer better?"

"Never hurts to get to know people."

"You didn't answer the question."

"Yes, I'm seriously considering buying the piece. I'm hoping it's within my range."

Sienna looked at Fin. "He's not into serial-killer art or anything like that, is he?"

"No," Fin said, laughing. Then he winced. "Wait, that's not funny right now, but no. Let's see, Ryder has a great painting he bought at Jackson Square of the cathedral. He has pics of his family on his mantel. His house is an old place he bought from his folks when they moved to Arizona. And he loved the *Blue Dog,* has several images in different forms. A few classic copies, *Lady in the Lake* among them. Let me think. No. No serial-killer art."

Sienna stopped in the street and stared at the two of them. "Has it occurred to either of you that this person you're looking for might not be associated with any of these people?"

"Sure," Ryder told her.

"Then?"

"Possible, but not probable," Fin said.

"But, according to the great Sherlock Holmes, when you eliminate the impossible you're left with what's possible even if it's improbable — or something like that," Sienna said.

"And there's no such thing as co-incidence," Ryder said. "Hey, let's see my art. Yes, sorry, I'm a big football fan, okay? But not to worry, I like figure skating, too."

Sienna let out a sound of aggravation and walked ahead of the two.

When they walked into the gallery, she saw Freddie was talking with a couple by one of his caricatures of a movie star. Thayer was sitting behind the counter, reading something on his phone. He looked up when they entered and offered them a smile.

"Hello. Welcome." He was genuinely glad to see them, but then his smile faded, and he looked worried. "Is anything wrong?" he asked.

"No, nothing, Thayer," Sienna quickly assured him. "Ryder is a football fan."

"Ah, yes, the Saints. I'm with you, my friend," Thayer said. "We can give you the 'old neighborhood' discount, since you're hanging around with a member of it," he told Ryder.

"Great. That's nice of you," Ryder said.

Freddie excused himself from the other conversation, leaving the couple to study the caricature that interested them. "Hello." He, too, seemed happy to see them, but then he asked quickly, "Is anything wrong? Man, what a shocker about old Mr. Berger!"

"Nothing is wrong, Freddie, and yes, a shocker for sure," Sienna agreed.

"Boy, sweetie, you were so young back then, getting people out of that house. Thank God he never went after you," Freddie said. "Or me. Or our families. I don't think he would have messed with Thayer. He was already tough as nails back then, but wow."

"We're here because I really like that piece," Ryder told him, pointing.

"Yeah?" Freddie said, pleased. "Not to be immodest, but I am proud of that one. I mean, there are a lot of problems in NOLA, but I believe the Saints are something good in the mix. Football can be rough, but people do come together over the game. I like things that bring people together."

Ryder laughed. "And you don't like people who tear people apart."

"Huh?"

He pointed at a caricature of a particularly discordant politician. It was one creation that enhanced certain flaws in the posturing man.

Freddie shrugged. "Peace and harmony. That's me." He laughed. "Well, I guess I'm grateful my parents came in. Usually, they are much more up on my siblings. They wanted me to go into politics, not art. Me — a politician! No, thanks. I think there are secret classes in the art of lying for politicians. Anyway, I guess I let some inner turmoil out when I was doing that piece. Not my favorite. But the one you like is a caricature that I'm really proud of, and I'll be delighted to have it go to a good home. Okay, I do this for a living, so I'm thrilled to have a buyer. We'll give you the —"

" 'Old neighborhood' discount," Ryder said. "And thank you. The price is right for art, but as a public servant, I appreciate the discount."

Ryder really was buying the piece. Sienna was surprised.

They all talked about the various works on display as Thayer rang up Ryder's credit card and arrangements were made for the piece to be wrapped up so Ryder could pick it up the following day.

They left Thayer's gallery then.

"You really bought art," Sienna said.

Ryder nodded. "I told you I like the piece."

"And we learned more about him and Thayer," Fin said quietly.

"From?"

"We're still dealing with possible and probable," Ryder said.

"But if you study Freddie's art, you see a lot of his personality," Fin said. "Hey, coffee and something before we head in for the night?"

"Sure, we can take it to go," Ryder said. "I know we still have agents watching the neighborhood, but the Craton family share a house with Sienna, so . . ."

"Got to watch out for vile rat murderers," Sienna said.

"You do," Ryder said and nodded.

Sienna winced. She should just be grateful she was protected with what was going on. And she should be happy: it sounded as if, for some reason, the little trip to Thayer's gallery had made Ryder and Fin believe more deeply in the innocence of the two men.

"One day, I'll understand you two . . . maybe," Sienna said. "It's late. I'll have tea and something deliciously sweet and sinful. Oh, they do a fantastic bread pudding filled with nuts and all good things. Let's go for it!"

They purchased their delicacies and headed for the car to drive to Sienna's.

Fin went to Grace's house with his little bag of goodies after he parked. He lifted a hand to say good-night, adding, "Remember, I'm just a burned-out lot away."

Ryder tapped at the door to the Craton residence. Ronald opened it.

"Just checking on you," Ryder told him.

"All is well, and thank you," Ronald said.

"Thanks. Let me know if you hear anything unusual," Ryder said.

"I thought the guy died by suicide?"

"We want to make sure there's no more danger here," Ryder told him.

"I like that. Taxpayer dollars at work. Seriously, thank you."

He looked past Ryder's shoulder to smile and wave at Sienna. She waved back and opened the door to her side of the house.

She set the goodies they'd bought on the table while Ryder checked over the place.

Ryder came to join her, looking at the plate of sweets.

"Hm. I thought we'd be eating in bed."

"No, food and then showers. Rats!"

"You have rats?"

"No! We were at rat autopsies — necropsies, sorry! Anyway . . ."

"All right."

He ate fast. Sienna studied him, then caught him smiling back at her.

"What?"

"Are you ever . . . just at ease?"

"Sometimes."

"But I'm sure you checked every closet and under the bed. Ryder, I might not be in any danger, you know. I mean . . . all right. So, someone paid Terry Berger and might pay someone else to murder people. But I'm not in tech, computer software of any kind, or the medical field."

He answered slowly and carefully. "Sienna, you now know a small percent of the population — maybe one percent — speak with the dead. Sometimes, others just sense things. And whoever is doing this might believe you have a sense for something — not even knowing what your sense actually is. But you got people out of burning houses twice. So for now . . . let me be diligent, okay?"

She smiled, reaching out to take his hand.

They didn't finish the goodies. They wound up racing up the stairs, laughing as they collided. They argued over the soap, towel-dried themselves and each other, and plummeted into the bed.

They made love, and it was still amazing, just as lying curled up together and falling asleep was.

But as she drifted, Sienna found herself going over so much in her mind again. She wished she could read all the thoughts that seemed to pass unspoken between Ryder and Fin.

But they didn't think it was Lightfoot.

And tonight, Freddie and Thayer had both behaved in a manner that had convinced both Ryder and Fin that they were not the kind of people to murder others.

She thought about those who lacked all empathy, who committed the most heinous murders without the least concern. Such as those in Murderers' Row . . .

She felt as if darkness surrounded her. She

was walking down the hall at the museum, entering Murderers' Row, and they were there, arrayed before her, some of the darkest murderers from the area's past.

Madame LaLaurie . . .

Leaving behind corpses that had been torn apart and put together, a legacy far worse than anything Mary Shelley's Dr. Frankenstein had imagined.

The Axeman, a phantom in the night, creating blood and death and destruction . . .

The vampire brothers . . .

Something was moving. Moving in the darkness. A dark phantom like the Axeman, just a shadow, a vampire, rising, and there was a soft cackle of laughter in the air, a whisper, perhaps a black widow, enjoying her kill from a distance, and yet knowing the horror of poison on the human body . . .

All of them, coming to life in a form, in a sound . . .

She knows . . .

The whisper was on the air. The wax figures were joining in one large shadow that grew and reached out with something that glittered in a thin threat of light that seemed to emanate from its eyes — a knife, glittering, and tipped with dripping blood . . .

She didn't know she had fallen into a real

sleep, that she had been dreaming.

She woke up screaming, sitting up in bed.

There was a form by her side, large in the night, but gleaming nicely in the moonlight. It was Ryder, naked as he stood by her side — except for his gun — as he protected her and looked for the danger that had brought about her terrified screams.

"Sienna, what? Where?" he asked. His voice was calm and level.

She swallowed hard and whispered, "Oh, my God, I am so sorry! I was dreaming."

She wondered if he would be furious. If he would think her ridiculous. If he would rethink the very idea of wanting to be near her.

But he lowered his weapon and leaped around the end of the bed to return it to the top of the bedside table.

Then he crawled in and took her into his arms.

"I'm here, you know," he told her. "And it's all right. We've all had nightmares."

"I feel so foolish."

"Never feel foolish for being afraid. Fear protects us. Just make sure that you use fear to have help around when you need it."

"Thank you," she said, happy to curl against the warmth of his chest again.

"Hey, this is what we all do."

"No," she said, "thank you for being you."

He held her; she knew that he lay awake until she slept.

This time, she did so without dreaming.

CHAPTER FOURTEEN

"All right, here's what I've discovered. Public holdings, obtained legally — with a bit of digging," Angela told Ryder.

He was in the hall just outside Sienna's office. He'd spent their first few minutes at the museum on his phone, going over his notes, trying to juggle all he knew and put the pieces of the puzzle together. When all else failed, what was improbable — but still possible — became the only truth to pursue.

But there was that other Sherlockian factor: he just wasn't a big believer in coincidence. And he'd been proven right. Terry Berger had most probably been guilty of both arsons.

He'd been hoping Angela would find the connection that might be the main factor in pointing out the truth he was seeking, maybe verify his instincts — or show him he was just downright wrong.

"Great. What? Am I crazy, or on the

mark?" he asked her.

"Quite possibly on the mark," she said. "Several players have interests in a parent company called American M Enterprises. One of their ventures, Up and Above, has been working on a machine that could revolutionize dialysis. Martin Kimball works for Delaney Enterprises. Their specialty is hospital machinery, specifically, the tech that runs it. They, too, are working on technology to revolutionize dialysis. Dr. Lester Mahoney was working with trial equipment. There was a lot of secrecy to it, and the hospital and his patients had to be informed they were working with experimental equipment and had to sign waivers. Up and Above and Delaney Enterprises are rival companies. Now, one would think a lifesaving situation would mean whoever had it first would just get it out there and everyone would want it all to work. But there is huge money in this kind of science and medicine. Back to Dr. Mahoney. He was part of the first controlled testing on human beings. There had been animal testing, though I'm not sure in what manner."

Ryder winced at that. Lightfoot? Had the man even known about it?

"But what about Brian McTavish? He was working in the financial sphere."

"Exactly. He was working with tech to help banking and the stock market. And his company was specifically associated with Delaney Enterprises. I've checked out everything about them, and they are above-board. I'm working on the rival company."

"But ten years ago —"

"Ten years ago, Brian McTavish was just about ready to go. What he was working on would prevent insider trading. I know this is a long shot —"

"But someone was afraid McTavish was ready to go, and given whatever medical breakthrough was imminent, he could prevent people from making big money?"

"Or losing huge money," Angela said. "Sad, but . . ."

"Possible!" Ryder told her. "Okay, so —"

"Those invested in the rival company include Joel and Mary Harrison, Thayer Boudreaux's parents, Hugh and Marlena Murray, Byron Mitchell, and of course, other names that don't mean anything to me, and one that is . . . strange."

"Angela!"

"Lawrence Patterson."

"Lawrence Patterson? As in Sheriff Lawrence Patterson?"

"Yes."

Ryder let out a long breath. Two people

he hadn't been expecting — a sheriff, and a man who spent his days giving away his money. But owning stock, of course, didn't mean anything.

And a killer was willing to wait ten years to strike again?

"Also, in the middle of all this," Angela continued, "I found an article in a magazine from ten years ago. They'd expected a breakthrough in the medical field that didn't happen. Now, apparently, two companies are neck and neck coming up with the results of their clinical trials with the equipment." She was quiet a minute. "The bad news is that I don't have any definitive answers for you. The good news is that your theory about it all being connected is probably solid."

"Yeah, thanks," Ryder said. "And thank you for being so good at —"

"Cyber-sniffing?"

He laughed. "Something like that. Hey, have we found anything else on Atlanta?"

"I can find no record of anyone on our list spending a night in Atlanta. There aren't many places that take cash these days, so whoever managed that hit-and-run on Brian McTavish was smart enough not to stay in the city or spend a cent there."

"And I still have nothing on what happened to Dr. Mahoney . . . except I believe the phone call the waitress told me about was from the same person who killed him. His cell phone wasn't found. Whoever made the call did it from a burner phone. Captain Troy pulled video from the casino and got records from his phone company. He left sight of the cameras, and that was it. Officers took his photo around but came up with nothing."

"I can keep combing through everything I can find on all these people," Angela said. "Maybe something will leap out. What is your plan? You have several people who stand to gain if Delaney Enterprises fails with their clinical trials."

"Well, I don't like Sheriff Patterson, so I'm telling myself that doesn't make him guilty. I think he just wanted the whole thing closed, wanted Berger's death to be a suicide and not a murder. He doesn't want guilty people in his territory. Again, that makes him lazy, not guilty. I met the Harrison couple only briefly, though I did spend some time with Freddie. In fact, I bought a caricature from him. Thayer . . . I guess he reminds me of Freddie. The antiexpectations guy, doing what he wants rather than following what everyone thought would be right."

"Byron Mitchell is damned rich. He has a major investment."

"I still haven't met him."

"Maybe you should."

"Right. I should."

They ended the call. For a moment, Ryder stood there in the hall, and the slashed rats came to mind. He wasn't sure who he could imagine being so violent, especially someone terrified of the disease-bearing rodents.

He needed to take another drive out to Terrebonne Parish.

And meet with Byron Mitchell. Maybe he'd have Captain Troy see if he could invite the man down to the station.

Fin was out back, but whether it was somewhat overkill or not, he didn't want to leave the area where Sienna was almost within arm's reach. He called Fin, asking him to come back to Sienna's office, then put a call through to Captain Troy.

Captain Troy agreed to see if Byron Mitchell would come. Ryder doubted the man would say yes. They had nothing against him and nothing to hold him on, and in truth, though Ryder didn't know him, he couldn't imagine a man with his Midas touch and massive donations to charity would be involved in a money scheme.

Troy agreed and assured him an officer

had escorted Martin Kimball to and from work every day, to lunch, and basically, stuck to the man like glue.

That was good. Ryder had been seriously afraid there was going to be another attack on Kimball.

When Fin reached the hallway, Sienna also popped out of her office. "Ah," she murmured, looking at Ryder. "You're taking off, and Fin is staying with me."

"Yes," he said. "I'll be back before closing, though." It was early. They had reached the museum by eight thirty that morning and it was just about nine now. He could easily get out to Terrebonne Parish and back before closing.

"I'm sorry," he told her.

But she smiled. "That's okay. Sometimes I like Fin a lot better."

Fin laughed. Ryder made a face at Sienna.

He left, reminding them to call him if needed.

As he was leaving, Artie came through the hallway, extolling the virtues of the Lafitte brothers in the hearts of many a New Orleans resident at the time, also stating that while he did bring supplies to the city, he was a pirate. He and Ryder exchanged waves. Artie was a good docent: he was passionate and talented in his presentation.

Out past the parking lot, he saw Tim Busby lounging against his car, wearing big, puffy earphones. That day, his choice of T-shirt plugged Queen.

He tapped his earphones when he saw Ryder and mouthed, "All for show. Are you taking off?"

Ryder nodded and tapped his watch. "Back before closing," he said.

In the car, he turned the radio on to an old rock station. An hour and a half drive with his own thoughts.

His own thoughts were making him crazy.

It was a busy day. Groups had been scheduled correctly, but the hours were full. Sienna took a group herself at ten. They were from the college, and college kids were usually pretty decent, and in truth, she hadn't been out of college that long herself.

As tended to be the case, they were fascinated with the wax museum. Luckily, they were attentive in the history area. Those who weren't from Louisiana listened, and now and again, those who were from Louisiana put in. Yes, it was true that the war had ended when the battle took place: the Treaty of Ghent had been signed on December 24, 1814, and the Battle of New Orleans had taken place January 8, 1815. The internet hadn't been invented, and the telegraph didn't even exist yet, so the two opposing parties met in battle. But the battle proved the ragtag American forces pulled together by Andrew Jackson could defeat one of the greatest naval forces of the day and cemented the power of the new American nation.

Many took pictures with the wax figure of Jackson. Some decried his treatment of Native Americans.

They moved on to Murderers' Row, Sienna aware Fin was never far from her.

She gave her speeches, studying each of the tableaux. She noted the platforms on which they stood again and found herself wondering what was beneath.

She had never thought much about it before. The tableaux were raised, she'd always reasoned, to keep people from causing damage to the figures. She started wondering about the person who had come after her and how they might have stayed in the museum.

Fin opened the door for the students to head out to the rescue center and petting zoo. She lingered just slightly behind the last student.

She thought she heard something again.

Someone whispering.

Two distinct voices.

"How?"

"How the hell do I know? But, somehow, she's dangerous."

The last student went out. They'd all been chatting. Maybe she had imagined the whispers, maybe hearing voices was part of her paranoia.

Fin was frowning as he looked at her.

He walked back to her, letting the door close as the last student went through.

"What is it?"

"Did you hear anyone whispering?"

He shook his head. "There are twenty kids there, I think. I heard them talking about the creepy figures and the past and, just in case it means something to you, Jimbo having a pool party this Saturday night."

She smiled and shook her head. "I think I imagine things."

She heard voices in the hall — real ones, she knew. Artie was coming through with a group, and he was chatting with Morrie, who had a group of grade-schoolers in the How Things Work section.

"They're still working on the security system today, right?" Sienna asked Fin.

"Yes, they're doing some inside work from six to eight tonight and finishing up from six to nine tomorrow morning."

"So tonight, after eight, only Dr. Light-foot will be on the property, right?"

"That should be true," Fin said.

"We have to come back here," Sienna said.

"Okay," he told her. "Why?"

"The platforms. I want to get under the platforms."

"Not a bad idea. You think the person who came after you might have been beneath the tableau, hiding, until the museum had emptied?"

"I think it's possible. I mean, I've never thought about the platforms before, but every time we came in here, something was bothering me. More than the figures."

"I'll let Ryder know," Fin said.

"Where exactly is he? Do you know?"

"Exactly? No."

"Okay, roughly, where is he?"

"Terrebonne Parish," Fin said.

Sienna stared at him. "I guess my parents are suspects, then," she said.

"No, I don't think so. They produced you."

She smiled. "Well, that's nice. But I doubt it really clears them."

"Let's say, then, they're at the bottom of the list." Fin grimaced. "Moncy. History has proven it to be the number-one motive for murder. When leads run dry, there's one thing left to do, and that's to follow the money."

It seemed most plausible to see Sheriff Patterson first.

He was in his office, and while his secretary was trying to dissuade Ryder from seeing him, Patterson came out.

He looked surprised at first, then annoyed, but he barked out, "Ryder. Big-city detective, checking on the little guys out here. Oh, wait. *Consultant,* right? You're not a fed yet. So, what are you doing out here? Did you go to medical school, find something we missed?"

"I'm here because I need your help," Ryder said.

Patterson didn't smile; he did look surprised.

"Come in," he told Ryder.

"Thank you."

Ryder didn't think he much liked Patterson. The guy seemed to have a chip on his shoulder, but maybe he just needed to play him right.

Patterson indicated Ryder should take the chair in front of his desk, and he did so while the sheriff walked around to his big swivel chair.

He waited for the detective to talk.

Ryder explained they knew Berger had attacked Martin Kimball in NOLA and they knew, too, he'd been the one to — at the very least — case the Kimball house before the fire had been set. He also talked about the money that had gone into Terry Berger's account a decade ago, when the McTavish house had burned.

Patterson appeared to be honestly confused. "Then, it is likely Terry was guilty of it all, though he was just a crusty old bayou man, loved the bayou and his boat and shrimp and crawfish. It's still hard for me to figure."

"Well, that's what is hard to figure. The ten thousand dollars into his account suggests someone was paying him. And his staged suicide suggests to me that when he failed with Kimball, it was time for him to go rather than be paid again."

"If he set the fire at the McTavish house, he failed there, too."

"But McTavish was struck and killed a year after. That suggests someone gave him time to right his wrong back then, but this time, when he failed, we were able to track him down through the clothing he discarded. The police were onto him. He was a liability."

"You're not one of those crazy conspiracy-theory guys, are you?" Patterson asked.

Ryder smiled. "No. But there's a lot of money involved. There's a company that rivals Kimball's that is on the same track."

Patterson leaned back. "Are you accusing me? I have stock in some company that invests in medical . . . stuff."

Medical stuff.

Ryder shook his head. "The Boudreaux family, the Harrison family, and the Murray family have all invested as well."

"Tons of people must have invested," Patterson said, frowning.

"What I was hoping was that you could tell me more about the fire years ago. Sienna was what, fourteen? That's not a little kid or a child, but you were there."

Patterson's face scrunched; he bit his lip and shook his head. "It was bad," he said. "The smoke was horrible. A few first responders needed treatment — Sienna needed treatment. I'll still never know how that kid saved the woman and the baby. Another few minutes and they would have died."

"Do you remember anything after the firefighters came, anything about the investigation that could help?"

Patterson drummed his fingers on his desk. "The street doesn't have much on it, a couple houses, the bayou side, the land side. Terry Berger was out, watching everything from his front yard. Of course, he was questioned. He swore he didn't see a thing until the flames shot up." Patterson grimaced. "I believed him. No reason not to believe old Terry. He was just . . . a bayou guy. Sienna's folks weren't there. They had gone out shopping, which was the reason Sienna was watching her grandmother. The old lady was sick, but she never had dementia. Smart as a whip. People loved her. She could tell them off and make them laugh while she was doing it." Patterson shrugged. "But Thayer Boudreaux is an only child. His folks were older when he was born. Mom was forty-three, and his dad was in his late fifties. He was their pride and joy. All three of them were on their lawn when I arrived. And the entire Harrison clan was out, too, picnic in their front yard. They were all questioned. All anyone could say was they suddenly saw the flames shooting up. Now, what any of them were doing when the fire was set, we can't say. But we believe Terry Berger set the fire and got back to his place."

"But no one saw him."

Patterson shook his head.

"Well, not that they were willing to say,"

Patterson told him. "And, what the hell? It was natural, or so it appeared. Flames were shooting out of a house. Neighbors who were stunned and scared by what was happening burst out onto their lawns. Trust me. We sure as hell weren't happy we never solved it."

Ryder nodded slowly. "Yeah."

"You're not asking. Spit it out. Where was I? Right here. I had an interview with a paper that day. You can ask anyone. I wasn't there until the emergency call went out. Oh, wait, that doesn't matter. Terry was paid, so I could have paid him and come up with an alibi for myself," Patterson said dryly.

"I'm not accusing you. I'm investigating," Ryder said.

Patterson leaned forward. "I have nothing to do with this, I swear."

Ryder nodded. "Thank you." He stood. "With your blessing, though, I'd like to stand on the street again, survey the houses, see what I see. I'm not sure how all those people were outside, but no one saw anything."

"You've got my blessing. And talk to anyone you like. Be careful about accusations, though," Patterson told him.

"Oh, accusations are bad. As soon as you accuse someone, they're wary. Much better just to talk, the way I see it."

"Hm," Patterson said, looking at him suspiciously.

"I really don't think you're involved," Ryder told him, smiling.

And it was true. Patterson had been a bit of a jerk to him before, but again, that didn't make him guilty. And now, he seemed to realize the events years ago might have stretched into the present, that a hit-and-run might have been a completed murder attempt, rather than a tragic accident.

He thought someone in one of the households had to have seen Terry Berger leaving the McTavish house to get to his own.

Not Sienna's parents. They had not been there.

He thanked Patterson again and left, driving to the street where Sienna had grown up. He parked at Terry Berger's empty house and judged the distance the man had gone to start the fire, and then to get back to stand in his yard and watch the blaze and the arrival of the police and the fire department and emergency services.

He had seen Sienna run down the street to the house.

He had probably just gotten back when she had taken off, hurrying for the McTavish place.

He looked at the Boudreaux house, the Murray house, and the Harrison house.

No one had mentioned seeing Terry Berger.

Because they hadn't seen him?

Or because they had seen him — but they had been the ones to pay him to do it?

Sienna was working but wondered if she should be.

Scheduling needed her attention, so she wouldn't double-book or cause events to overlap, but she couldn't keep her mind off Murderers' Row.

The museum was busy. People were coming and going. They'd be seen inspecting the platforms.

She sat back in her chair. Fin was concentrating on whatever files were on his phone. She started to speak to him when there was a knock on her door.

"Come in!" she called.

She expected Morrie or Artie, or maybe even Dr. Lightfoot or Lori.

But it was Byron Mitchell.

"Hi!" she said. She was always happy to see him.

No one would look at Byron when he was in casual attire and think the man was as rich as Croesus — or just about as giving as a saint. He was in his early sixties, tall and fit, with a round, almost cherubic face, dark brown eyes, and a headful of salt-and-pepper hair. He was wearing jeans that weren't a name brand, sneakers, and a denim jacket over a theme-park shirt.

He smiled. "Couldn't be in the area without stopping in to see my number-one girl!" he told her.

Fin had risen; Sienna had, too, and walked around her desk to give him a hug.

"I'm always happy to see you!" she told him. She turned to Fin. "Byron, this is Special Agent Finley Stirling. Fin, Mr. Byron Mitchell."

They shook hands, Fin telling Byron it was a pleasure, Byron saying he was grateful Fin was there, as the museum meant a great deal to him.

"And maybe we were plagued by a mischief-maker, but I'm glad you and the police are watching over the museum — and Sienna," Byron said.

Fin nodded. "We'll definitely be around until your security system is fully functioning," he said.

"That's great. Anyway, I'm going out to check on all the creatures, check in with Lightfoot, and then head to the police station."

"The police station?" Sienna said.

"Going to see if I can help in any way," he said. "Would you two care to join me and pet some critters?" he asked.

"Sure," Sienna said.

"Never a bad thing to pet a few creatures," Fin agreed.

Byron smiled and held the door for Sienna and Fin, but then he took the lead. Sienna noted with a small smile that even then, even there, Fin brought up the rear, as if sandwiching her between safety nets.

Morrie had a group in the hands-on area. Artie was telling a group that French fur trappers had first come to the area in 1690.

Seeing Byron, both smiled and waved, and he returned their greetings.

They passed into the hallway that held Murderers' Row, and Byron paused there.

He shook his head. "I guess hiding in plain sight among the figures was an easy thing for someone."

"It wouldn't be again," Sienna said.

Byron turned to her. "I know you know this place like the back of your hand. No, I don't think anyone could hide on you again — and you did see the trespasser right away!"

"I saw movement right away — quickly enough to run the other way," she explained.

"And a cop was here, right?"

"Yes, Ryder Stapleton was here."

Byron nodded thoughtfully again. He shook his head. "Someone should have noticed before they closed the place up, but I admit, I wouldn't have checked through everything myself. We're just not big enough for real trouble, and I wouldn't expect it."

Sienna noted Fin was staring at the tableaux, and she wondered if he was studying the platforms, preparing for whatever time they might get to investigate what lay beneath.

She stared at them, too. And at the platforms. And noting one, she thought she saw a crack running along one of the support beams.

A way to slide it open?

"Byron, were you here when you had all this put together?"

He gave her a rueful smile. "No, I handed it over to the architect and the contractor doing the restructuring on the old building. I saw the plans and approved them, but no, I'm not into saws and dust."

"What lies beneath the platforms?" Fin asked him.

"Nothing. It could be storage space. We just haven't needed it yet. Well, onward to cute, cuddly animals."

"And Ruff! You haven't met Ruff yet," Sienna said.

When they arrived outside, Lori was putting the dog through his paces for a group of children.

Jared Lightfoot was on a bench with the bear cub, talking to another group of children.

Lori saw them and smiled. She finished her demonstration and hurried over to them with the German shepherd.

"Byron, meet Ruff. Ruff, this is the man who makes it all possible," she said. "Ruff, these people are friends," she assured the dog.

Ruff wagged his tail. Byron petted the dog and then rose to talk to Lori, asking her how she was doing, thanking her for all she did.

Sienna squatted to pet the dog. He was such a beautiful animal, so well trained, and so responsive to affection. Fin hunkered down beside her, scratching the dog, too.

Lori's group of kids was eagerly entering the petting gate. She excused herself to hurry over. "Most of the time, kids are good. Every once in a while, you get a kid who thinks it's funny to pull a tail."

"Right. Good to see you, Lori," Byron said.

They walked over to the bench where Dr.

Lightfoot sat, stroking the cub and telling the children they were never to approach an animal in the wild. The cub would remain with them, but even then, they'd have to be very careful once he reached adulthood.

He had a great group of students. They all nodded somberly.

"Go see the birds, kids," he told them. "I'll be right there."

The kids ran off. Lightfoot stood and beamed at Byron and greeted him with a hug much like Sienna had done.

"Hey, Byron, thank you," Lightfoot said. "I don't think any of us ever thought much about security. I mean, we had security, but . . ."

"But it was outdated and needed replacement," Byron said. "I'm glad I got a wake-up call that was minor, before something bad did happen." He shook his head. "To be honest, I should have worried long ago."

"I should have spoken sooner. We all should have spoken sooner. We just tend to assume that people are decent when it isn't always so. And I take a pretty strong stance against anything that has to do with animal testing, and I've caused some problems for some people. You just never know who you might upset!"

"I don't think someone running around with the wax figures had anything to do with you, Jared," Byron said.

"Well, still, I wasn't any help to you on that," Lightfoot said. "I mean, I always thought with someone on the property at all times, we had the police just minutes away. But after what happened, I realized that not only might someone hide in the museum, but I could sleep through someone breaking in. Anyway, that won't happen with Ruff, not out here, anyway. And with the new cameras connected straight to the security company, it's all good."

Ruff, who had trailed after Lori, came running up to their group, nudging Sienna on the thigh. She bent down to pet the dog again.

"Hey, what am I, chopped liver?" Lightfoot asked the dog. He laughed. "I think he's partial to women. He seems to choose Lori over me every time," he said. "But that's good. I'd never want anything happening to her."

"I would never want anything happening to any of you," Byron said.

Lightfoot smiled. "Well, we've had cops and the FBI the last few days. That's felt good." He grinned at Fin.

"Spending time here has been a great assignment," Fin returned. "And we're just helping out, of course."

"Regardless, we're grateful for your time," Byron said. "Speaking of time, I've got to get going, but I will be back in tomorrow afternoon for an inspection with the company redoing the security system. I'll see you all then."

"Great!" Lightfoot said.

They started back inside, Fin once again making sure he followed after Byron and Sienna. Again, Byron paused in Murderers' Row.

He shook his head. "We know these figures. How did someone hide in them? That's why the figures are on platforms, to discourage people from wanting to play with them."

When they reached Sienna's office, he told her, "I will be back in tomorrow. I've got to get to the police station."

Sienna said goodbye to him as he waved. She headed into her office, and Fin followed. When the door was closed, she looked at Fin.

"Byron? Really? Trust me, he never lived in my neighborhood. He couldn't possibly need more money than what he has, and . . . Byron? Really?"

"Eliminate all you can," Fin told her. He

looked perplexed.

"What?" she demanded.

He shook his head then, at a loss.

"Something just bothered me. Something someone said. But I can't figure out what, who, or why. But, hopefully, I will."

Sienna just shook her head. "I thought I saw a door."

"A door?"

"Like a sliding door that led beneath the platforms. Byron says there's nothing under them, but there has to be a crawl space, and if what I saw is a door, then —"

"We can go beneath and see what's there. But you're going to have to be the one to close, and we're going to have to work fast if you don't want anyone seeing what you're up to."

"As in other museum workers?" she asked.

"Yes."

"You and Ryder are convinced that —"

"We are," Fin said. "Convinced that, at the least, someone here knows something. And someone here is involved in some way."

She wanted to argue with him. She wanted to believe her friends and coworkers were just what they appeared to be: nice people with no hidden agendas.

But she had heard the strange whispers.

And she couldn't quite convince herself
the whispers had been a lie.

CHAPTER FIFTEEN

"Frankly, I asked you in here not just because of the intruder at the museum," Ryder told Byron Mitchell, "but because of your investment portfolio."

The man looked shocked. "I — what? Listen, I swear to you, I've either been smart or lucky. I don't engage in insider trading. I —"

"Sir, it's because you're largely invested in a company that is neck and neck with Delaney Enterprises on a machine that could transform the dialysis process. I don't know anything about medicine, but we've been doing a great deal of research. Martin Kimball is lead on the project from the technical side, and a doctor, murdered after his arrival in New Orleans, was the key man on the clinical trials taking place."

Byron sat back, staring at him.

"My God!" he said. "But I'm confused. Do you think this also has something to do with the break-in at the museum?"

Ryder was honest. "Yes. We think it has to do with the attack on the Kimball family, the attack on Martin Kimball in the street, and even the burning of a house ten years ago and the death of Brian McTavish."

Byron frowned, shaking his head. "But the man who attacked Kimball was found dead on his boat, and from what I read, he set the fire, too. I can tell you I'm not involved in any way. The break-in . . . How or why would that connect?"

"I think someone may think Sienna Murray knows too much," Ryder told him.

He was still confused. "Why?"

"Because she saved people ten years ago in Terrebonne Parish, and again, recently, right here."

"Well, if she knows something, wouldn't she just tell the police and be done with it? I know Sienna, and she wouldn't let anyone get away with something like that."

"She doesn't know anything," Ryder told him. "But perception and fear can be motivating forces."

"I need to put her on a plane to Tahiti or somewhere far, far away!" Byron said.

"She wouldn't go," Ryder said. "She's not the kind of person who would spend her life running. We both know that."

"What can I do?" Byron asked him.

"Well, forgive me, but we had to speak with you. Because of your investment port-folio, plus you do own the museum. And something is going on with someone there."

Byron shook his head again, letting out a long sigh. "I was so careful. I had everyone investigated before I hired them. They all have clean records and impressive résumés. I don't know how to help you, or what to say."

"I'd like your permission to have free rein with the museum."

Byron nodded solemnly. "Whatever you need to do." He hesitated. "You know, I was speaking with Jared today. He was mention-ing the fact he might be hated by some people."

"Because he's so anti-animal-testing?"

"Yes. He's written articles about the hor-ror of it," Byron said. He frowned. "You don't think that Jared Lightfoot could be . . ."

"I don't think so, no," Ryder assured him. "But I'm still weighing all the evidence. The person hiding in the wax museum went after Sienna. He ran out back. Jared says he saw him. There's always the possibility it was Jared — or that he allowed him in through the back."

"My God, no!"

"It's just a possibility."

"I don't think Jared owns a cent of stock."

"We didn't find any records suggesting he did," Ryder said.

"So, what do you want at the museum?"

"First, to be there," Ryder told him. "At any time," he added. He leaned back. "Also, I'd like you to announce the new system is going to take a little longer than you expected. That it won't be on tomorrow, but maybe the next day."

"Artie works with the security people. He'd know."

"I'll need you to ask them to stall Artie as well," Ryder said.

"I will do whatever you need."

"Do you trust your security company? You said Artie works with them. With what I need right now, no one in the museum can know anything. Artie might inadvertently talk."

"Oh, don't worry. I'm the one who pays the bills."

"It's important."

"And I'll see it's handled properly. I swear it."

"I believe you."

Ryder thanked him, and the wealthy man rose to leave. Captain Troy came out to the hall and thanked him as well.

When Byron was gone, Captain Troy said, "Well?"

"I don't get *money-grabbing killer*. My instincts say he's not our man. But that's an instinct, not anything solid to go on."

"Then?"

"I still think someone who was an adult when the first fire happened had to have been in on this. I walked the street where the first fire took place. And —"

He stopped, realization coming to him.

"I have to make a call to Terrebonne Parish. And I need you to make an announcement. Say that a suspect, an accomplice in the crimes carried out by Terry Berger, has been arrested."

"But we haven't arrested anyone. And we don't have a suspect."

"Right. But if everyone believes there is a suspect in custody, others may come out from under the rocks, wanting to know just what it is that we know. And when we find the main power behind all this, I'm pretty sure we'll find one or more coconspirators." Ryder hesitated again, wincing. "I'm just wondering if . . ."

"What?"

"What if this became something like a family business?"

■ ■ ■ ■

Sienna was restless. They were waiting, of course. Ryder hadn't talked to her, but he had called in and spoken with Fin.

He was held up with Captain Troy.

Of course! He was after Byron Mitchell.

Which, of course, was why he hadn't called her. He didn't want to hear her protests.

He would get to the museum as soon as he could; there were matters he had to deal with at the station. The hour was growing late, and the museum would close soon.

But as she sat there, agitated, Clara came bursting into her office without knocking.

She stared at Sienna and Fin. Glancing at Fin, Sienna saw he had been reaching for his Glock, but seeing Clara, he quickly dropped his hand.

Clara didn't notice.

"Did you hear? Oh, my God, it's so horrible!"

"Oh, God, what?" Sienna asked. "What's happened?"

"They've just arrested someone. That awful Berger guy who started the fires and tried to kill your next-door neighbors wasn't working alone! They've arrested someone.

The police captain just announced it. They believe Terry Berger was hired to murder people, but they think they have the person who hired him in custody."

"Who?" Sienna demanded.

"They're not releasing his name yet," Clara said. "But to think someone hired that man to do horrible things . . ."

"Sad, yes," Fin said.

"You didn't know?" Clara asked him.

"Must have just happened."

"Well, I'm going to tell the others. They'll be relieved. Byron just called, and there's going to be a delay on the security system being finished. That nice cop, Tim, will be around tonight. That will make Dr. Lightfoot feel better. While they have a suspect in custody, they said it's still an ongoing investigation, so they won't say more. I'm going to make sure that Lori and the doc know, and Morrie and Artie. Then I'm gone for the night."

She hesitated.

"Sienna, tomorrow morning, I'm going to wait in my car for you and your escort to get here before I come in. Is that all right?"

"Of course. We'll make sure we're on time," Sienna promised.

Clara left the room, and Sienna stared at Fin.

"Okay, what the hell is going on?" she asked him.

Fin's phone was ringing as she spoke. He answered it. She could hear Ryder's voice but couldn't make out the words.

Fin ended the call.

"It's a ruse," he told her.

"What?"

"Rest assured about Byron. He's helping with it. The idea is to see who crawls out from beneath the rocks, wondering what the heck has happened."

She shook her head, confused.

"Ryder got Byron to agree to hold off on the security so we could tear this place apart tonight."

"But someone paid Terry Berger ten years ago when most of the people working here and my friends from the neighborhood were too young to have ten thousand dollars to throw around."

"True."

"Then?"

Fin looked uncomfortable.

"What?"

"According to Ryder, well, you know how sometimes your dad is a doctor, and you want to be a doctor, or your mom is in politics, so you go into politics?"

"What are you saying?"

413

"Family business?" Fin said softly.

Sienna let out a sigh of weary exasperation. She loved going home with Ryder, sleeping with him, waking with him. She loved his humor, his understanding, his compassion, and his strength.

But this was driving her crazy.

"I guess it's a good thing Terry Berger didn't have any children," she said.

"Sienna, let's follow this lead."

She stood up. "You're right. Let's follow it."

"Look, Ryder and I are both getting to know you. And we all know the truth has to come out. Byron wanted to send you to Tahiti so you'd be safe. We don't believe you want to hide the rest of your life."

"I don't. I said, let's follow through."

"And what do you mean?"

"Follow me!" she said.

"Sienna, what —"

She was already out the door. Fin followed her.

Clara was hurrying back down the hall.

"They're all outside, getting ready to make a last sweep and head out, if you want to catch them. And good night, my lovelies!"

"Thanks, Clara. Good night," Sienna said.

She kept moving with Fin at her heels, though he, too, bid Clara a good-night.

She moved fast, determined. Of course, her determination might prove nothing, but in proving nothing, might she prove something?

She ignored the figures in Murderers' Row and barged outside.

As Clara had said, her fellow employees were gathered around the bench between Lightfoot's apartment and the rescue center.

"Hey," Lori said, seeing Sienna and Fin. "Clara told you, too, right? Fin, you didn't know?"

"Remember? This stayed a NOLA case," he told her.

"Oh," Artie said, disappointed. "Then you don't know who they nabbed?"

"I don't," Fin said.

"Regardless," Sienna said brightly, "it's great news for us! I mean, Fin won't have to hang around, Ryder can move on as he intended to . . . and we can be free! Oh, no offense, Fin, but you know, it is creepy having cops or agents on you every second."

"Big Brother," Morrie commented ruefully.

"I can't wait to work in relief, freedom, and happiness," Sienna said. "Again, no offense, Fin."

"Well, I for one am still glad I have Ruff and that we are getting a good security

415

system," Jared Lightfoot announced. "Then again, I'm here alone when you all go away. I thought I had it covered out here before, but now with new cameras and Ruff, I am good."

"Well, the cameras aren't ready for a bit," Sienna said. "But my faith is in the police, even if we don't know what went on. I may just enjoy the peace and quiet of coming in here and working all alone. Oh, and no offense to you guys. When we're open, I wind up with a few tours, and there are people all over. I always did love my off-hours."

"So, Fin, does that mean we won't be seeing you anymore?" Lori asked. "We've really enjoyed your company, you know."

"Thanks. But our headquarters aren't here, so . . ."

"You'll be heading back," Artie said.

"I will be," Fin confirmed.

He looked at Sienna. He knew what she was trying to do, and she doubted he agreed with it. But he didn't say more. He didn't suggest to them he'd still be around anytime Sienna was there.

Then again, he didn't say he wasn't leaving.

"Well, I have a few things to tie up. Dr. Lightfoot, you're on your own, and I'll give you guys and Special Agent Stirling a chance to get out, then lock up for the night," she said. "Heaven! Working all on my own."

"Well, that's antisocial," Morrie teased. "I'm going now. Lori, mind helping Artie make sure no one is hanging around?"

"No problem," Lori said. "Clara is gone, so the front door is locked. We'll have to escort people out if anyone is still inside."

"Yep, let's get to it," Artie agreed. "Morrie, you go ahead. Doc, good night."

"If you need me, Dr. Lightfoot, I will be in my office," Sienna said. "Call me. I can always head out to you."

She spun around, calling, "Fin, come on. I'll show you out so Artie and Lori can clear the place."

She took off back to the main building.

Fin followed her.

She hurried through the halls with him on her heels, but when she went into her office, she didn't close the door. She encouraged him to get in quickly.

Then she shut it. She brought a finger to her lips. "Stay."

"Sienna," he said, "Ryder knows nothing about your plan to see if anyone comes after you. And if they don't, you think you'll prove they're all sweet and innocent, but it doesn't work that way. They could wait. You don't know —"

"Warn Ryder, then. He put his plan into action and then told us. You can tell him about my plan."

"Sienna —"

"You guys put your lives on the line every day. You believe my life is being threatened. Well, I can't cower anymore. I must take something into my own hands with your help," she said a little desperately.

"I'll call Ryder and hide here, but you'd better be right back."

"Just this hall," she said.

She stepped out and hurried down to the hallway branches that led to the hands-on area and the wax museum. She was ready to ask if they needed help making sure the place was cleared out, but before she could, the main lights went out, and the smaller, eerie auxiliary lights came on.

Looking down the long hall, she saw the photo-op figure of Andrew Jackson was a strange, tall shadow against the green light that now permeated everything.

They were just doing the usual measures that were a part of closing. They had made sure all their visitors were gone for the day, and in preparation to leave, they had locked the back and turned off the lights.

But then . . .

She heard voices. Whispering again.

Strange, hushed whispers, barely discernible. She couldn't tell the sex of the speakers from the whispers because they were so hushed in the strange green light that seemed misty as well. Her imagination, she knew. There was no mist there, just green.

Maybe the whispers were part of her imagination, too!

"Who the hell did they pick up?"

"I don't know! Not —"

"Shush! We need to make sure he's gone. And it's important, because if they did pick up —"

"You hush! I hear something!"

The whispers fell silent.

Where the hell was Granny K when she was needed?

Sienna didn't call out: she hurried back to her office as silently as she could.

She opened her door, and for a moment, she thought Fin had left her. But he had been behind the door, watching for whoever came in.

With her new bravado, she hoped her sigh of relief wasn't too loud.

"What's going on?" he asked her.

"Lights are out."

"But people aren't?" Fin asked.

"I'm not sure," she said, and then she

419

admitted, "Fin, I thought I heard whispering."

"From where?"

She shook her head. "I just went to the fork in the hallway. It might have been from the hands-on gallery or the wax museum."

"Okay, then. We'll sit tight. If they want you, they'll come here eventually. What did you hear?"

She let out a soft sigh. "Someone wondering who had been picked up, and somebody starting to say who hadn't been picked up, and then shushing. There still might have been someone from outside in the museum."

"We were out back with Lightfoot and the others. There was no one in the back then. If the main lights were turned off, that would mean your friends cleared the place."

"But they might have missed someone! Like the other night."

He hesitated. "We need to see if Lightfoot is in his place. And make sure Morrie did leave, and that Artie and Lori are out, too."

"We never got a chance to check beneath the tableaux. If we try to walk through —"

"I do have a gun, and I do know how to use it," Fin told her dryly.

"I know, I know —"

She broke off.

They suddenly heard a strange sound, a cry for help so loud and panicked it came through the walls in a strange echo, like the shriek of a banshee.

"Get under your desk," Ryder told her.

"What?"

"Your desk! Lock your door. Put your phone on silent. Now. Then get beneath your desk. And do not move unless you hear it's me or Ryder at your door. Me or Ryder only!"

He'd pulled his Glock. She scrambled to do as he ordered.

Ryder was still a block from the museum when he saw Granny K standing on the street, desperately trying to flag him down.

He was already growing anxious. He had finally called Sienna.

She hadn't answered. Then, when he tried Fin, he didn't answer, either.

It had grown late. The day had naturally been long, but he'd planned on being back at the museum before closing.

It had now been closed for half an hour.

"Get there!" Granny K said, pausing by the window. "I'm just going to run in and see if . . . Well, ghosts aren't much help, but maybe I can do something."

"What's happening?" Ryder demanded.

"I don't know. I just heard something horrible! A cry . . ."

"It's locked up now. I can't reach Fin or Sienna —"

"Hop the damned wall, lad! Show me those muscles aren't just for looks."

"Right!"

Ryder left the car where it was, running around to the back, to leap the fencing into the neighbor's property, thankful he already knew the fellow wouldn't come out with a shotgun, nor sic a guard dog to get him.

He ran from the barn roof to leap over to the museum's petting zoo, pausing for just a second to survey the yard.

Quiet.

He leaped in, jumping down to join the sheep and goats and miniature pony.

He made his way through the paddock, seeing nothing. Then he heard a whining sound, and in the night-lights and glow of the moon, he saw a creature coming toward him.

Not to attack.

To seek help.

It was Ruff.

And the dog was covered in blood.

Dragging his left hind leg, Ruff reached him.

Ryder quickly ripped a piece of fabric

from his shirt and bound up the wound that was flowing, surveying the area at the same time.

Nothing was moving.

Friend. Ruff had been taught Ryder was a friend. But the dog had also been taught the others there were friends.

He wouldn't attack them unless . . .

Unless they attacked Lightfoot.

The dog whined and moved toward the front of the paddock. Ryder followed. The dog couldn't make it over the fence so Ryder opened it.

Then he heard commotion from behind the bird sanctuary and sped that way. Two men were on the ground, struggling.

One, he realized, was Officer Tim Busby, but he was rolling and grunting with someone else. They were so closely entangled he didn't dare use his gun in case he killed the cop and alerted anyone else to what was going on.

He holstered his Glock and threw himself into the fray, dragging a man off Busby, and catching him with a good right to the jaw. He went down, out cold.

Ryder winced. He'd been right.

But that meant there was more.

"Busby," he said, reaching down to help up his friend. But Busby was out cold, too.

Ryder squatted quickly and discovered Busby had a pulse, but it was faint.

And he had a serious knife wound to the right side of his chest.

Ruff whined, looking hopefully at Ryder.

"Someone is still inside, boy. Wait here. Watch out for Tim, for me, and yourself, buddy."

Ryder stood quickly, whispered in a call to Captain Troy, looking at the man he'd knocked out cold as he did so. Now it seemed obvious.

He dug in his pocket for his plastic restraints, cuffing the man who had attacked Tim Busby in case he woke and finished the job.

Help would come, but not in time.

Where is Fin?

And worse . . .

Where is Sienna?

He got an answer from the dog: Ruff was whining and heading toward Lightfoot's apartment. Ryder drew his weapon again and raced for the front door, slamming it open, ready to shoot.

There was no danger: he'd found Fin, who was bandaging a wound on Jared Lightfoot. The woman who had attacked him was on the floor, and a gun across the room, kicked out of the way.

424

Mary Harrison was knocked out, too. She and her husband had to have been in the area. Lori had probably called them right away, and they'd arrived quickly.

But Mary Harrison was cuffed. Fin was trying to stanch the flow of blood pouring from Lightfoot.

He looked up and saw Ryder. "Get in, get in! Sienna is in the main museum. I told her to hide. They could be there by now, if she heard them . . ."

"How many?"

"At least two more. All armed. Go!"

He didn't need more.

He had to find out what the hell was going on — and pray he got to Sienna in time.

Sienna heard her whisperers moving down the hall.

Fin hadn't returned, and she didn't dare call him. She might be heard.

"Yeah, we'll try the hands-on," someone said.

"If she's not there —"

"She might have lied and left. We'll search under every moving waterwheel and then go back. Her office."

"It will be locked."

"Then we'll break the damned door down!"

Her office. They were coming back, and they'd surely look under her desk.

She waited until they were gone. Whether Fin liked it or not, she had to get out. If she could reach the petting zoo and rescue area . . .

She scrambled out from under her desk and hurried down the hall. She could hear movement in the hands-on area and raced past.

But before she could reach the back, she heard movement there, too.

Swearing, she leaped up on the tableau with the vampire brothers, then crossed over quickly to steal the large black cape from the Axeman of New Orleans figure.

Then she rushed back to the tableau where there were victims lying on the floor and covered herself with the cape.

No good . . .

They were coming.

One of them was heading down through the historic figures, coming through to Murderers' Row.

"Come out, come out, wherever you are! Come on, Sienna, we just need to talk."

She lay utterly still, stunned.

The speaker was Lori Markham.

Did that mean that she and Lightfoot were in it together?

426

What had happened to Fin?

"Come on, Sienna, I know you're in here. All alone, your detective and agent gone. Come on, come out and play!"

Lori jumped up on the tableau that featured the infamous NOLA black widow, Minnie Wallace.

"Come on, Sienna, let's talk! I mean, we could implicate your mom and dad, you know. But if you want to just come out . . ."

She heard the other whisperer calling from the back, not caring anymore if they were heard.

"Screw it! Just find her and get rid of her."

Lori Markham laughed and agreed. "We will find you, Sienna. Make it easy on yourself. Come out, come out!"

Lori posed for a minute, standing dead still next to the wax image of Minnie Wallace. Then she jumped across to another platform, crying out dramatically and falling on the floor like a victim of the Axeman.

"Man, can you imagine?" Lori said. "Being hacked to death by an axe? Oh, it must have been horrible and so gruesome. Come on, Sienna, come out and make this easy. A bullet to the head, it's over in two seconds. Imagine the fear and agony of being axed to death!"

She hopped to another platform, waving her gun around.

"Oh, well, you don't have to worry about the LaLaurie thing. I mean, there's no time for connecting and reconnecting your limbs, or anything like that. Though, that could be fun. Ugh! Can't imagine. The one that always haunted me the most was the Axeman. It sure was scary when we had a copycat, huh? You wouldn't want to die that way. Bloody, bloody flesh chopped, lying there, lumpy, horrible, sticky, agonizing!"

She listened to Lori, thinking it had been forever since Fin had left her; it had been minutes. But Ryder was on his way, she knew.

But . . .

"Lassie, there's a poker there by the fireplace. I'll lead her astray the best that I can. She'll come after you, and you bean her! You wallop her, that's the way. Quick, reach for the poker, and I'll distract her."

It was Granny K.

Back at last!

And from where she lay, Sienna could see the poker by the hearth.

She had to stretch and move to reach it. She was so afraid Lori would hear her . . .

Who had Lori been whispering with? Freddie? Sam? Maybe Lili? Had she let her

428

cousins in? And still, they couldn't have done what was done years ago. They'd been too young . . .

Family business.

Ryder had known. Ryder had been right.

"There you are!"

Lori jumped to the wrong display. She stood with a wax figure cop, looking down at the body of Addie Hall, so viciously killed before her slayer had died by suicide.

"Oh, come on!" Lori cried angrily.

She hopped onto the tableau where Sienna lay.

"You know, I have a gun and a knife. I can shoot your kneecaps and then slowly slice you to bits, let you die in agony. And get this — Uncle Joel already took care of all the rest! He went out back and had Dr. Lightfoot write up the most wonderful murder–suicide confession! He saw you mistreating our animals, and he couldn't bear it! You were going to kill his bear cub. You told him he was refusing to return it to the wild, and we couldn't keep it. I mean, everyone knows how he loves that bear cub." She started to laugh. "He was so happy with Ruff, and he was even happy Ruff loved me so much. But that dog started out believing Uncle Joel was a friend because of me, and well, there went Ruff and Dr. Lightfoot. So sad!"

She was moving closer and closer.

Granny K leaped onto the vampire brothers' tableau, too. She stood right in front of Lori and breathed in her face.

Lori noticed something. She swatted at her face, as if she thought a flying insect had been around her.

Granny K managed to make a noise by the hearth.

Lori spun around, aiming her gun in that direction.

Sienna sprang to her feet, poker raised.

And before Lori could turn, Sienna slammed her hard on the head.

Lori went down without a whimper.

But then Sienna heard applause.

"Bravo!"

She turned.

She hadn't expected to see the man she saw.

Artie Salinger.

And he was aiming his gun straight at her.

"I told them even without your law-enforcement support, you weren't going to be that easy."

"Artie," she said, then shrugged. "I was expecting Freddie or Lili or Sam. You know, someone in the family dynasty."

"Aw, you've got to be kidding me! Artsy-fartsy Freddie? He and Thayer are both lost causes. You know, Thayer could have been among the best. He could have been famous. But you know those artistes!"

"And Sam and Lili?"

Artie shook his head. "No, their folks knew them for a loss, too. But Lori here, well, she has what it takes! Tough as nails, devious, fun . . . My kind of girl!"

"I see that now. But Artie, you know Fin is out back."

"Fin is dead by now."

"You think Joel Harrison is a match for an FBI agent?"

"And a cop. That idiot plainclothes guy who looks like a delinquent hippie was back there, but he's not now," Artie said, grinning. "Hey, kid, sorry. The money in this is just going to be too good. So, you gotta go. This could have been a whole lot simpler. I mean, if Terry Berger hadn't been such a dolt, we would have been okay. You'd think Joel would have given up on him after he failed in Terrebonne Parish, but Terry got it done in Atlanta. So, he screws up another fire. But he screws it up because of you. Damn it, girl. Are you a fire hound or something?"

"No, my grandmother told me."

431

"Your dead grandmother?" he inquired skeptically.

"Yep. She's breathing on you right now. Whatever happens, you'll be sorry. She'll haunt you the rest of your days."

He laughed, but he swatted at his neck.

"Time's up!" he told Sienna, taking aim.

But at that moment, a figure leaped out from a tableau — a figure that had been wax just moments before.

The figure of the Axeman.

Artie never got a chance to shoot.

The Axeman flew against him, slamming him down to the ground and sending his gun flying to a stop in front of Sienna's feet.

She nearly screamed.

But it was no Axeman. It was Ryder . . .

How the hell had he gotten in? How in hell had he gotten up on the platform where the wax rendition of the Axeman had stood?

"Arthur Salinger, you are under arrest for conspiracy to commit murder, for attempted murder, for conspiracy to commit arson . . ."

Ryder began reading him his rights. He used plastic restraints to cuff him and then walked over to Sienna, looking from her to Lori Markham on the floor.

"Damned good — with a fire poker," he said.

He knelt down to cuff Lori, too.

432

And by then, the sound of sirens was like a beautiful melody on the air.

EPILOGUE

They had all the pieces to the puzzle; they just had to put them together.

That night, at the hospital — both Ryder and Sienna wanted to make sure Dr. Lightfoot and Officer Tim Busby were going to pull through — Ryder tried to explain what he believed to be true, even before he returned to the museum.

"Terry Berger went up and down the street when the McTavish house burned," he said.

"Well, obviously."

"Wait. Thayer and his folks claimed to have just come out of the house when they heard the sirens. At the time, Terry Berger claimed the same thing. Now, we know he was lying. But when I went over it all in my head, I couldn't fathom what you had told me. The Harrison family had been having a picnic. The kids might not have noticed, but the parents most surely would have seen

434

their neighbor, and they would have denied seeing anyone if they had been the ones to pay him to do it."

"But it could have been someone else."

"If anyone was lying, I thought it was them."

"But you questioned Byron."

"I had to. He stands to make money when Martin Kimball finishes his work. Because he's playing both sides, pitting the devil and the demon against one another. And while Lester Mahoney was the key doctor on the first clinical trial, he did work with others. And they will pick up where he left off. That means Delaney Enterprises' investors will make the money, and the other stock will —"

"Plummet?"

"No, but it won't bring in what those who invested in Delaney Enterprises will make. Some will be sitting extremely pretty."

Sienna shook her head. "All that for money."

"A lot of money," Ryder said quietly. "Anyway, I was wrong in one aspect."

"You were wrong?" she said dryly.

"I thought the Harrison children were involved. Captain Troy and Fin have been interrogating Joel and Mary Harrison and Artie and Lori. Apparently, none of the kids wanted in on their dad's stock-trading advice. I believe Joel quickly realized he didn't have a single child interested in the machinations it would take to make sure his investments went right. But Lori was a frequent visitor, and she didn't grow up with much. Joel told Fin when he saw Lori set fire to a cat's tail one day, he knew she was his girl."

"And Artie?"

"Lori reeled him in. Sex and money."

"I had no clue!" She frowned again. "So they believed your ruse. Joel and Mary were delighted to think someone else was going to take the fall. They decided to end their worries once and for all. Stage a murder–suicide for Dr. Lightfoot. All in one. Good plan, I guess. I mean, in a way I didn't think my ploy would work. If they'd come after me while someone else was in custody, how would they explain it?"

"Exactly." He grimaced. "And Lori introduced Joel and Mary Harrison to Ruff. It wasn't until Mary went after Dr. Lightfoot that Ruff turned on them and was slashed for his efforts."

"Oh, the dog! Did anyone —"

"Fin saw to it that he went to one of the vets our department uses. She's an amazing woman, and I'm sure Ruff is going to be fine," Ryder reassured her. "I don't think they expected Tim Busby would be *in* the museum or the petting zoo and rescue areas. But he and Lightfoot hit it off. They figured Mary could handle Lightfoot and Joel would take on the cop. But Tim is a strong, well-trained cop."

"All right. I have to ask. Who slashed the rats to pieces — Lori Markham?" Sienna asked. After her last encounter with Lori, she could well imagine her committing such a deed.

Ryder shook his head. "Mary. She got here really quickly, and I guess she has a streak of mean. Meaner than others, anyway. Bizarre. Given Lori's violence, it's pretty amazing she took on a job at the museum, working with Lightfoot and animals."

"What will happen?"

"I'm not an attorney, but they will all be charged with conspiracy to commit murder."

"McTavish was killed when Lori and Artie were still young."

"But not Dr. Mahoney," he reminded her. "And they're all facing four counts of attempted murder. I believe they'll go away for a long, long time, no matter what kind of drama Lori comes up with for a jury."

"Okay, here's the big one — to me, at

least, since I'm so grateful to be living and breathing," Sienna said. "How did you sneak into Murderers' Row and get up on the platform in a position to bring Artie down?"

"The back door was unlocked. I barely opened it to slip in. You weren't facing that way, and Artie and Lori were intent on killing you. And there is a crawl space beneath the platforms. I inched my way in and then up. I would have had to take a shot at Lori, except you proved to be adept with that fire poker. And then you had Artie talking. I let him talk, until I couldn't let him talk anymore. I'd have shot if I'd had to. I prefer the justice system, though. I believe in it. But if I hadn't known I could get him down, I'd have taken the shot."

She smiled, leaning back in the chair at the hospital. It was sometime in the early morning by then. Even with Fin and Captain Troy taking on the arrests and the interrogation, they'd been at the museum a long time, getting some information down on paper.

Now, both Jared Lightfoot and Tim Busby had been in surgery for hours.

But they waited. They both wanted to wait, and they didn't need to tell the other how they felt.

He took her hand. She leaned her head back on the seat and closed her eyes.

She had barely done so when the first surgeon came out.

Tim Busby had suffered some internal injuries, but he had been sewn up nicely and was doing well. They wouldn't be able to see him, though, until the following afternoon.

Ryder had believed Tim Busby would make it.

Sienna knew they were both more worried about Jared Lightfoot.

But they were soon to be relieved. Not a half hour passed before his surgeon came out. The man had lost a great deal of blood, the doctor reported, but miraculously, none of his vital organs had been hit. It had been touch-and-go for a while, and he'd be spending some days in intensive care, but he was a strong man, and he would make it.

Again, they couldn't see him until the following afternoon. Ryder put calls through to Captain Troy and Fin, and then they left the hospital.

"They're survivors. It's a miracle everyone is going to make it," Sienna said. But then she looked at Ryder worriedly. "But we have to find out about Ruff!"

"I'll call."

"It's almost five in the morning."

"They're open twenty-four hours. Someone will know how he's doing."

Ruff, too, was going to recover. It was the one leg that was injured, but no arteries or veins had been hit and he was going to be fine.

"Busby is a tough cop. So is Ruff," Ryder told her.

"We can go home," Sienna said. Then she sighed again. "No, we can't. There is no one watching the animals and —"

"Byron is there. He'll stay at Lightfoot's place until he gets someone to come in for as long as the vet is in the hospital. You can relax. It's all handled."

"And Grace and her family can come home, and I can tell my housemates that Whitney and Noah really are safe this time."

He smiled. "Let's go home."

They headed to Sienna's. She hurried into the house. She was anxious to tell Judy and Ronald the case had been solved and it was over, but she also wanted to get in without any more explanations to anyone.

They made it.

She thought they'd both just crash on the bed and sleep.

They didn't. It suddenly seemed too important now that it was over and they were both all right, and that Sienna had found the courage and faced down her demons — with help from Ryder and Fin — and that she was alive and well and breathing.

They made love.

They didn't talk about the events of the night, and they didn't talk about the future.

They just made love.

And then they slept.

The museum was closed for several days as the new security system went in, and Byron interviewed for new employees.

He was deeply disturbed he had hired Lori and Artie. He was worried in his hiring the next day that, as he'd told Ryder, he'd "had the instincts of a rat's ass."

But Clara was going to be with him during the process. "Morrie told me once that Artie Salinger could be pompous, but Morrie is a good guy — the best. Lori was always a little too cheerful, you know? I had my worries about that girl."

Ryder had come to the museum to thank Byron for his cooperation. Byron had apologized to him up and down and was grateful the detective had taken control.

"Not exactly the way I'd planned it," Ryder assured him. He would never have set things in motion if he'd suspected he'd start the ball rolling so quickly. But then, Sienna had been guilty as well, by making herself a target and giving Artie a chance to let his partners know it was time to strike, before discussing it all with Ryder and Fin.

Ryder was grateful they were able to see both Jared Lightfoot and Tim Busby the next day.

"Lori!" Lightfoot moaned. "You know, I would be dead if not for Ruff. Poor dog!"

"Ruff will be fine," Sienna assured him, smiling at Ryder quickly. "He's with a wonderful vet — not as wonderful as you, but pretty darned wonderful."

"How could I have been so fooled?" Lightfoot murmured.

"We all were," Sienna told him.

Thayer came to the hospital, white and pale as he assured them he'd had no clue of what had been going on. Neither had his folks.

Ryder believed him. Ryder wished him well and wondered if what had happened would mean Freddie's work wouldn't sell — or would instead go through the roof.

Finally, it grew close to dinnertime, and Sienna asked, "Should we get takeout and go to my place, or should we eat out somewhere?"

"I have plans for dinner, if you don't mind."

"Oh, I didn't mean to presume —"

"No, you're included, of course! Fin's wife is back in town. She has two weeks before her next project. And another friend from the Krewe is here, too, the man who handled the Axeman's Protégé case, along with his wife. And," he said, then paused. He'd been ready to go full blazes, but his words failed him instead.

"And?" she said.

"I'm between jobs now," he told her. "My resignation was accepted the minute we finally ended this whole thing, and I leave for the academy soon. I want you to come with me."

She stared at him. For a minute he thought she must think he was crazy.

He smiled ruefully. "I'm sorry. I'm not good with words and explanations and getting what I want to say out —"

"That's an understatement," she said wryly.

"Okay, so I'm not good with words. But . . . I love you."

Her smile deepened. She didn't speak a word. She kissed his lips instead. A light kiss became a deep one, and then they broke apart.

It was too deep for the sidewalk in front of the hospital.

"I love you, too," she told him. "I've been afraid to say so. I was afraid it would sound ridiculous."

"Definitely not. I'm not sure of many things in life, but I am sure I love you."

She smiled and nodded with her arms still locked around his neck. "But Byron! Poor Byron, losing so many people . . ."

"You can keep working for him. You can do media long-distance, just report into your office once a month. You can have an assistant working in-house if you want."

"You talked to Byron?"

"He talked to me. Apparently, others have seen . . . what we hadn't."

"Oh, goodness!" they heard suddenly, and they both smiled.

Granny K had joined them. She clapped her spectral hands together.

"Finally! I mean, you can lead two stubborn mules to water, but sometimes it's darned hard to make them drink."

They both laughed.

Ryder asked her to join them for dinner. They met up with Fin and Avalon, and Katie and Dan Oliver. Granny K was delighted to have been asked to the meal and was even more excited to be seen by six living people at one time. They all talked about their love for New Orleans and the Krewe of Hunters and how things that were meant to work out did work out.

Dinner was lovely. Knowing they would head back together was wonderful.

Granny K wouldn't get into the car with them.

"I have some walking and some thinking to do," she told them.

Sienna looked frightened, concerned. "Granny K, you're not —"

"Thinking of leaving you? I do miss your grandfather something awful, and I really feel my work is done. I've taught you so well."

"Granny K," Sienna said.

"Oh, gracious, child! I was thinking about the move. Though, I hope you will understand when the day comes and I . . . well, I believe the day will come when I do feel something call me, and I get to see Grampa again."

"I'll understand," Sienna promised her.

Granny K waved to them, walking off. "Not coming to the house tonight, children. I have some friends, and I want to do some bragging!"

Ryder laughed. "She wants us to know we

have privacy," he said.

When they reached Sienna's house, he went to speak with the Craton family. Sienna had told him she had to make a phone call, so it seemed like a good time to check in with them.

They were relieved, of course.

And happy.

When he headed over to Sienna's half of the house, he discovered she had finished her call.

"My parents," she told him.

"And?"

"Well, my father is happy that we're safe and that you seem to have the integrity to want to make an honest woman out of me."

"Ah! When is the wedding?" he asked her.

"That sucks as a proposal," she chastised him.

"Yeah, you could have asked me with chocolates and roses or something," he teased.

"Wiseass."

"But I'll do," he reminded her.

She laughed. She was in his arms. But then he fell to his knees before her.

"I don't have a ring yet, but knowing you, you'd rather pick it out yourself, anyway. Sienna Murray, if you'd consent to be my wife, I'd . . ."

He paused.

She lifted his chin. "You'll still be an agent. Stubborn as a mule. But you'll start telling me everything you're thinking when you're thinking it. And I will listen. I won't always be determined I know better than you."

She was smiling; she was serious. He loved the truth and honesty and beauty in the green of her eyes. He loved her. Everything about her.

"And I will love you all the days of my life," he said softly.

She knelt, too, facing him, twining her fingers with his, and then she kissed him.

He stood, lifting her into his arms.

And the night was a promise of their tomorrows to come.

ABOUT THE AUTHOR

New York Times and *USA TODAY* bestselling author **Heather Graham** has written more than 200 novels. She is pleased to have been published in over 25 languages, with 60 million books in print. Heather is a proud recipient of the Silver Bullet from Thriller Writers and was awarded the prestigious Thriller Master Award in 2016. She is also a recipient of Lifetime Achievement Awards from RWA and *The Strand,* and is the founder of The Slush Pile Players, an author band and theatrical group. An avid scuba diver, ballroom dancer and mother of five, she still enjoys her South Florida home, but also loves to travel. Heather is grateful every day for a career she loves so very much. For more information, check out her website, TheOriginalHeatherGraham.com, or find Heather on Facebook.

The employees of Thorndike Press hope you have enjoyed this Large Print book. All our Thorndike, Wheeler, and Kennebec Large Print titles are designed for easy reading, and all our books are made to last. Other Thorndike Press Large Print books are available at your library, through selected bookstores, or directly from us.

For information about titles, please call:
(800) 223-1244

or visit our website at:
gale.com/thorndike

To share your comments, please write:
Publisher
Thorndike Press
10 Water St., Suite 310
Waterville, ME 04901